THE STONE MAN MYSTERIES

BOOK THREE

Breaking Out The Devil

JANE YOLEN AND ADAM STEMPLE
ILLUSTRATED BY ORION ZANGARA

GRAPHIC UNIVERSE™ • MINNEAPOLIS

To David Francis Stemple, who knows Edinburgh well enough —JY

For my favorite trilogy: Betsy, Ari, and David —AS

To Katie (my beautiful wife), Lisa and Mark (my wonderful parents),
Troy (my incredibly smart brother), and Richard and Sarah (my great
in-laws). I couldn't do any of this without you! —OZ

Story by Jane Yolen and Adam Stemple
Illustrations by Orion Zangara
Front cover coloring by Steve Canon
Lettering by Bill Hauser

Graphic Universe™
An imprint of Lerner Publishing Group, Inc.
241 First Avenue North
Minneapolis, MN 55401 USA

For reading levels and more information, look up this title at www.lernerbooks.com.

Main body text set in CCWildWords. Typeface provided by Comicraft.

Library of Congress Cataloging-in-Publication Data

Names: Yolen, Jane, author. | Stemple, Adam, author. | Zangara, Orion, illustrator.
Title: Breaking out the devil / Jane Yolen and Adam Stemple ; illustrated by Orion Zangara.
Description: Minneapolis : Graphic Universe, [2019] | Series: Stone man mysteries ; book three |
    Summary: "Silex and his assistant Craig must prevent one of the Devil's lieutenants from
    overtaking both the underworld and Earth" —Provided by publisher.
Identifiers: LCCN 2018038303 (print) | LCCN 2018043375 (ebook) | ISBN 9781541561151 (eb pdf) |
    ISBN 9781467741989 (lb : alk. paper)
Subjects: LCSH: Graphic novels. | CYAC: Graphic novels. | Gargoyles—Fiction. | Supernatural—
    Fiction. | Demonology—Fiction. | Scotland—History—20th century—Fiction. | Mystery and
    detective stories.
Classification: LCC PZ7.7.Y65 (ebook) | LCC PZ7.7.Y65 Br 2019 (print) | DDC 741.5/973—dc23

LC record available at https://lccn.loc.gov/2018038303

Manufactured in the United States of America
1-36195-16979-5/1/2019

Previously in THE STONE MAN MYSTERIES

Edinburgh, Scotland. The early 1930s. Young Craig, a desperate runaway, goes to the top of a church to throw himself off. But he is saved by a strange stone man, a gargoyle named Silex, who can move and speak but cannot leave the church parapet. Silex runs a detective agency and hires Craig to be his chief clue finder, since his last assistant has departed and the church's priest, Father Harris, is getting old.

Craig is shocked, but he signs on. Together, the gargoyle and the young lad solve the mysterious murder of an earl, as well as the deaths of several street people. But the solution points to a deeper, uglier conspiracy. One that involves freeing the Stone Man from his bonds, which will turn him from a force for good back into the evil demon he once was. In that form, he would threaten not only the church, Edinburgh, and Scotland, but indeed the entire world.

Father Harris gives his life to thwart the conspiracy. But troubles at the church continue. When a girl, Ealasaid—an innocent, yet guilty of a terrible crime—makes her way out of Hell, she begs the church for sanctuary. And a fallen angel comes to return her to the Underworld.

Once again, Craig and Silex push back against the darkness, sending the girl to Heaven with the aid of the new priest, Father Walker. But now the last battle is about to commence.

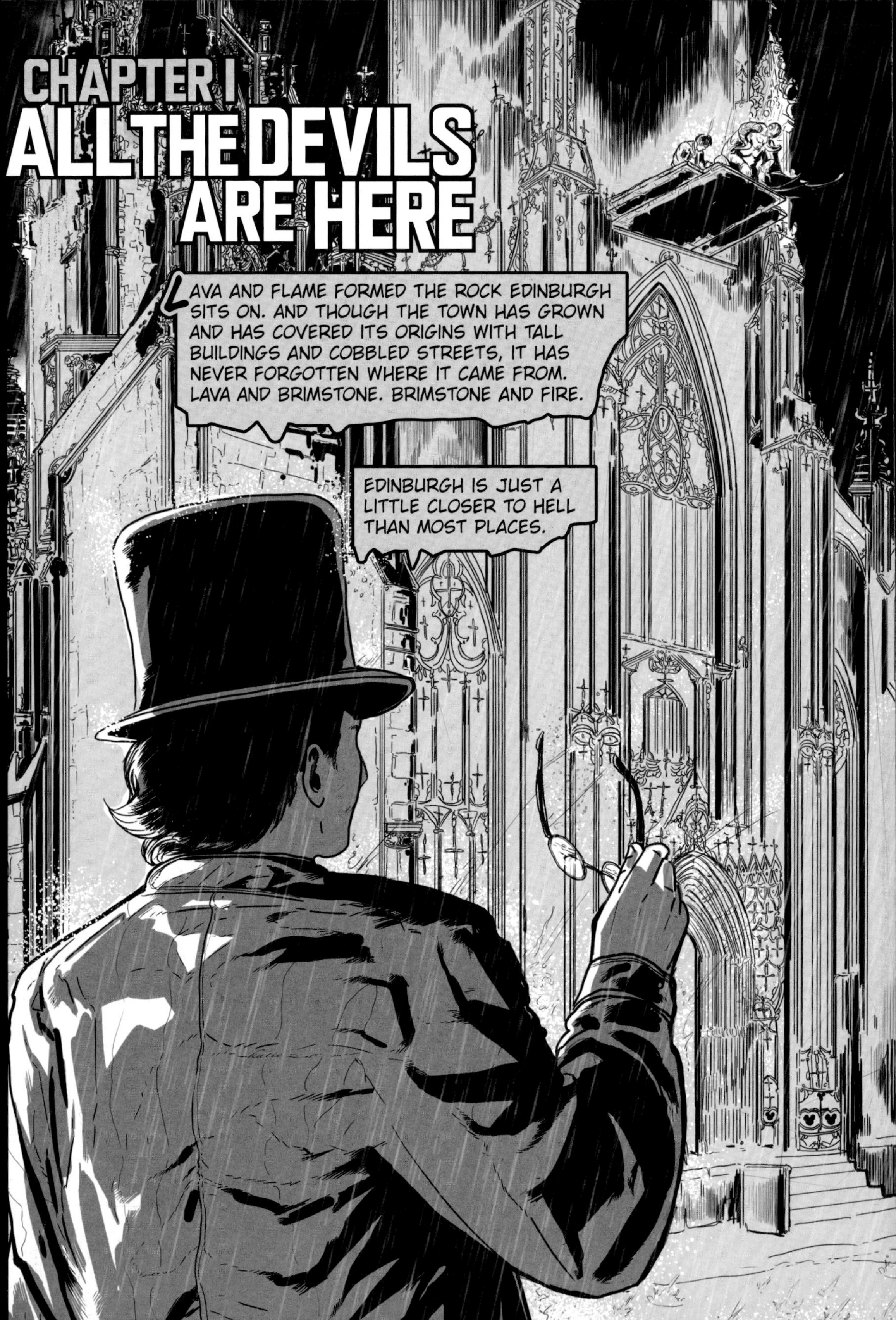
CHAPTER I
ALL THE DEVILS ARE HERE
LAVA AND FLAME FORMED THE ROCK EDINBURGH SITS ON. AND THOUGH THE TOWN HAS GROWN AND HAS COVERED ITS ORIGINS WITH TALL BUILDINGS AND COBBLED STREETS, IT HAS NEVER FORGOTTEN WHERE IT CAME FROM. LAVA AND BRIMSTONE. BRIMSTONE AND FIRE.
EDINBURGH IS JUST A LITTLE CLOSER TO HELL THAN MOST PLACES.

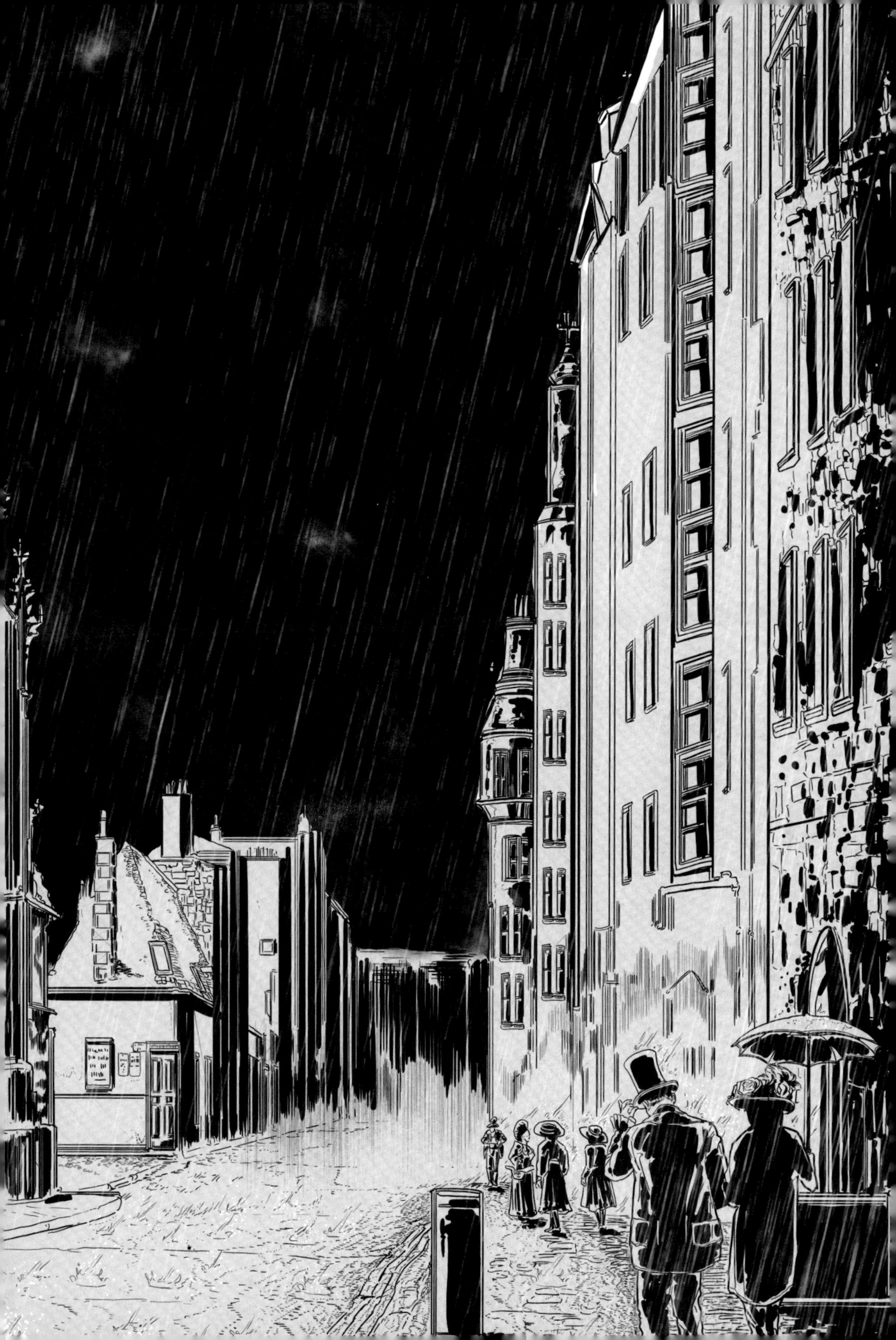

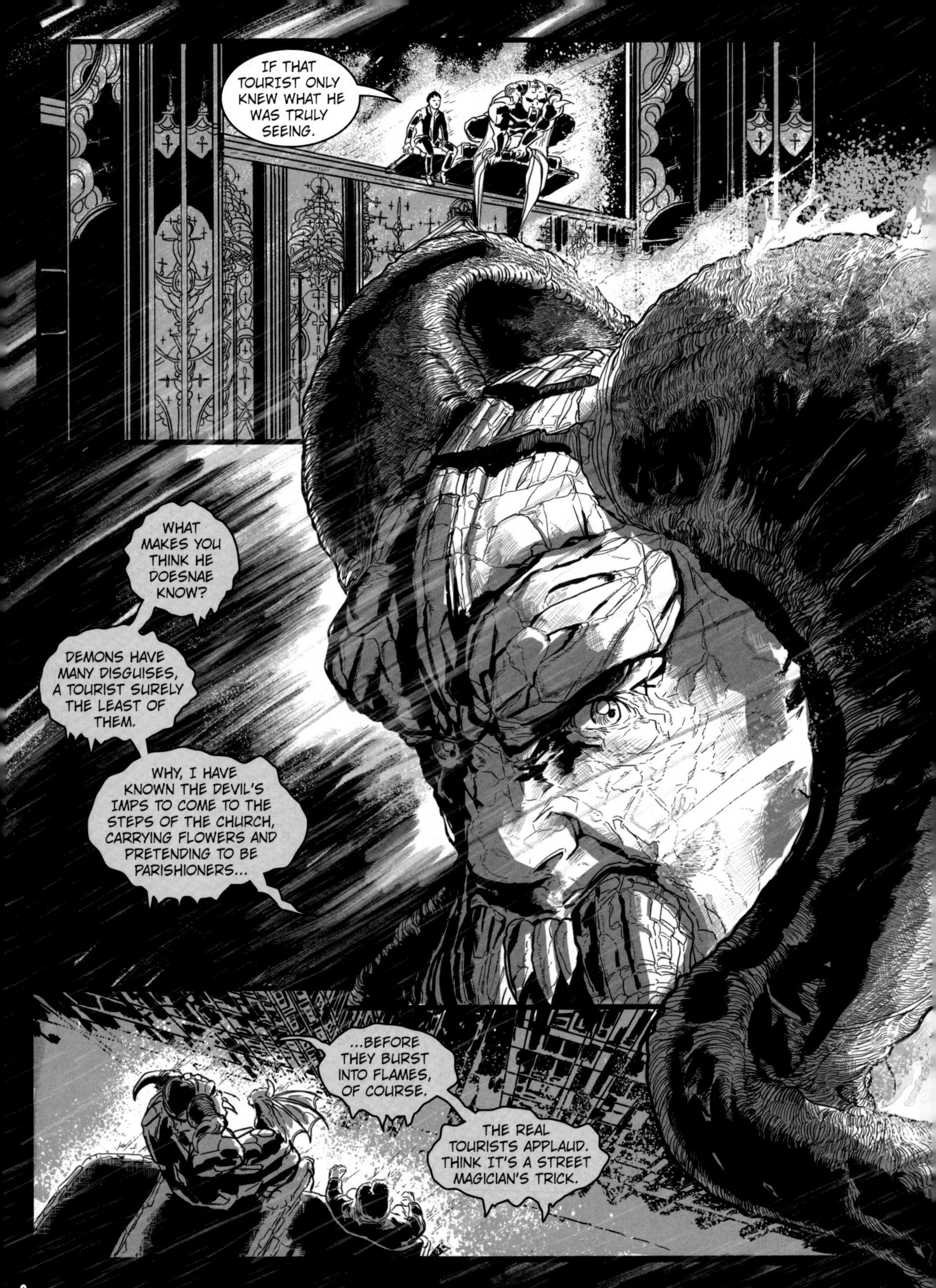
IF THAT TOURIST ONLY KNEW WHAT HE WAS TRULY SEEING.
WHAT MAKES YOU THINK HE DOESNAE KNOW?
DEMONS HAVE MANY DISGUISES, A TOURIST SURELY THE LEAST OF THEM.
WHY, I HAVE KNOWN THE DEVIL'S IMPS TO COME TO THE STEPS OF THE CHURCH, CARRYING FLOWERS AND PRETENDING TO BE PARISHIONERS...
...BEFORE THEY BURST INTO FLAMES, OF COURSE.
THE REAL TOURISTS APPLAUD. THINK IT'S A STREET MAGICIAN'S TRICK.

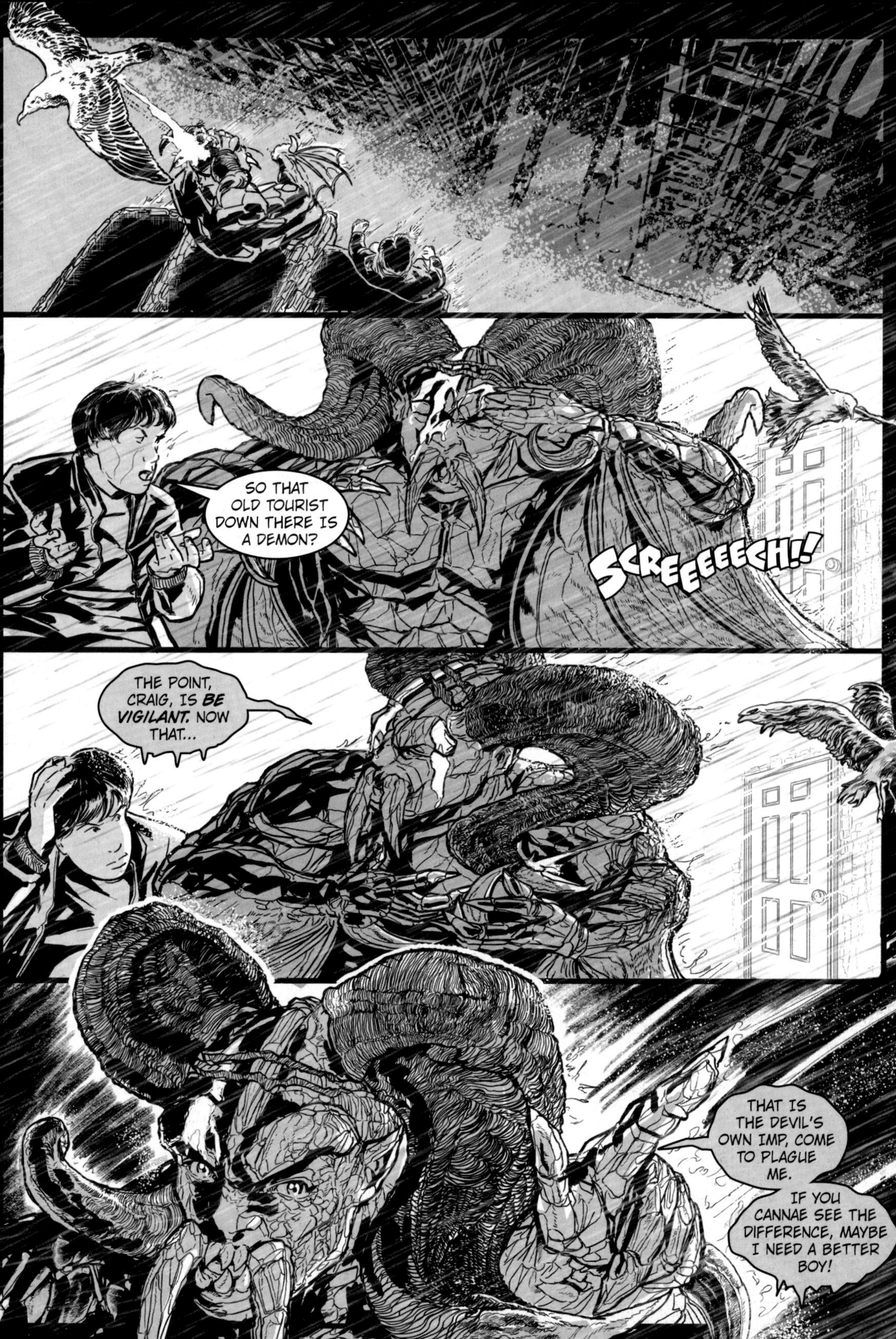
SO THAT OLD TOURIST DOWN THERE IS A DEMON?
SCREEEEEECH!!
THE POINT, CRAIG, IS BE VIGILANT. NOW THAT...
THAT IS THE DEVIL'S OWN IMP, COME TO PLAGUE ME.
IF YOU CANNAE SEE THE DIFFERENCE, MAYBE I NEED A BETTER BOY!

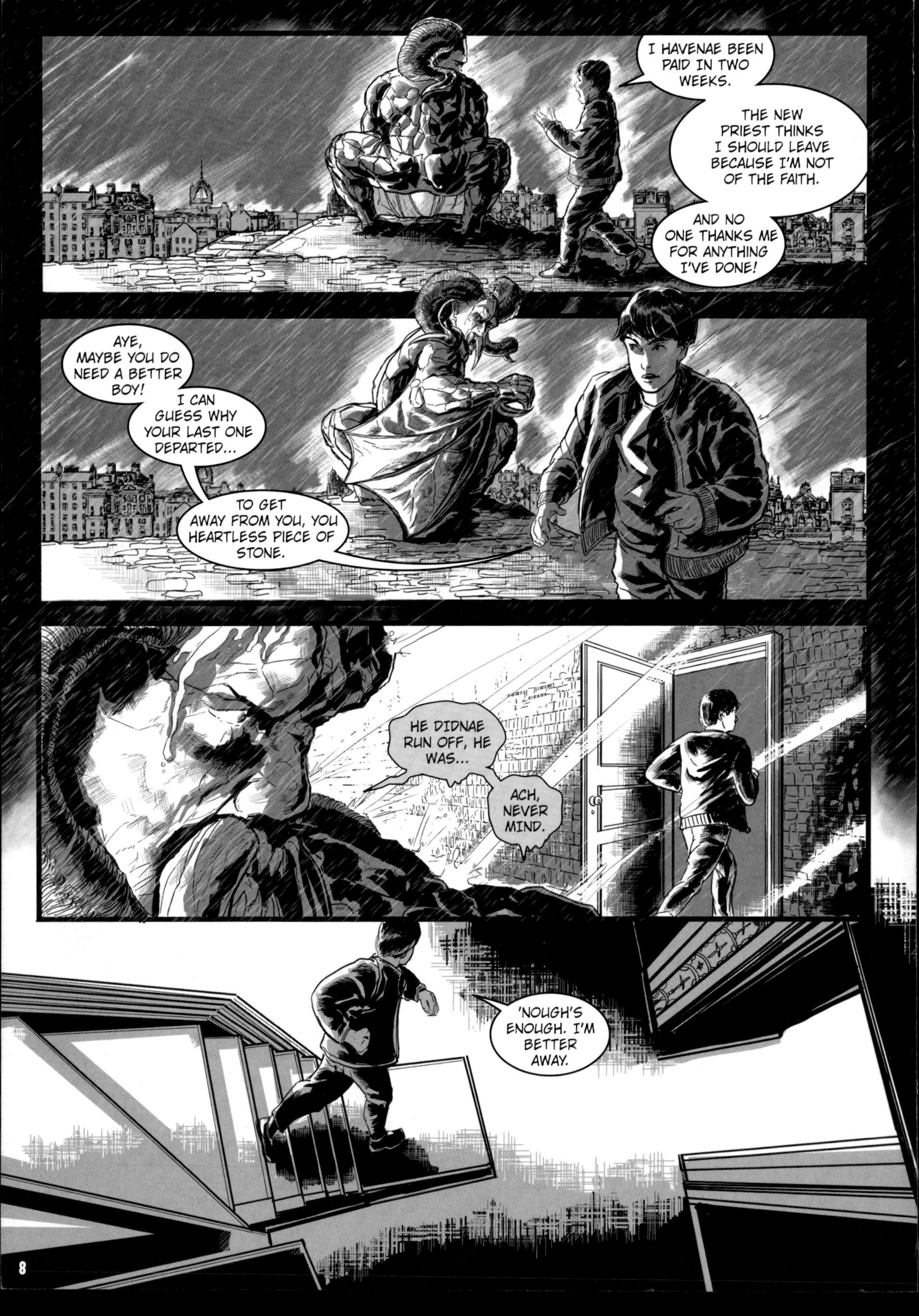
I HAVENAE BEEN PAID IN TWO WEEKS.
THE NEW PRIEST THINKS I SHOULD LEAVE BECAUSE I'M NOT OF THE FAITH.
AND NO ONE THANKS ME FOR ANYTHING I'VE DONE!
AYE, MAYBE YOU DO NEED A BETTER BOY!
I CAN GUESS WHY YOUR LAST ONE DEPARTED...
TO GET AWAY FROM YOU, YOU HEARTLESS PIECE OF STONE.
HE DIDNAE RUN OFF, HE WAS...
ACH, NEVER MIND.
'NOUGH'S ENOUGH. I'M BETTER AWAY.

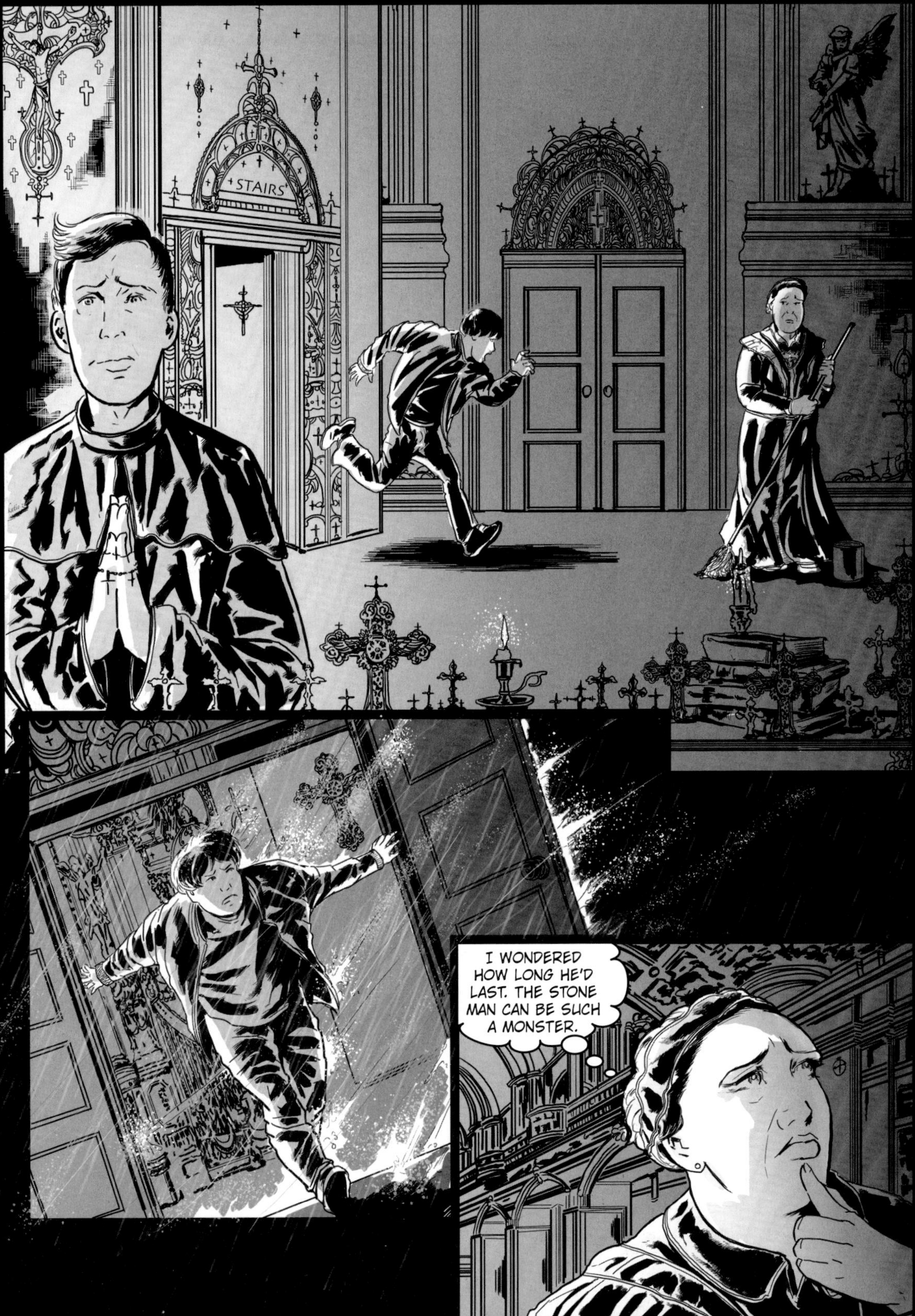
STAIRS
I WONDERED HOW LONG HE'D LAST. THE STONE MAN CAN BE SUCH A MONSTER.

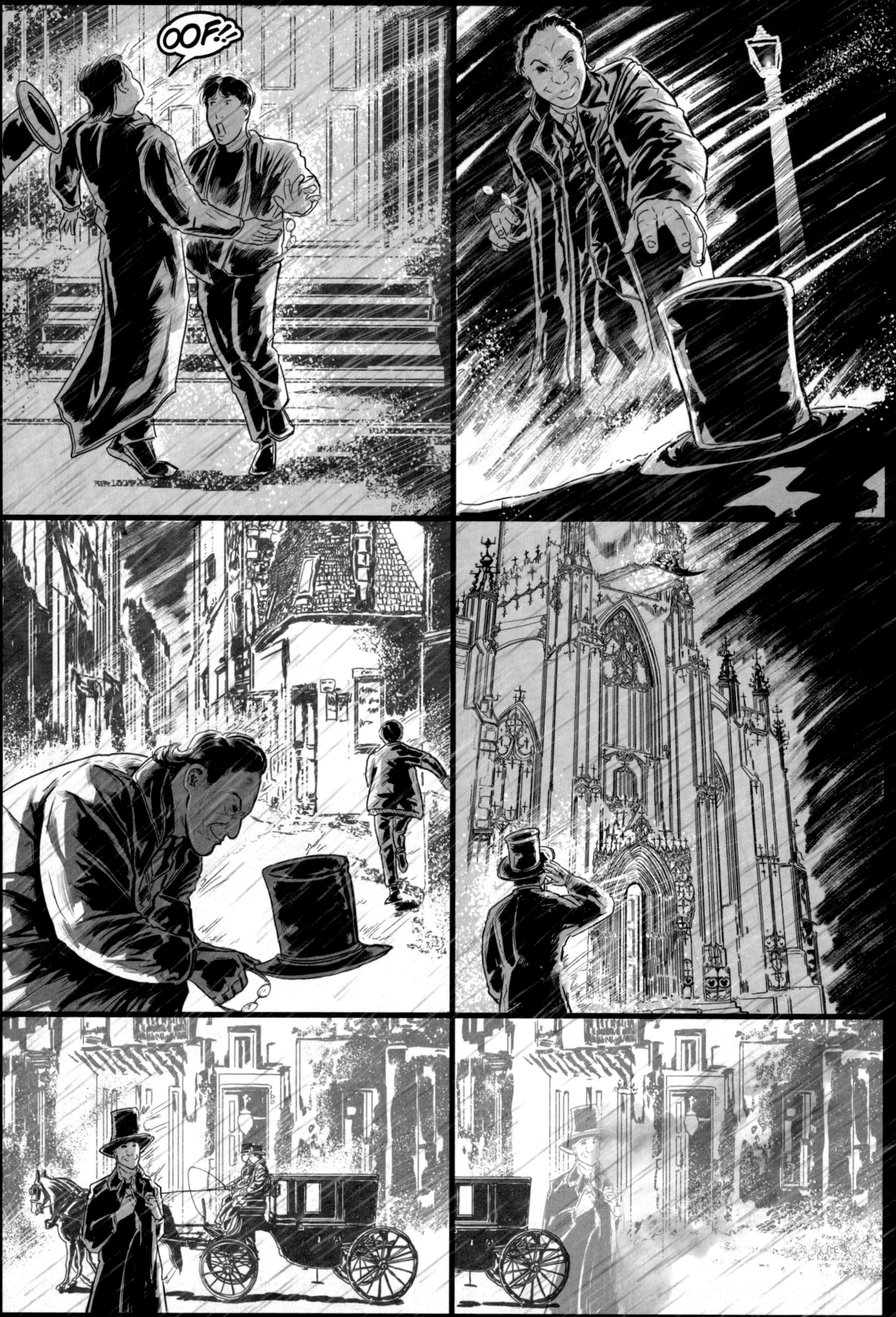
OOF!!

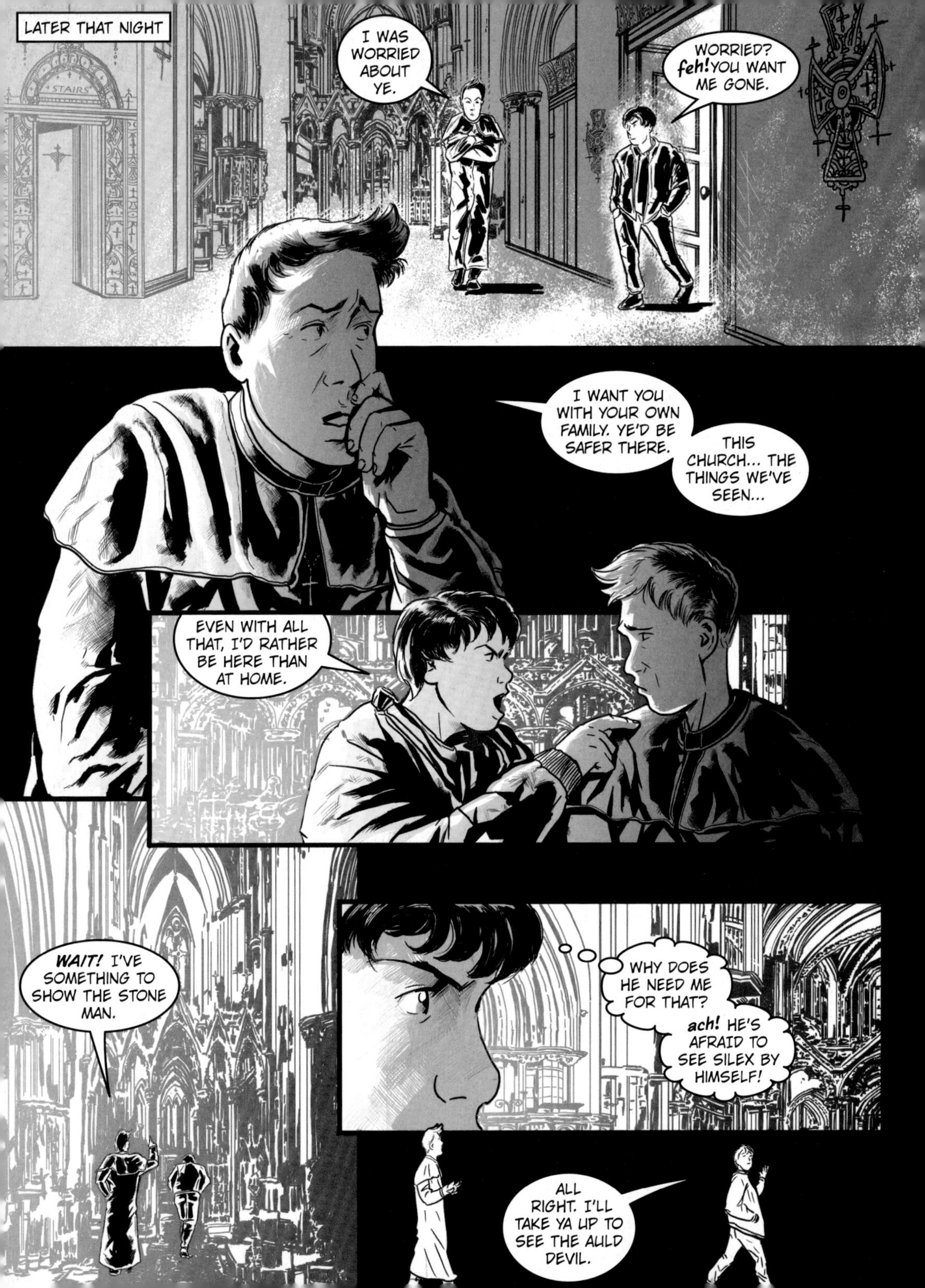
LATER THAT NIGHT
STAIRS
I WAS WORRIED ABOUT YE.
WORRIED? feh! YOU WANT ME GONE.
I WANT YOU WITH YOUR OWN FAMILY. YE'D BE SAFER THERE.
THIS CHURCH... THE THINGS WE'VE SEEN...
EVEN WITH ALL THAT, I'D RATHER BE HERE THAN AT HOME.
WAIT! I'VE SOMETHING TO SHOW THE STONE MAN.
WHY DOES HE NEED ME FOR THAT?
ach! HE'S AFRAID TO SEE SILEX BY HIMSELF!
ALL RIGHT. I'LL TAKE YA UP TO SEE THE AULD DEVIL.

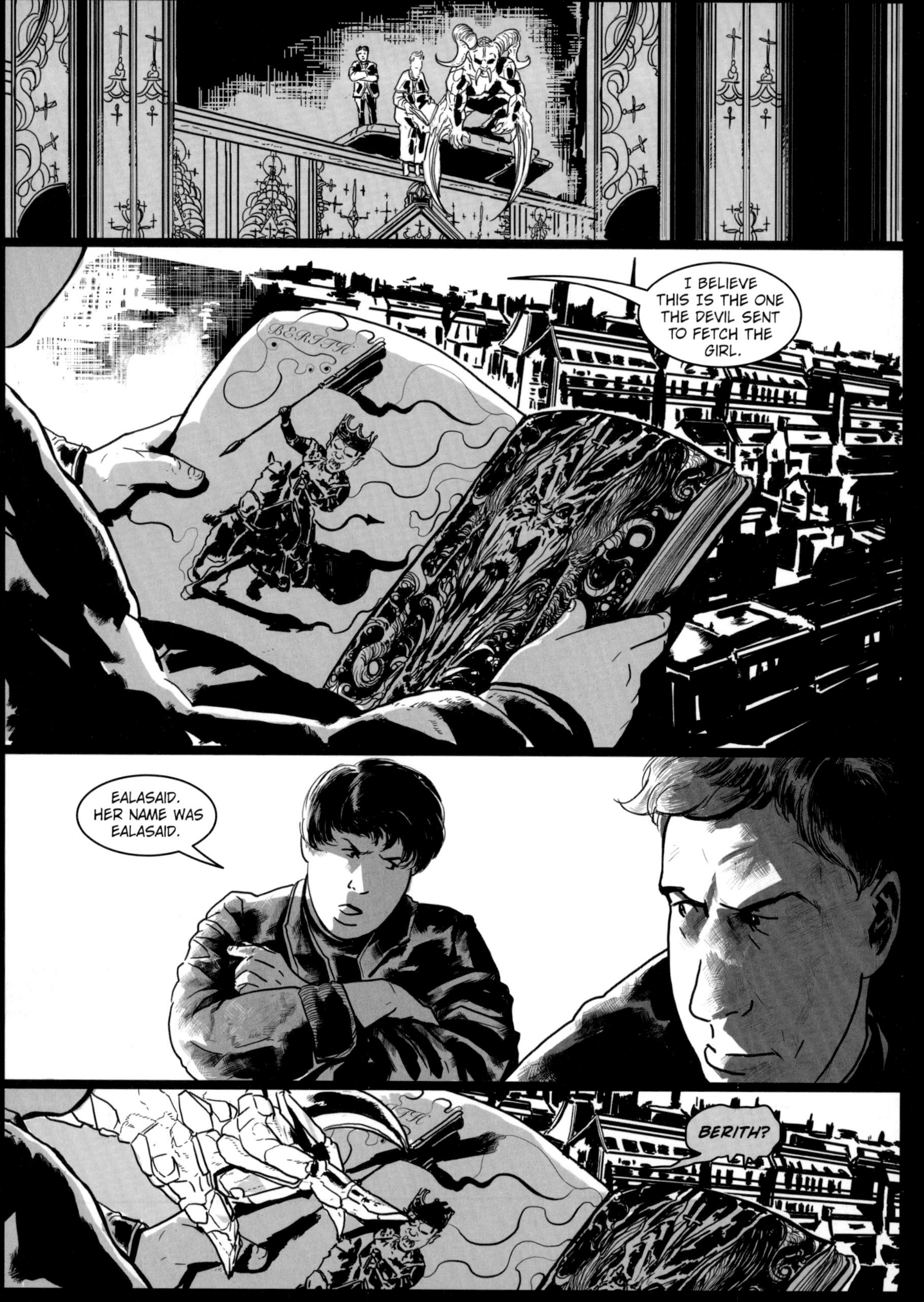
BERITH
I BELIEVE THIS IS THE ONE THE DEVIL SENT TO FETCH THE GIRL.
EALASAID. HER NAME WAS EALASAID.
BERITH?

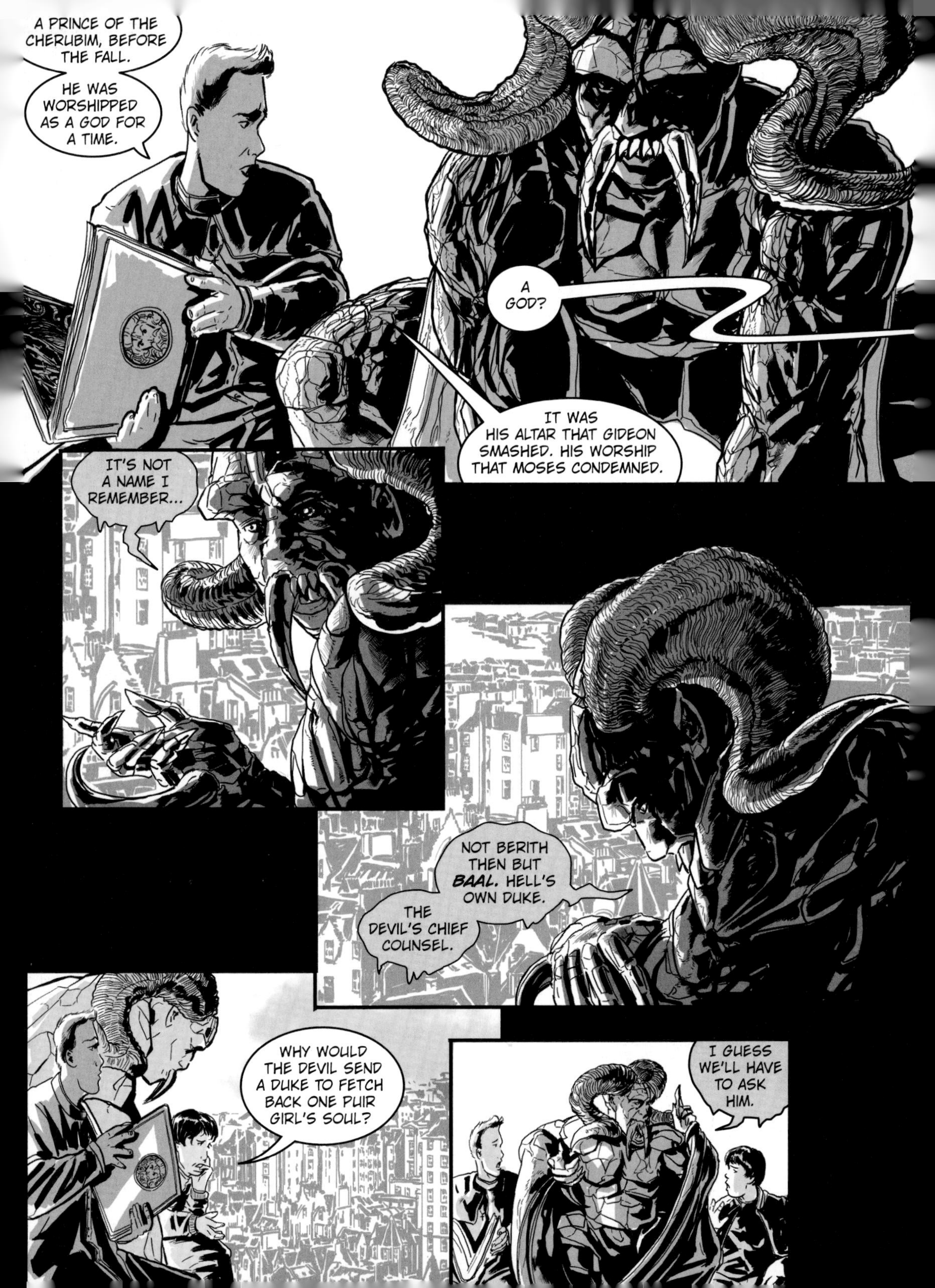
A PRINCE OF THE CHERUBIM, BEFORE THE FALL.
HE WAS WORSHIPPED AS A GOD FOR A TIME.
A GOD?
IT WAS HIS ALTAR THAT GIDEON SMASHED. HIS WORSHIP THAT MOSES CONDEMNED.
IT'S NOT A NAME I REMEMBER...
NOT BERITH THEN BUT BAAL. HELL'S OWN DUKE.
THE DEVIL'S CHIEF COUNSEL.
WHY WOULD THE DEVIL SEND A DUKE TO FETCH BACK ONE PUIR GIRL'S SOUL?
I GUESS WE'LL HAVE TO ASK HIM.

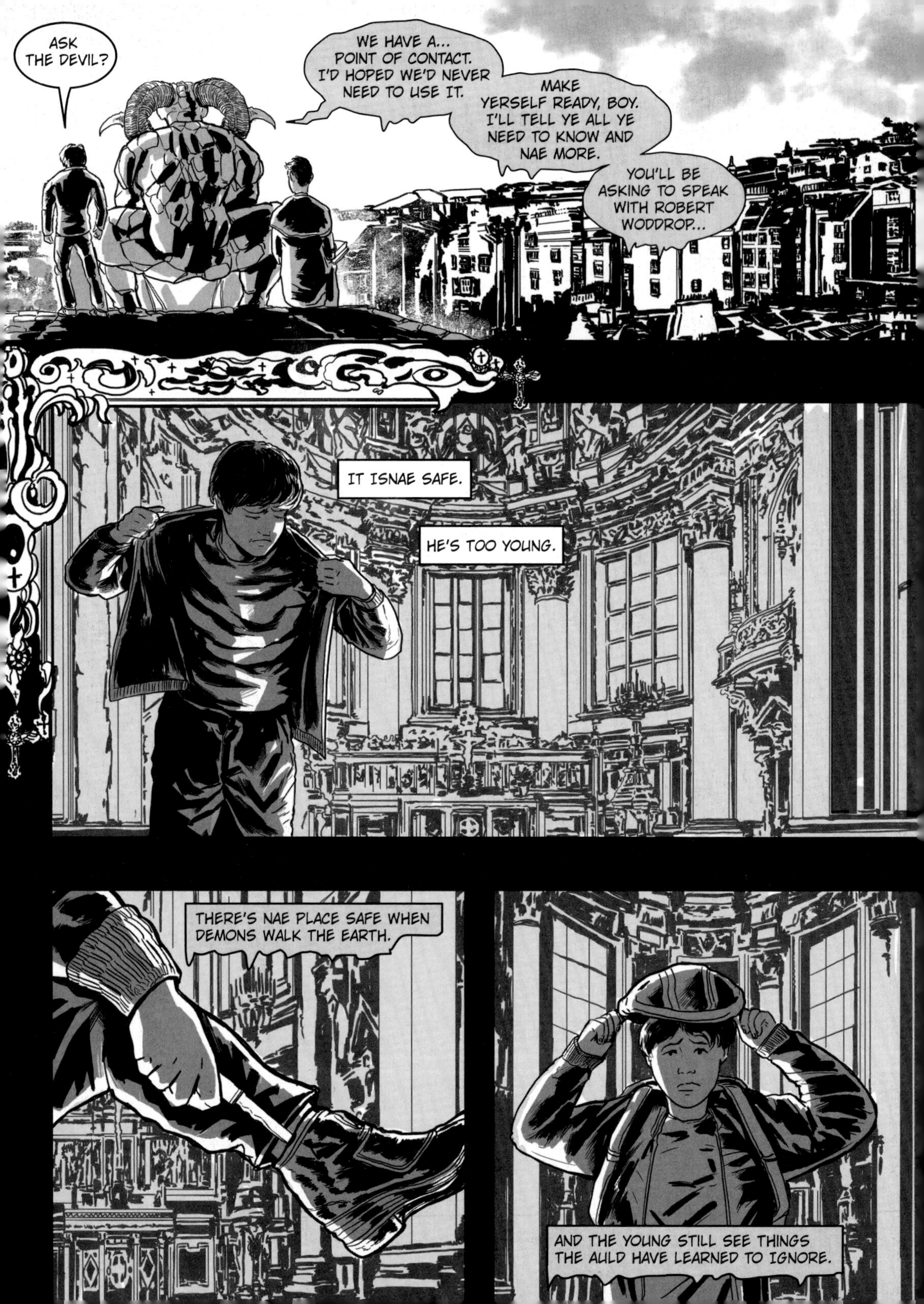
ASK THE DEVIL?
WE HAVE A... POINT OF CONTACT. I'D HOPED WE'D NEVER NEED TO USE IT.
MAKE YERSELF READY, BOY. I'LL TELL YE ALL YE NEED TO KNOW AND NAE MORE.
YOU'LL BE ASKING TO SPEAK WITH ROBERT WODDROP...
IT ISNAE SAFE.
HE'S TOO YOUNG.
THERE'S NAE PLACE SAFE WHEN DEMONS WALK THE EARTH.
AND THE YOUNG STILL SEE THINGS THE AULD HAVE LEARNED TO IGNORE.

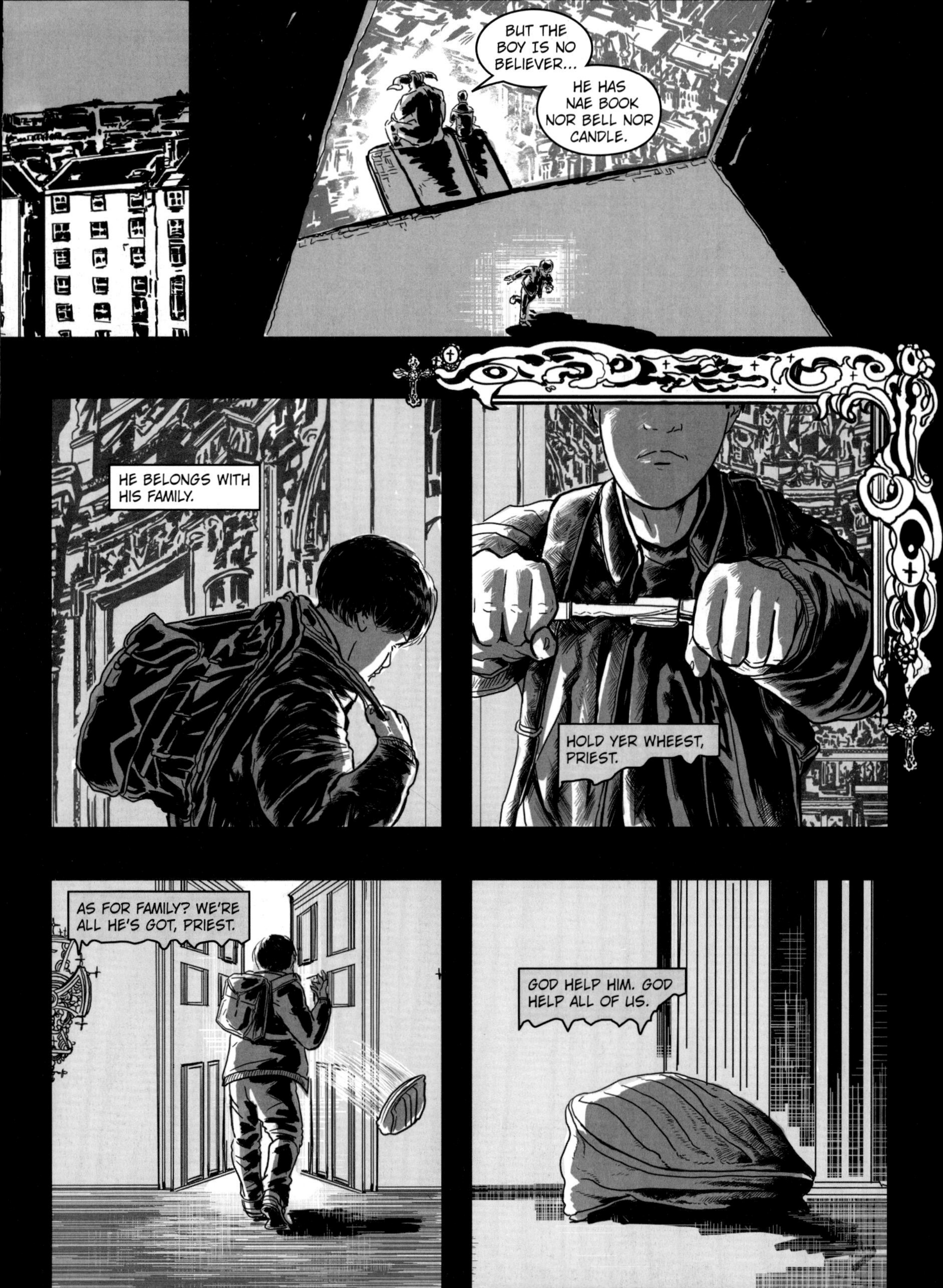
BUT THE BOY IS NO BELIEVER...
HE HAS NAE BOOK NOR BELL NOR CANDLE.
HE BELONGS WITH HIS FAMILY.
HOLD YER WHEEST, PRIEST.
AS FOR FAMILY? WE'RE ALL HE'S GOT, PRIEST.
GOD HELP HIM. GOD HELP ALL OF US.

CHAPTER 2
ASYLUM

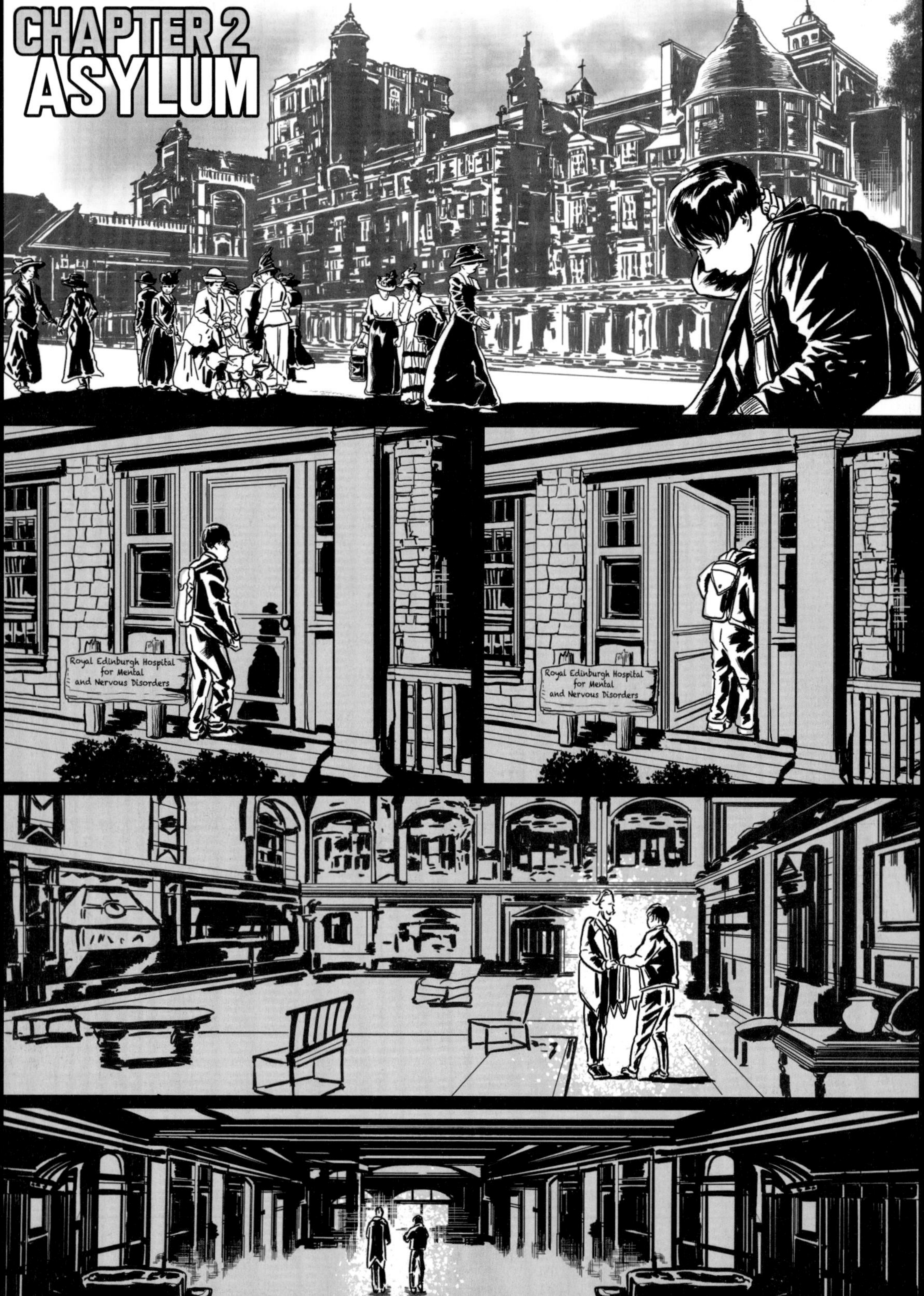
Royal Edinburgh Hospital
for Mental
and Nervous Disorders
Royal Edinburgh Hospital
for Mental
and Nervous Disorders

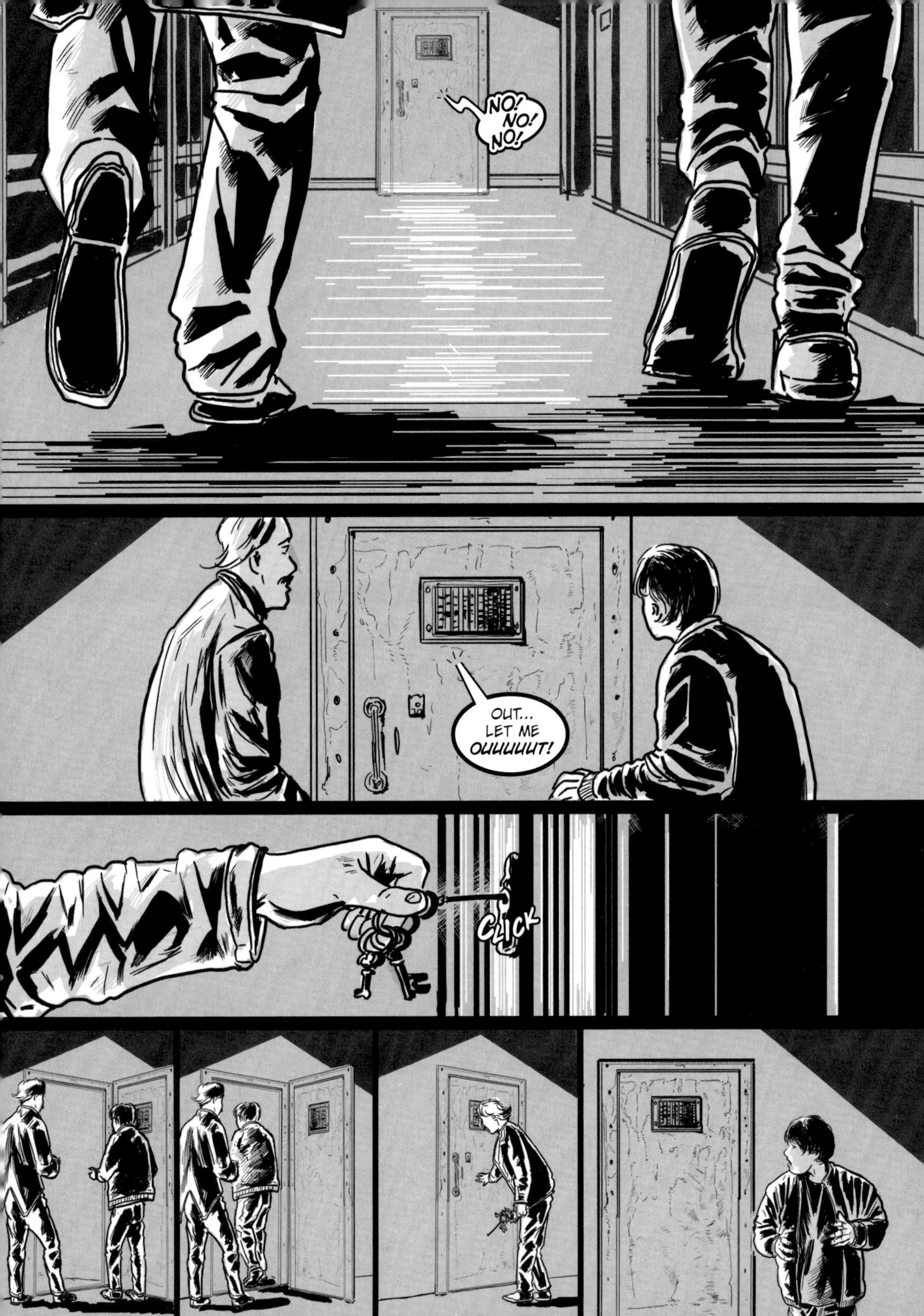
NO! NO! NO!
OUT... LET ME OUUUUUT!
CLICK

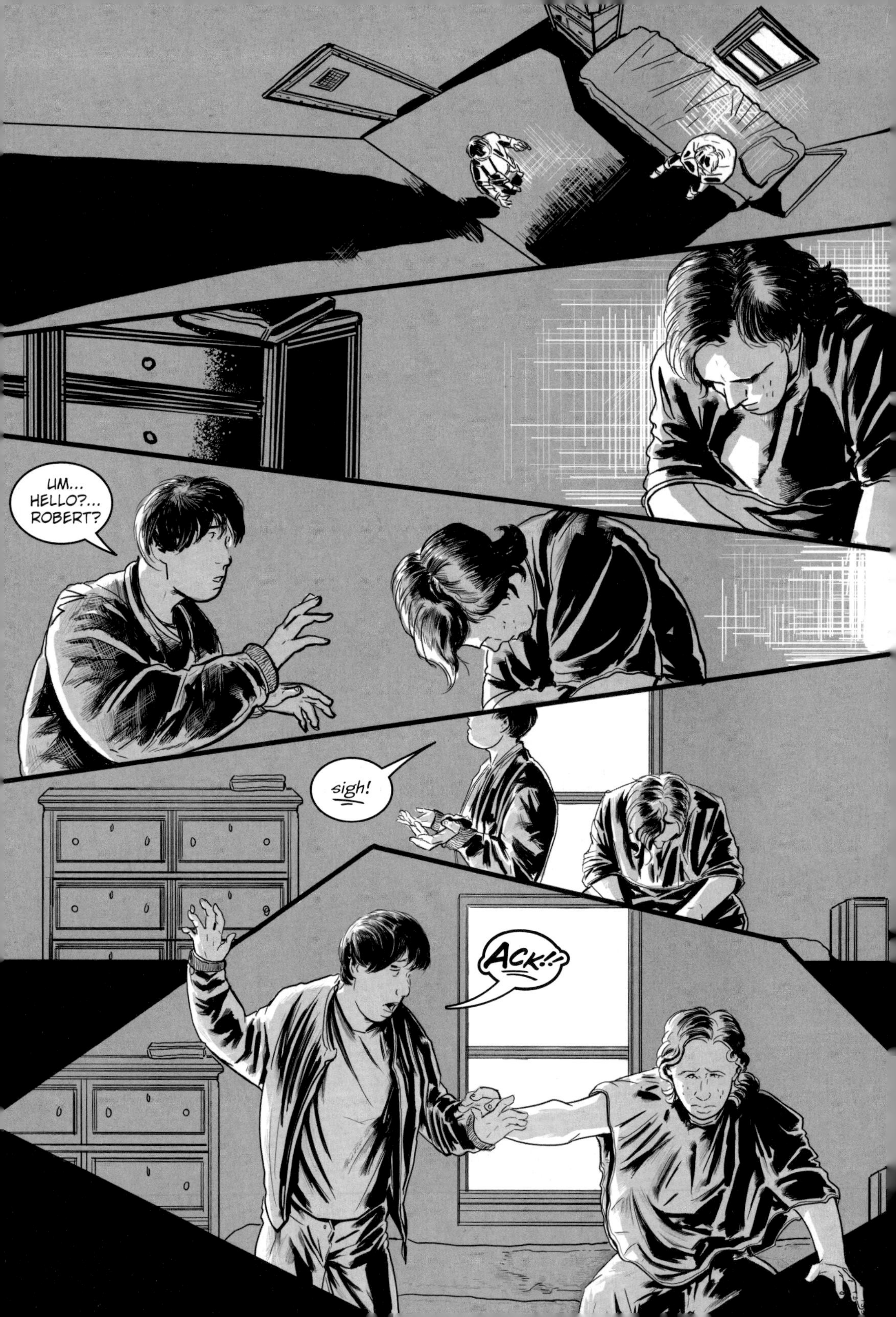
UM... HELLO?... ROBERT?
sigh!
ACK!!

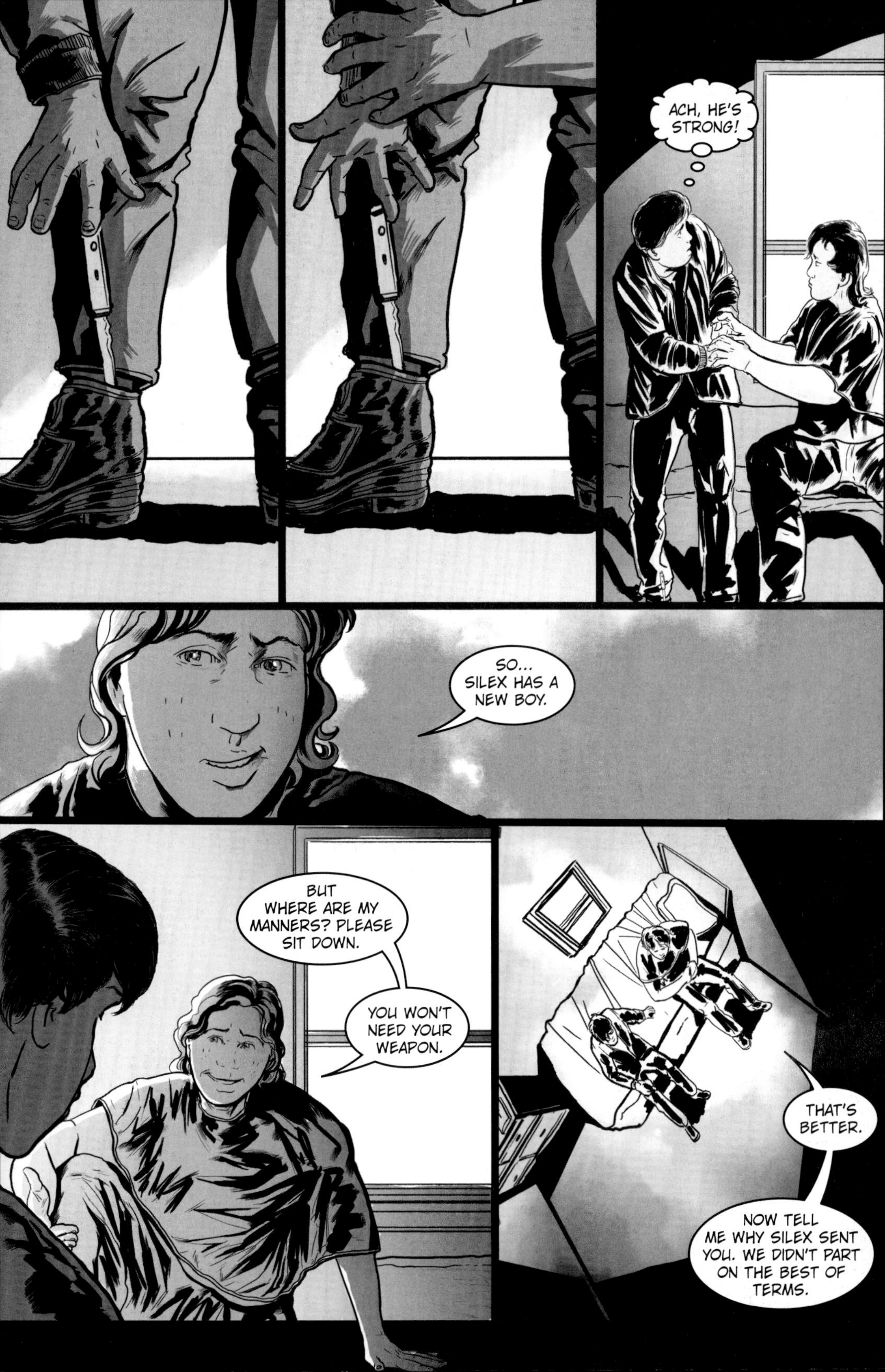
ACH, HE'S STRONG!
SO... SILEX HAS A NEW BOY.
BUT WHERE ARE MY MANNERS? PLEASE SIT DOWN.
YOU WON'T NEED YOUR WEAPON.
THAT'S BETTER.
NOW TELL ME WHY SILEX SENT YOU. WE DIDN'T PART ON THE BEST OF TERMS.

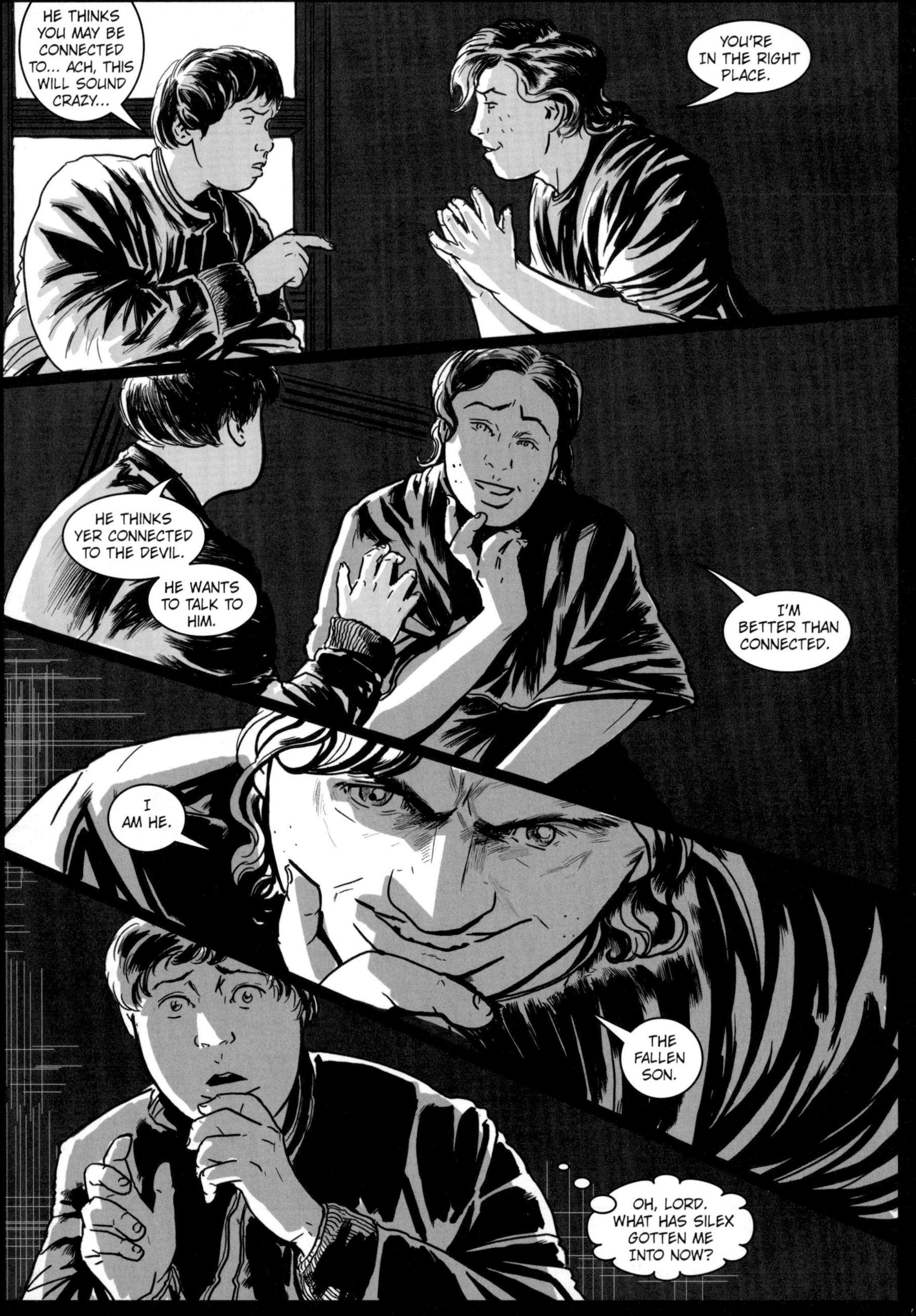
HE THINKS YOU MAY BE CONNECTED TO... ACH, THIS WILL SOUND CRAZY...
YOU'RE IN THE RIGHT PLACE.
HE THINKS YER CONNECTED TO THE DEVIL.
HE WANTS TO TALK TO HIM.
I'M BETTER THAN CONNECTED.
I AM HE.
THE FALLEN SON.
OH, LORD. WHAT HAS SILEX GOTTEN ME INTO NOW?

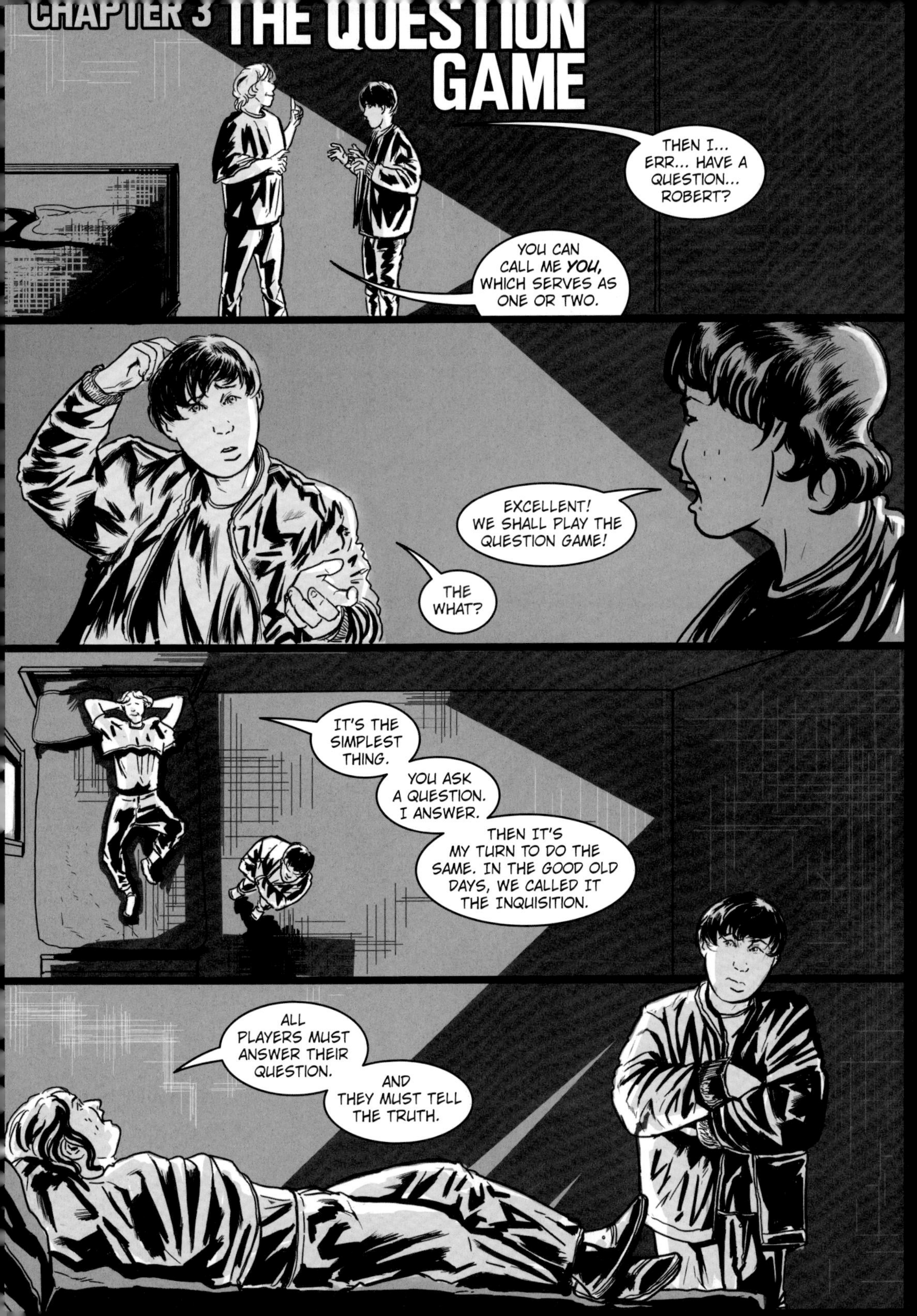
CHAPTER 3 THE QUESTION GAME
THEN I... ERR... HAVE A QUESTION... ROBERT?
YOU CAN CALL ME *YOU,* WHICH SERVES AS ONE OR TWO.
EXCELLENT! WE SHALL PLAY THE QUESTION GAME!
THE WHAT?
IT'S THE SIMPLEST THING.
YOU ASK A QUESTION. I ANSWER.
THEN IT'S MY TURN TO DO THE SAME. IN THE GOOD OLD DAYS, WE CALLED IT THE INQUISITION.
ALL PLAYERS MUST ANSWER THEIR QUESTION.
AND THEY MUST TELL THE TRUTH.

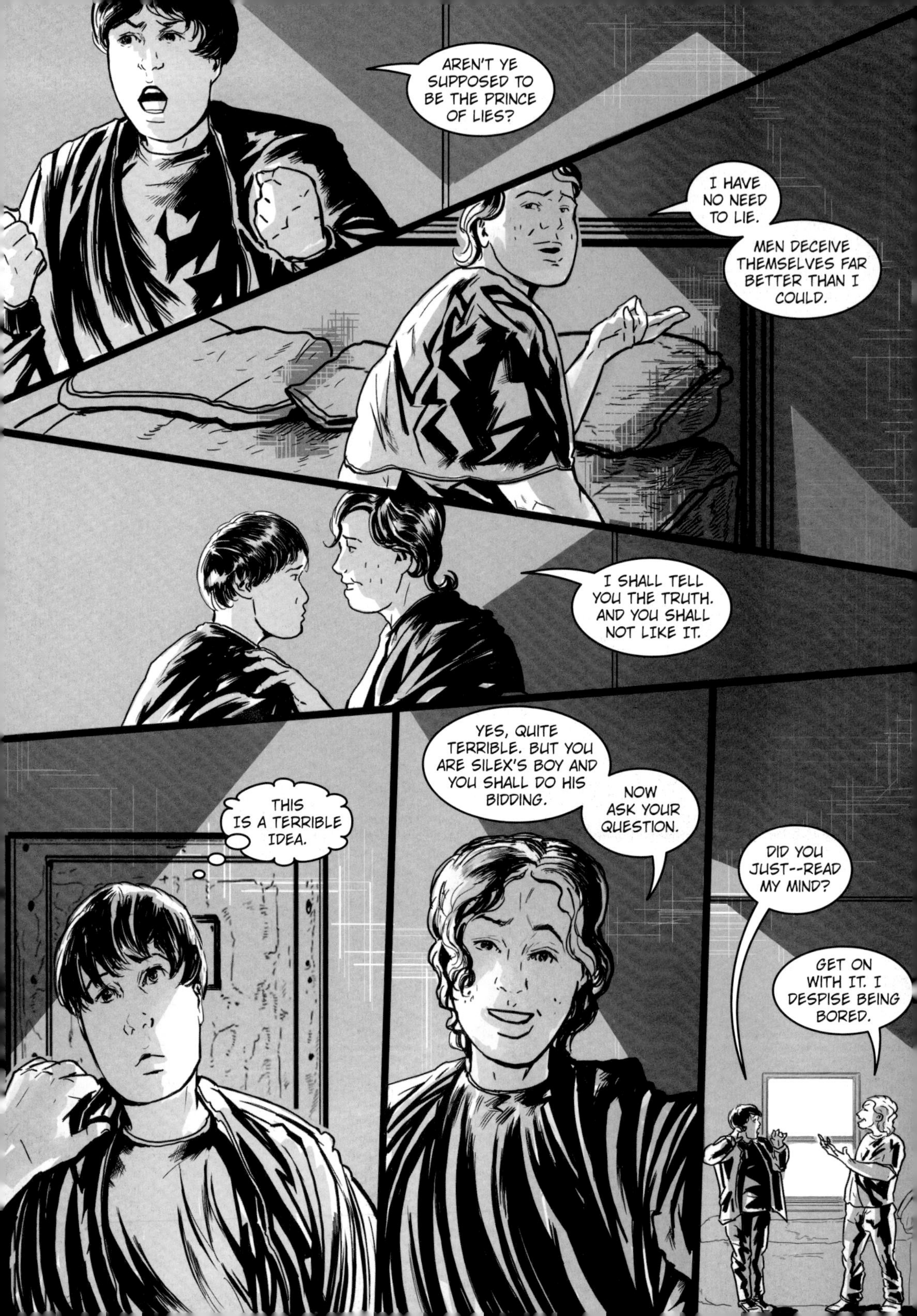
AREN'T YE SUPPOSED TO BE THE PRINCE OF LIES?
I HAVE NO NEED TO LIE.
MEN DECEIVE THEMSELVES FAR BETTER THAN I COULD.
I SHALL TELL YOU THE TRUTH. AND YOU SHALL NOT LIKE IT.
THIS IS A TERRIBLE IDEA.
YES, QUITE TERRIBLE. BUT YOU ARE SILEX'S BOY AND YOU SHALL DO HIS BIDDING.
NOW ASK YOUR QUESTION.
DID YOU JUST--READ MY MIND?
GET ON WITH IT. I DESPISE BEING BORED.

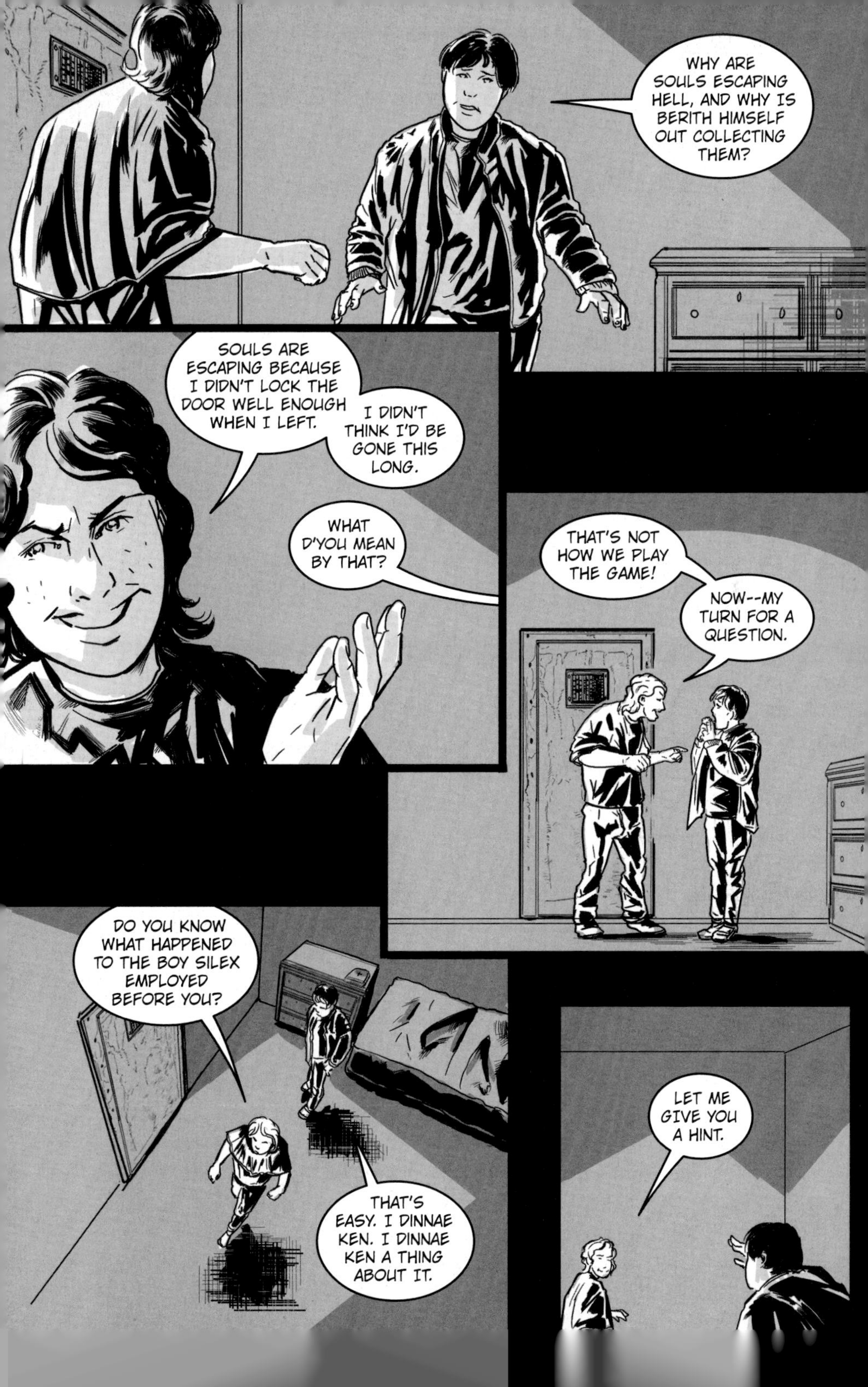
WHY ARE SOULS ESCAPING HELL, AND WHY IS BERITH HIMSELF OUT COLLECTING THEM?
SOULS ARE ESCAPING BECAUSE I DIDN'T LOCK THE DOOR WELL ENOUGH WHEN I LEFT.
I DIDN'T THINK I'D BE GONE THIS LONG.
WHAT D'YOU MEAN BY THAT?
THAT'S NOT HOW WE PLAY THE GAME!
NOW--MY TURN FOR A QUESTION.
DO YOU KNOW WHAT HAPPENED TO THE BOY SILEX EMPLOYED BEFORE YOU?
THAT'S EASY. I DINNAE KEN. I DINNAE KEN A THING ABOUT IT.
LET ME GIVE YOU A HINT.

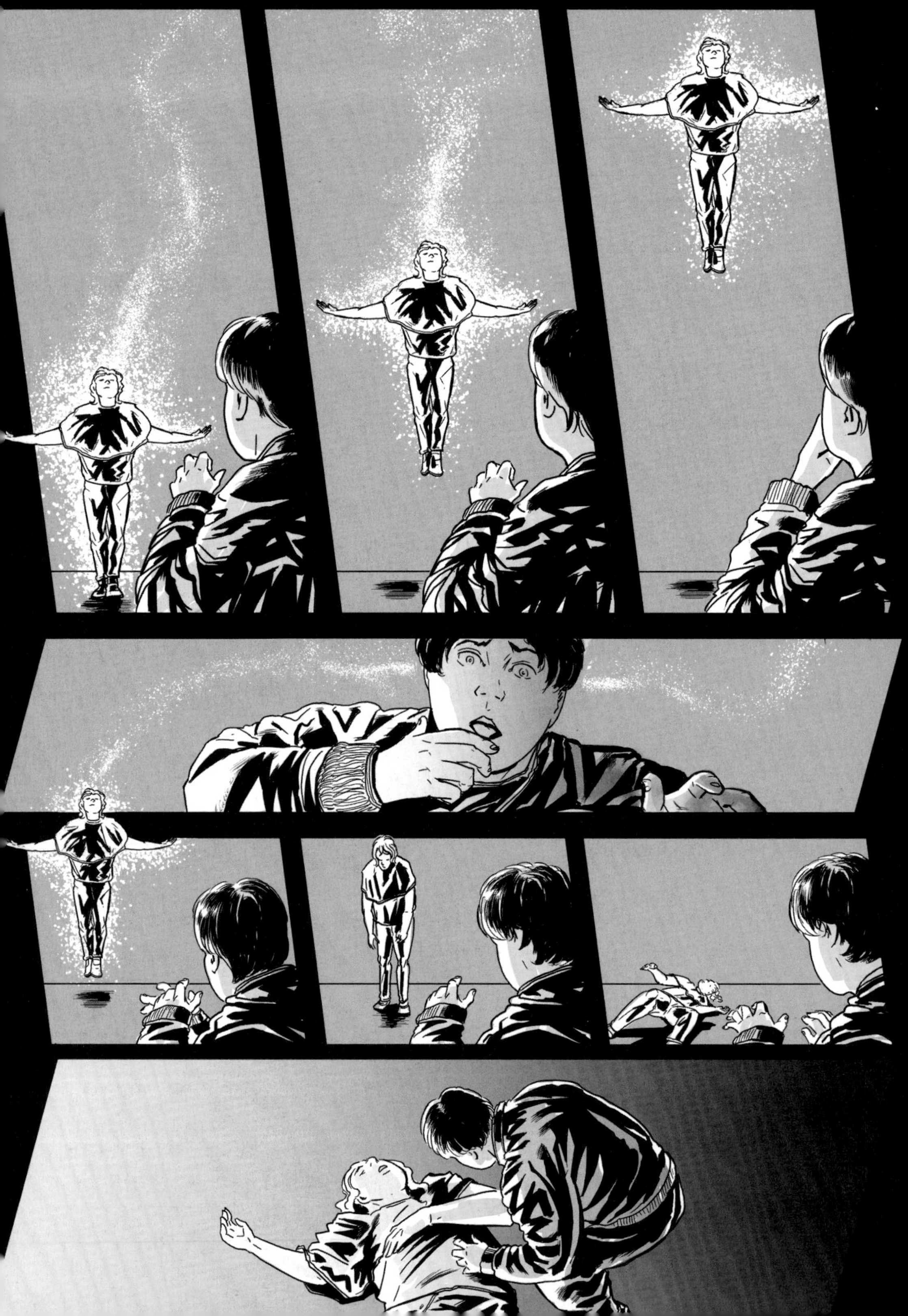

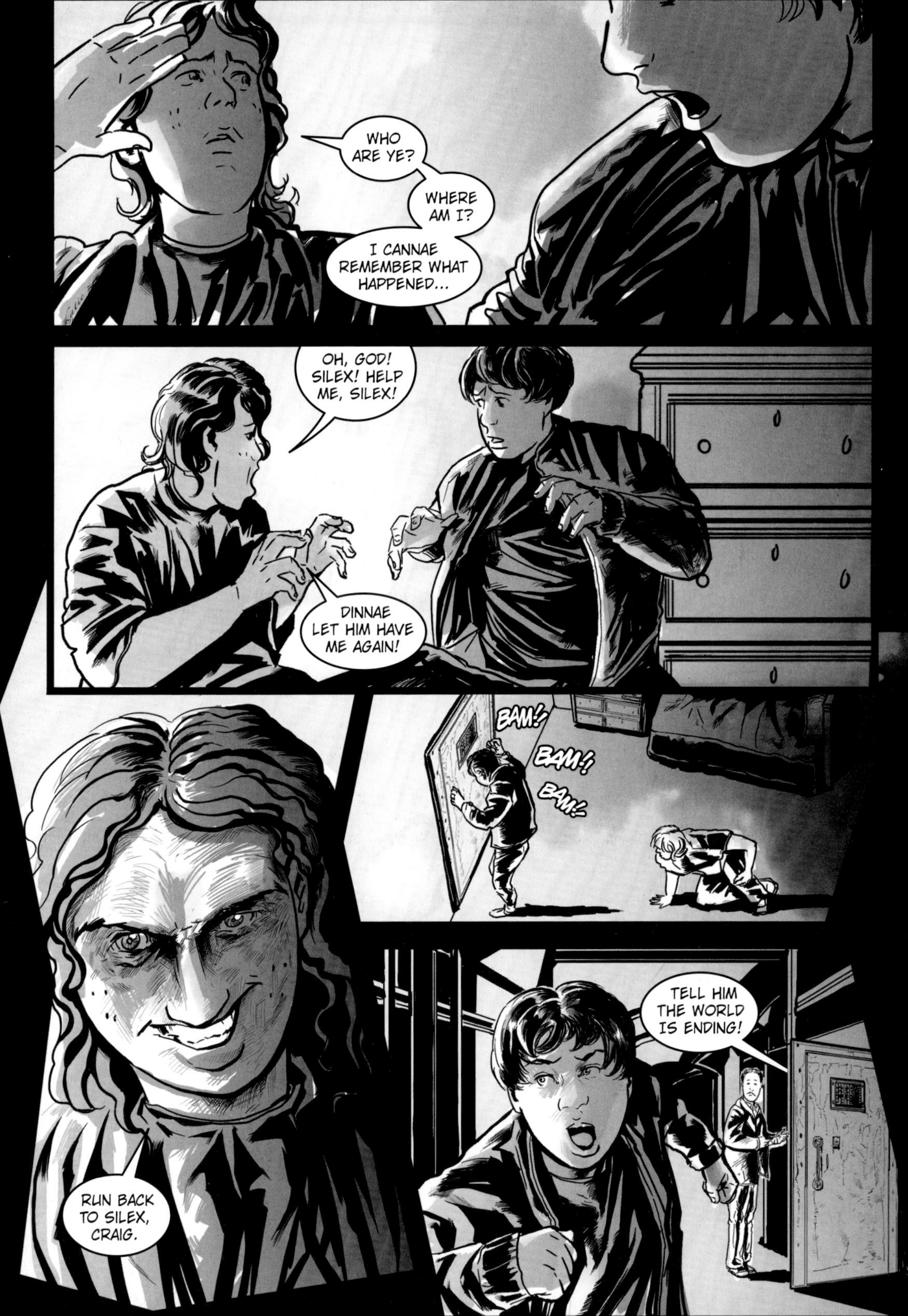

WHO ARE YE?
WHERE AM I?
I CANNAE REMEMBER WHAT HAPPENED...
OH, GOD! SILEX! HELP ME, SILEX!
DINNAE LET HIM HAVE ME AGAIN!
BAM!
BAM!
BAM!
RUN BACK TO SILEX, CRAIG.
TELL HIM THE WORLD IS ENDING!

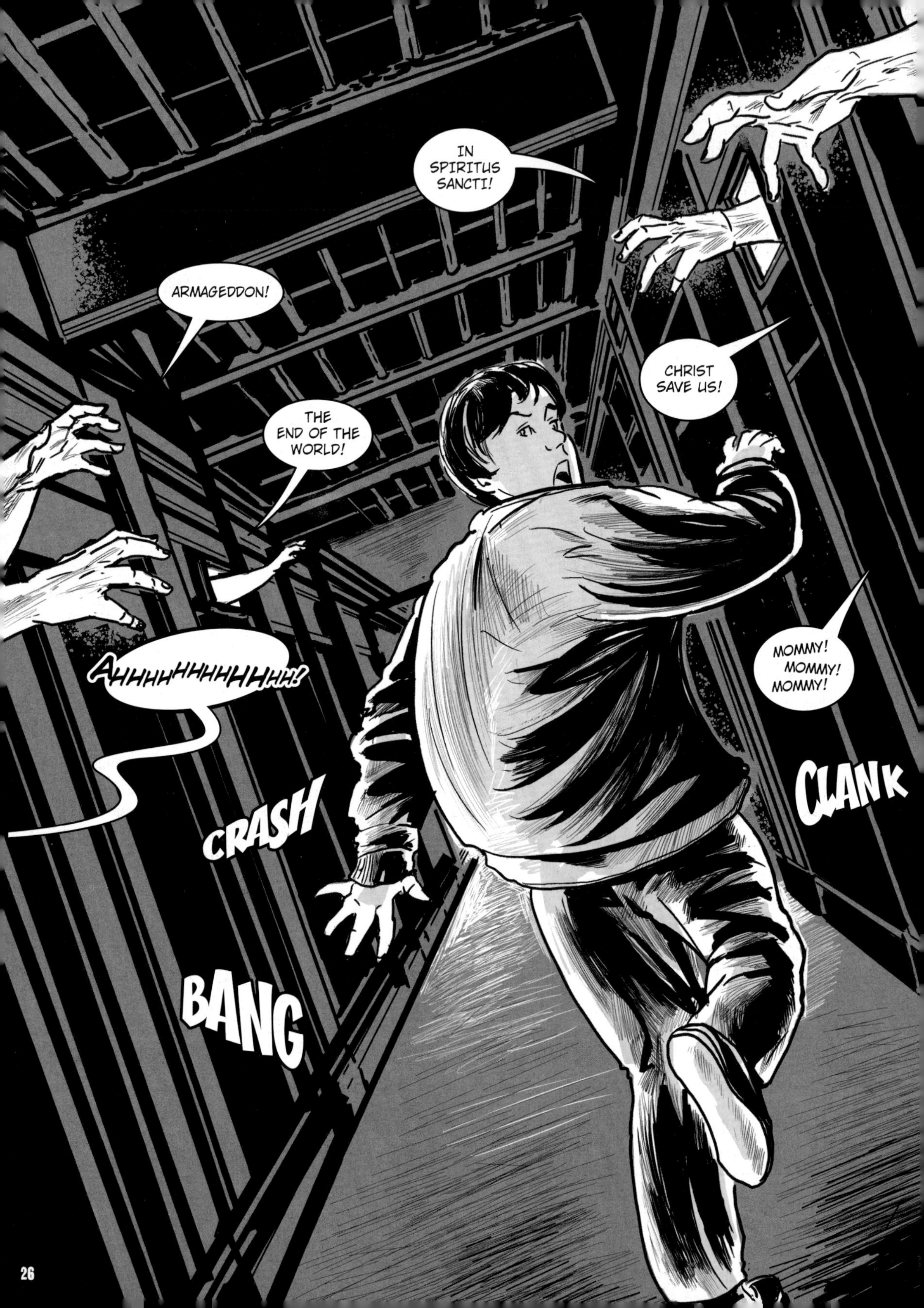
IN SPIRITUS SANCTI!
ARMAGEDDON!
CHRIST SAVE US!
THE END OF THE WORLD!
AHHHHHHHHHHH!
MOMMY! MOMMY! MOMMY!
CRASH
CLANK
BANG

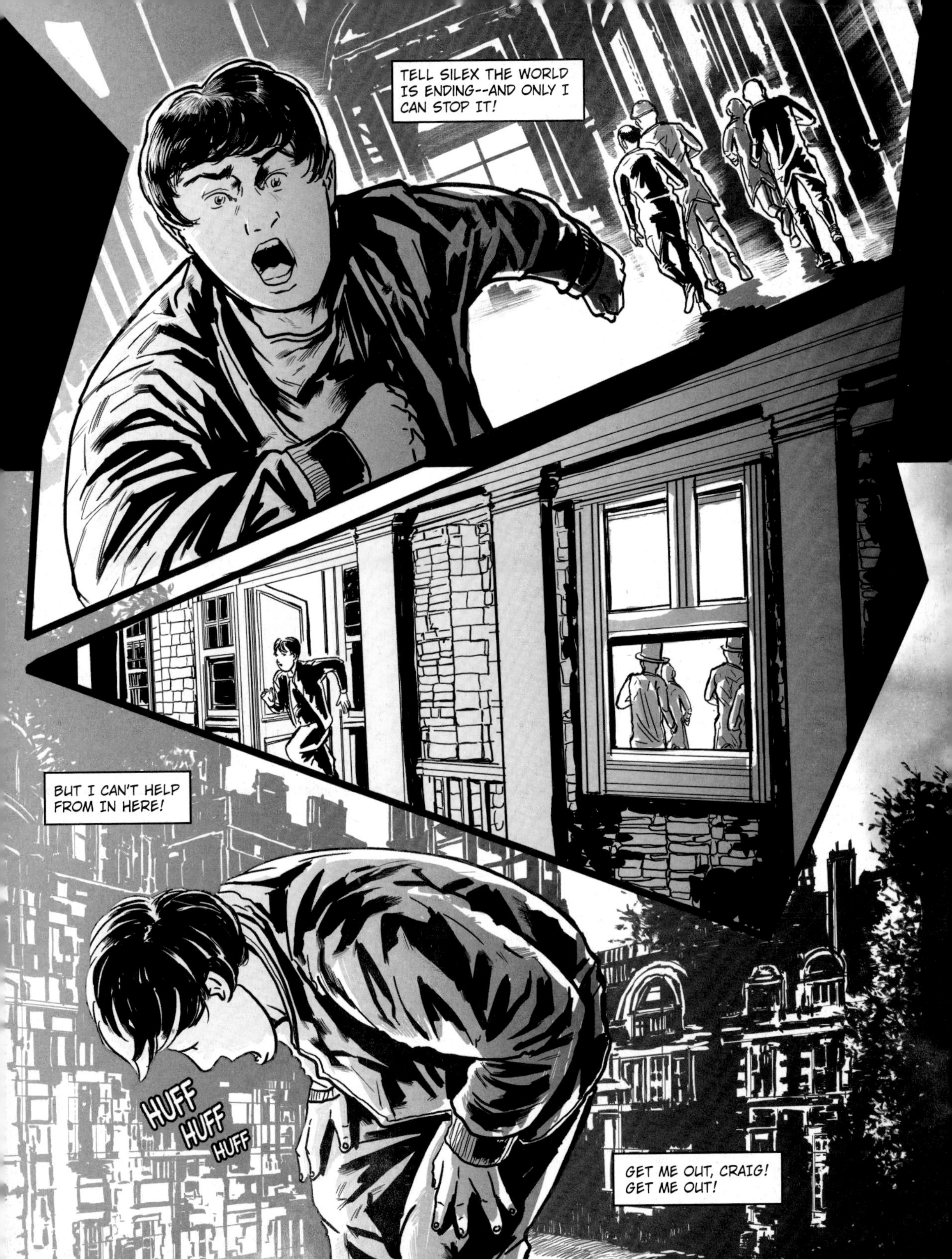
TELL SILEX THE WORLD IS ENDING--AND ONLY I CAN STOP IT!
BUT I CAN'T HELP FROM IN HERE!
HUFF HUFF HUFF
GET ME OUT, CRAIG! GET ME OUT!

CHAPTER 4
ROOFTOP PLANS

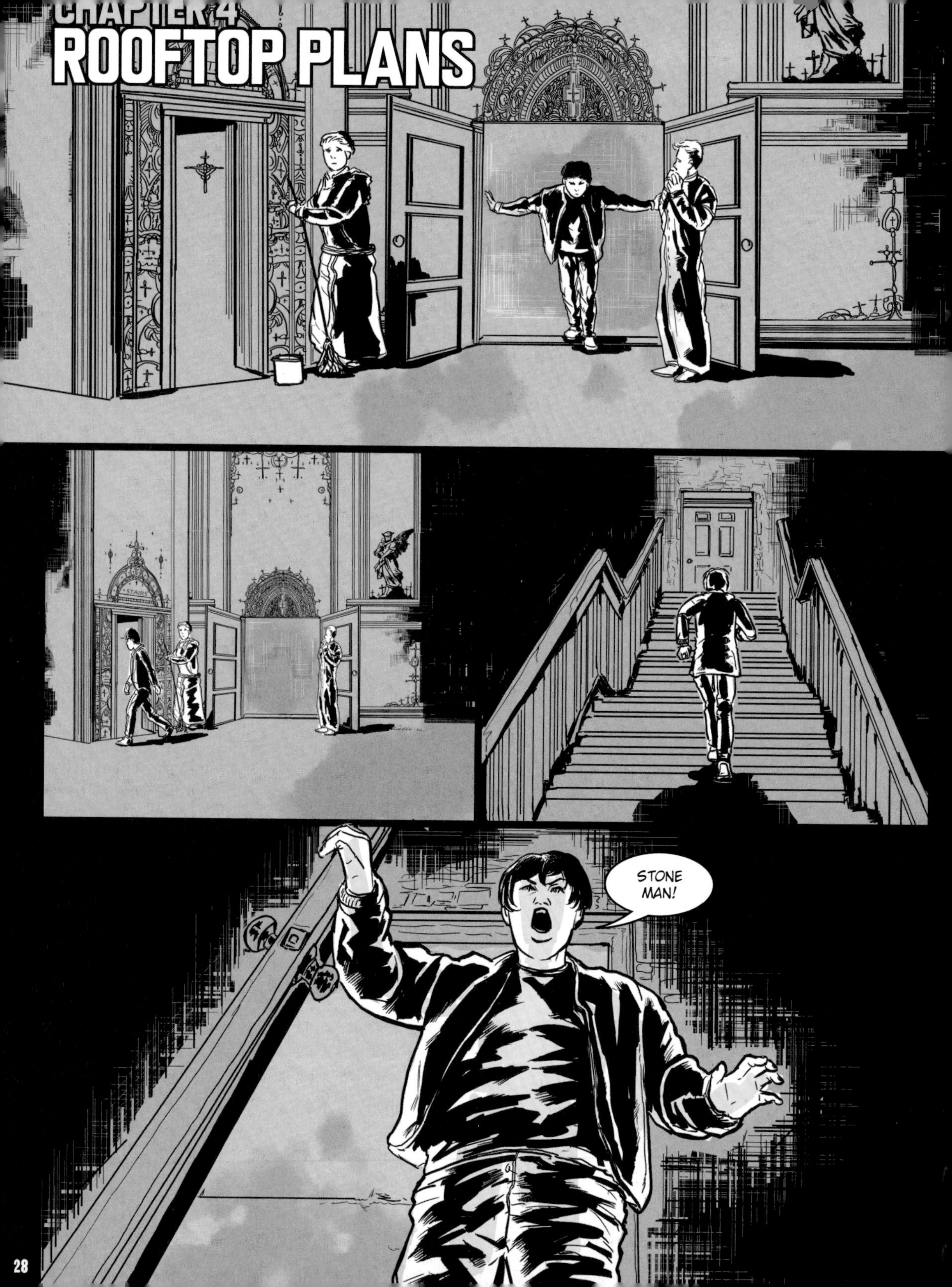
STAIRS
STONE MAN!

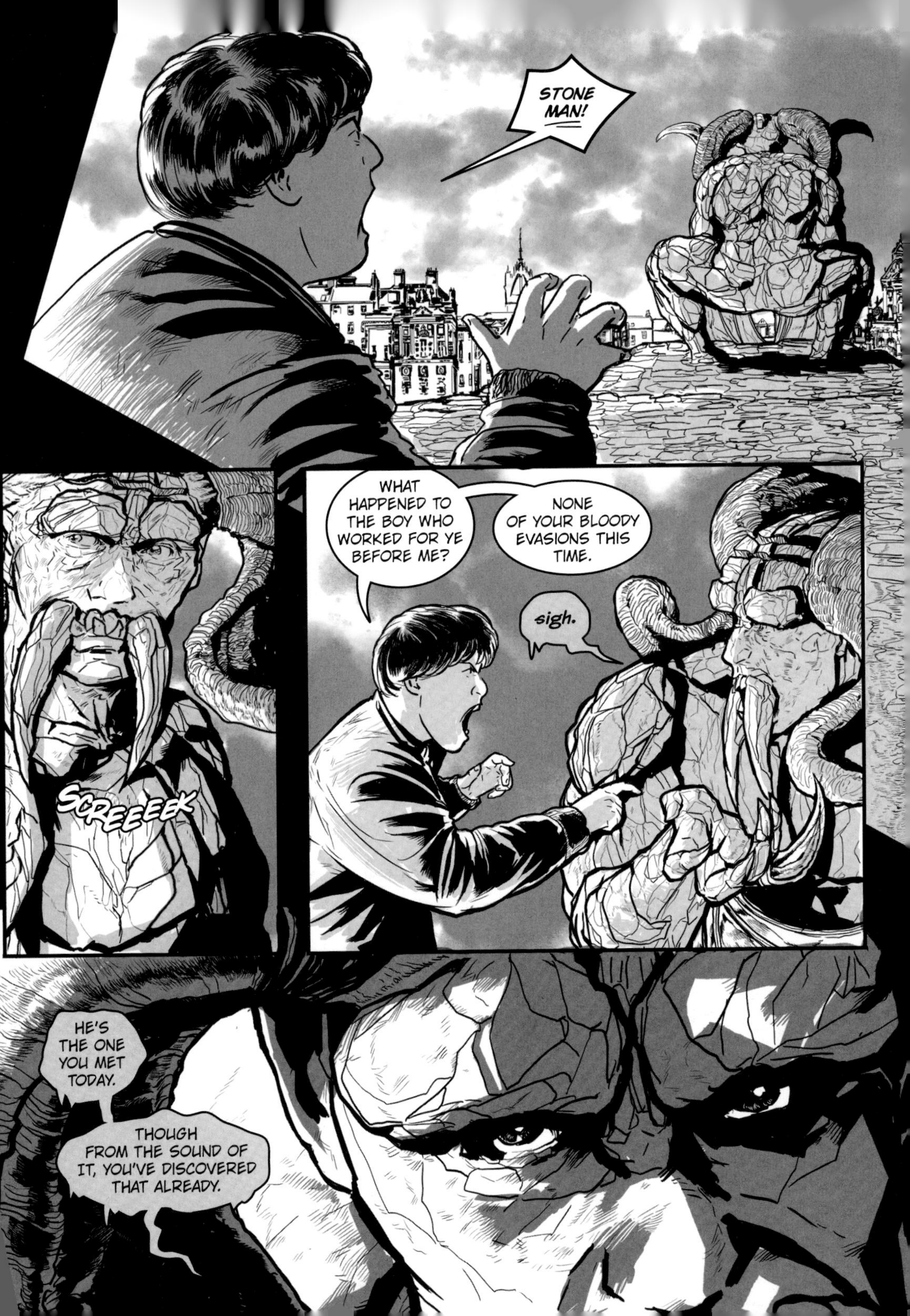
STONE MAN!
WHAT HAPPENED TO THE BOY WHO WORKED FOR YE BEFORE ME?
NONE OF YOUR BLOODY EVASIONS THIS TIME.
sigh.
SCREEEEEK
HE'S THE ONE YOU MET TODAY.
THOUGH FROM THE SOUND OF IT, YOU'VE DISCOVERED THAT ALREADY.

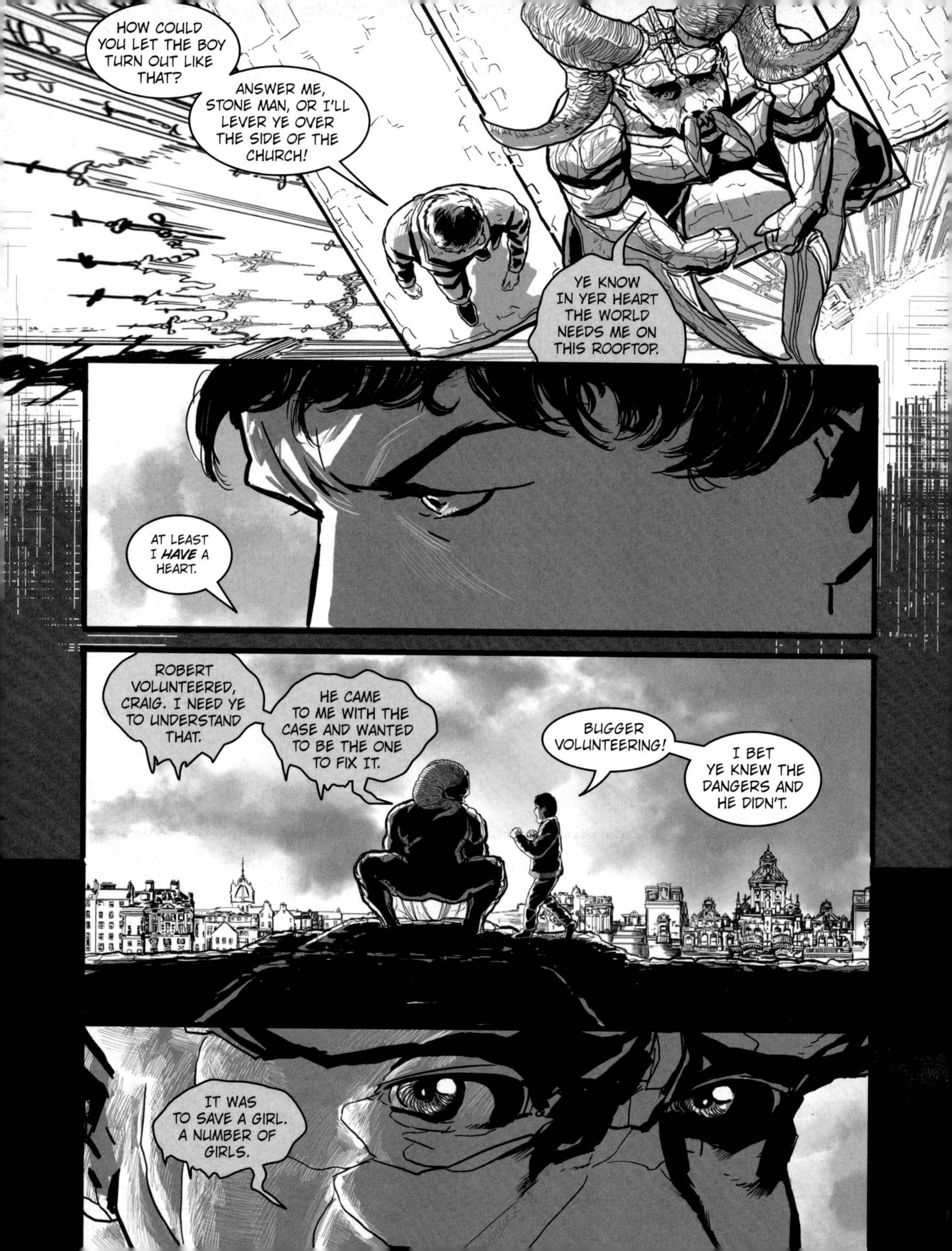
HOW COULD YOU LET THE BOY TURN OUT LIKE THAT?
ANSWER ME, STONE MAN, OR I'LL LEVER YE OVER THE SIDE OF THE CHURCH!
YE KNOW IN YER HEART THE WORLD NEEDS ME ON THIS ROOFTOP.
AT LEAST I *HAVE* A HEART.
ROBERT VOLUNTEERED, CRAIG. I NEED YE TO UNDERSTAND THAT.
HE CAME TO ME WITH THE CASE AND WANTED TO BE THE ONE TO FIX IT.
BUGGER VOLUNTEERING!
I BET YE KNEW THE DANGERS AND HE DIDN'T.
IT WAS TO SAVE A GIRL. A NUMBER OF GIRLS.

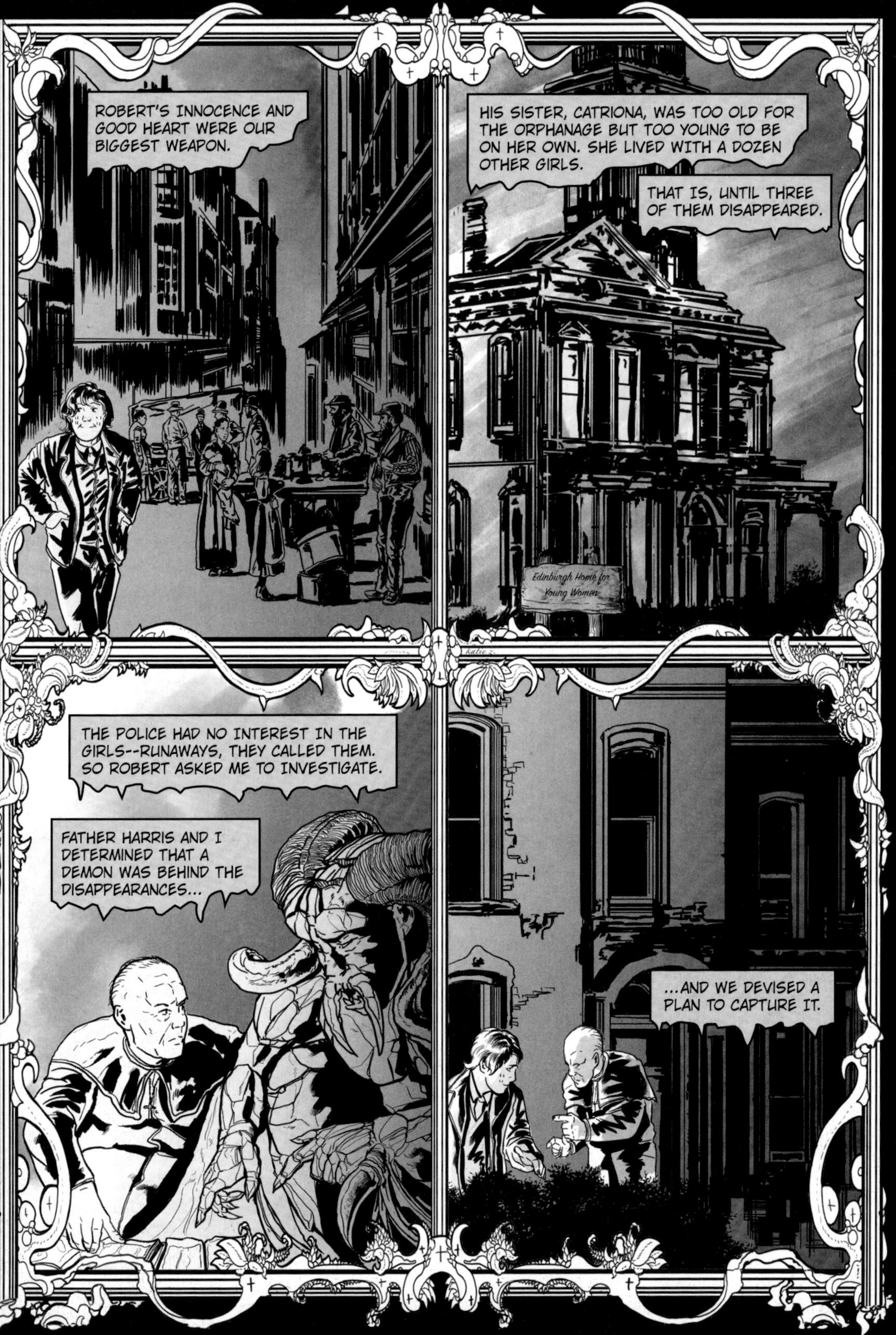

ROBERT'S INNOCENCE AND GOOD HEART WERE OUR BIGGEST WEAPON.
HIS SISTER, CATRIONA, WAS TOO OLD FOR THE ORPHANAGE BUT TOO YOUNG TO BE ON HER OWN. SHE LIVED WITH A DOZEN OTHER GIRLS.
THAT IS, UNTIL THREE OF THEM DISAPPEARED.
Edinburgh Home for Young Women
THE POLICE HAD NO INTEREST IN THE GIRLS--RUNAWAYS, THEY CALLED THEM. SO ROBERT ASKED ME TO INVESTIGATE.
FATHER HARRIS AND I DETERMINED THAT A DEMON WAS BEHIND THE DISAPPEARANCES...
...AND WE DEVISED A PLAN TO CAPTURE IT.

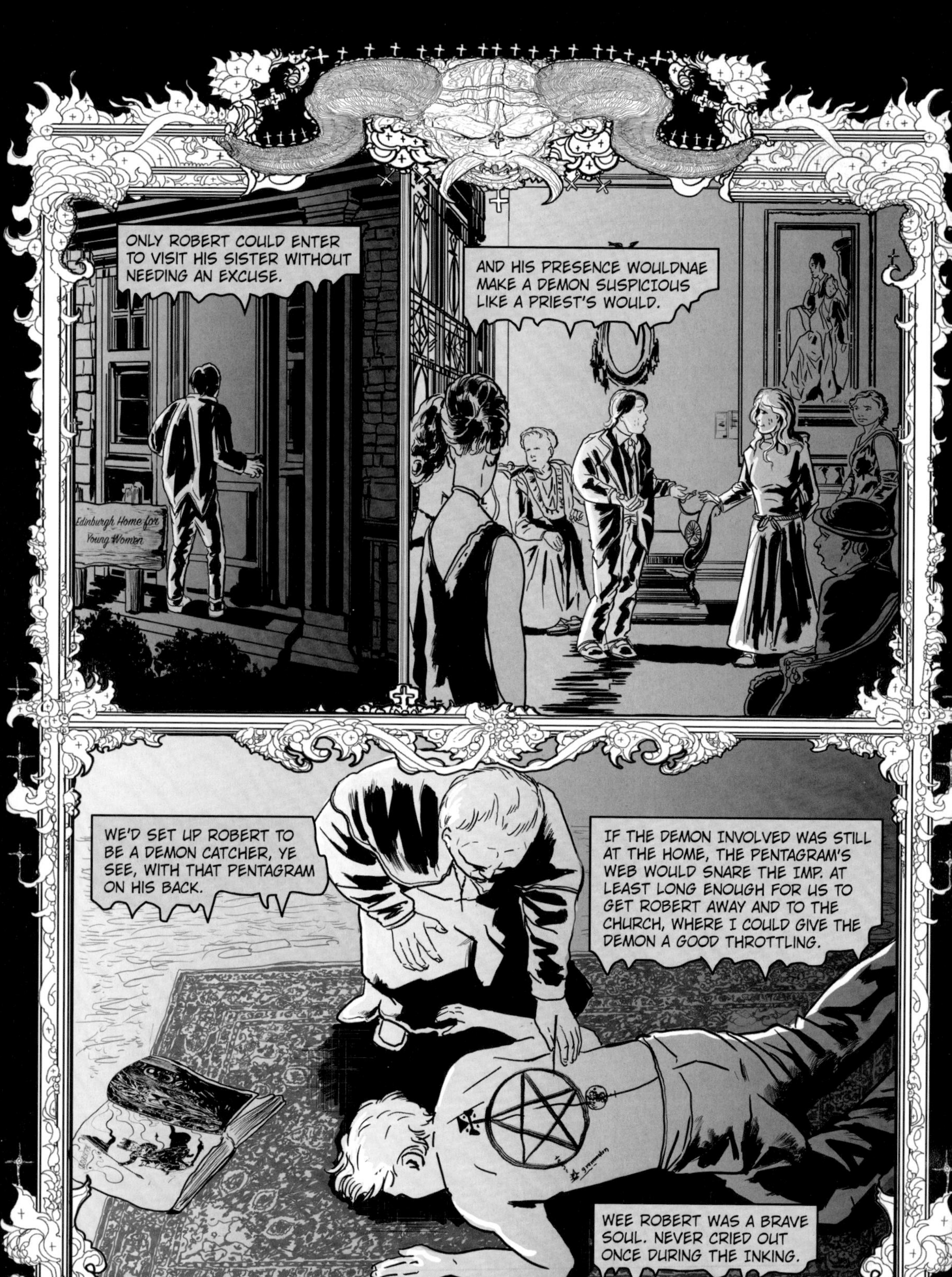
ONLY ROBERT COULD ENTER TO VISIT HIS SISTER WITHOUT NEEDING AN EXCUSE.
Edinburgh Home for Young Women
AND HIS PRESENCE WOULDNAE MAKE A DEMON SUSPICIOUS LIKE A PRIEST'S WOULD.
WE'D SET UP ROBERT TO BE A DEMON CATCHER, YE SEE, WITH THAT PENTAGRAM ON HIS BACK.
IF THE DEMON INVOLVED WAS STILL AT THE HOME, THE PENTAGRAM'S WEB WOULD SNARE THE IMP. AT LEAST LONG ENOUGH FOR US TO GET ROBERT AWAY AND TO THE CHURCH, WHERE I COULD GIVE THE DEMON A GOOD THROTTLING.
WEE ROBERT WAS A BRAVE SOUL. NEVER CRIED OUT ONCE DURING THE INKING.

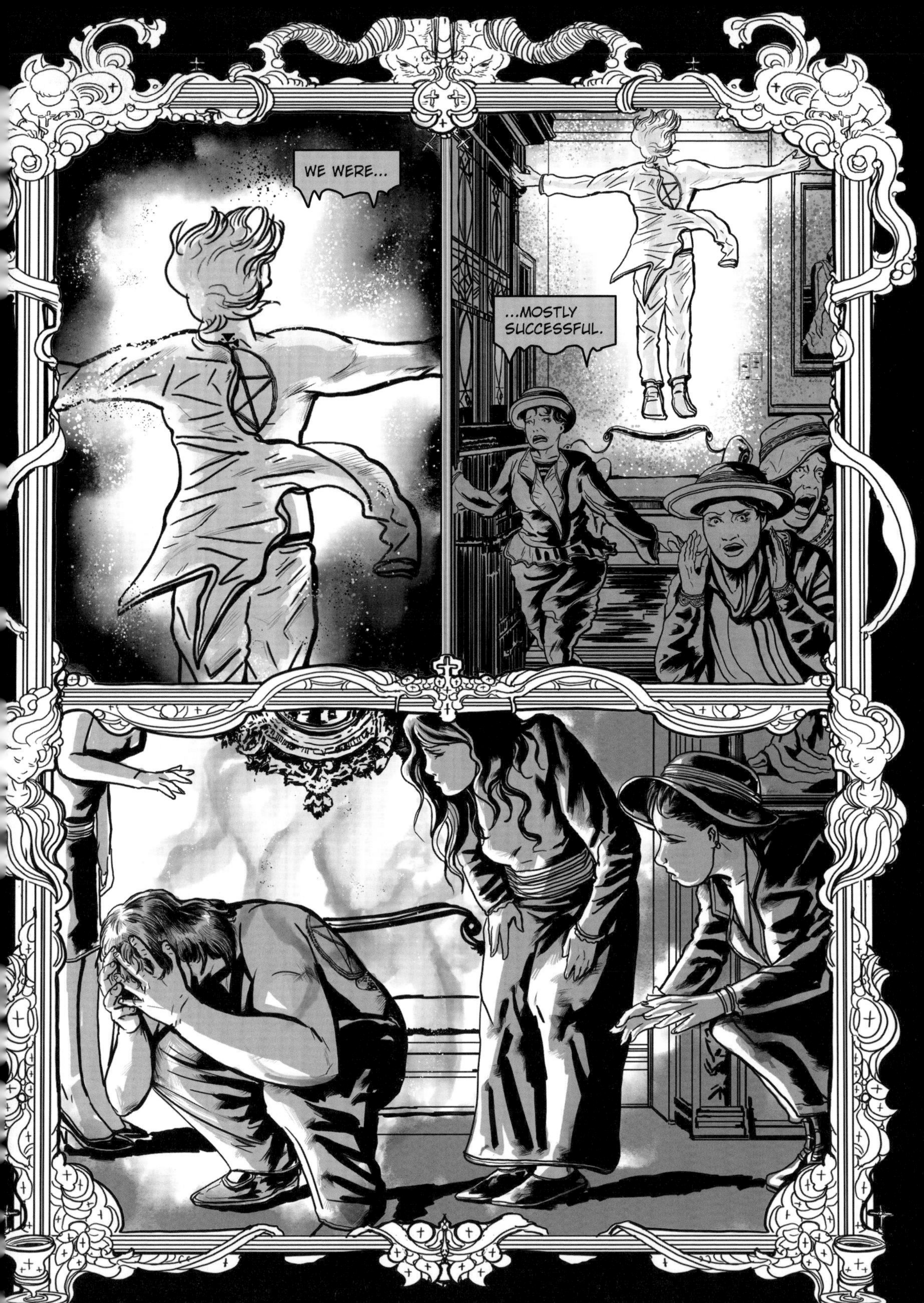
WE WERE...
...MOSTLY SUCCESSFUL.

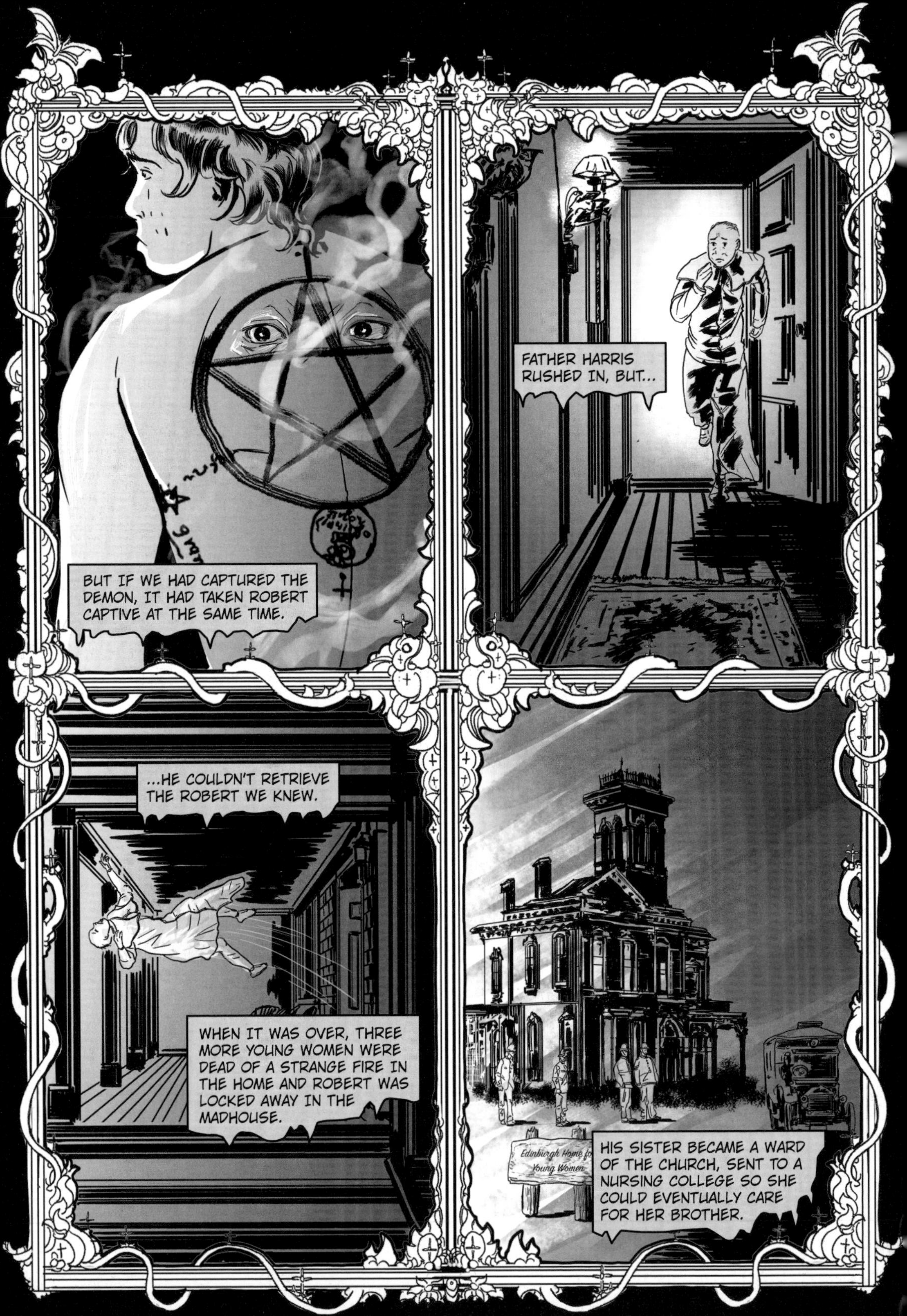
BUT IF WE HAD CAPTURED THE DEMON, IT HAD TAKEN ROBERT CAPTIVE AT THE SAME TIME.
FATHER HARRIS RUSHED IN, BUT...
...HE COULDN'T RETRIEVE THE ROBERT WE KNEW.
WHEN IT WAS OVER, THREE MORE YOUNG WOMEN WERE DEAD OF A STRANGE FIRE IN THE HOME AND ROBERT WAS LOCKED AWAY IN THE MADHOUSE.
Edinburgh Home for Young Women
HIS SISTER BECAME A WARD OF THE CHURCH, SENT TO A NURSING COLLEGE SO SHE COULD EVENTUALLY CARE FOR HER BROTHER.

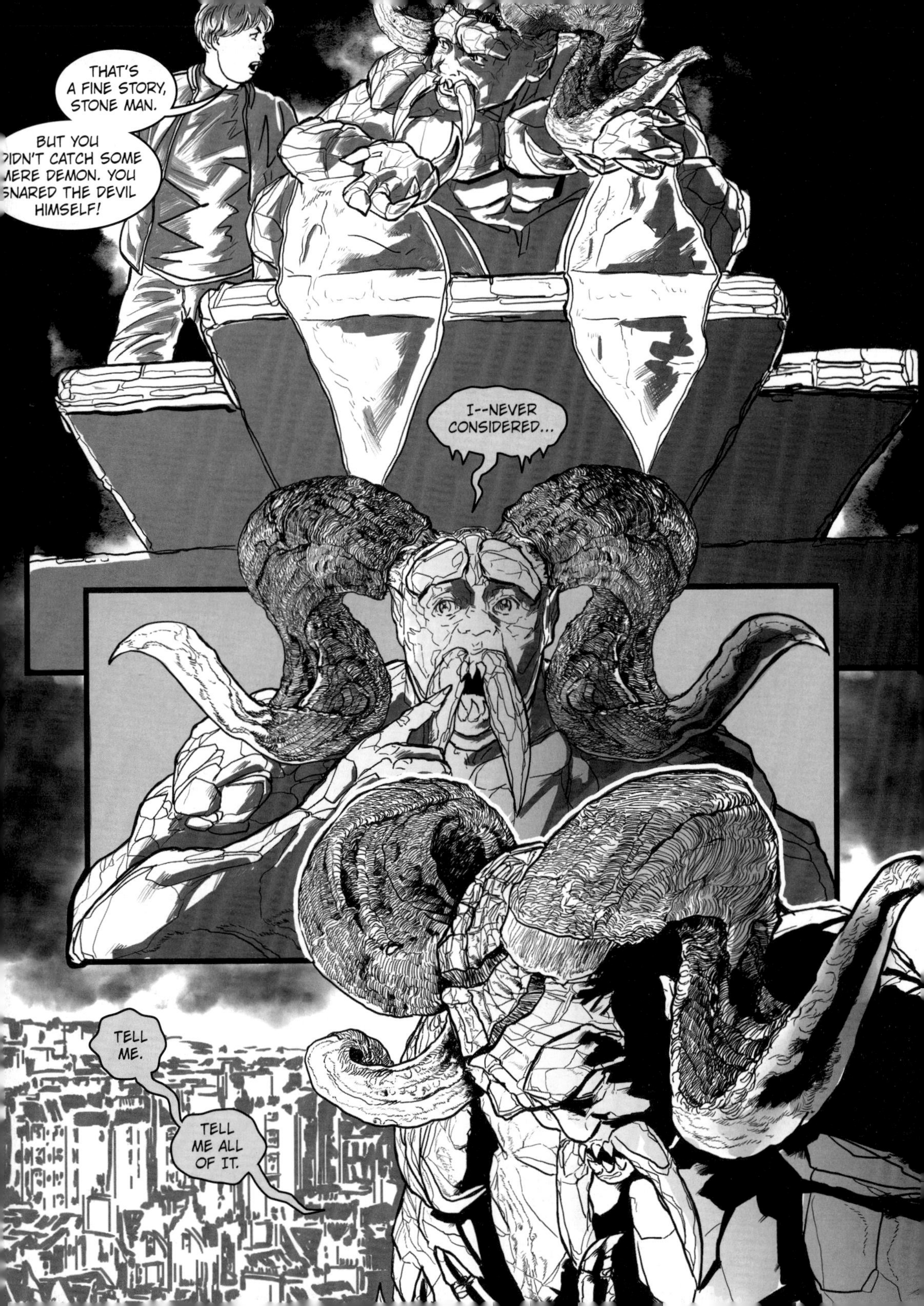
THAT'S A FINE STORY, STONE MAN.
BUT YOU DIDN'T CATCH SOME MERE DEMON. YOU SNARED THE DEVIL HIMSELF!
I--NEVER CONSIDERED...
TELL ME.
TELL ME ALL OF IT.

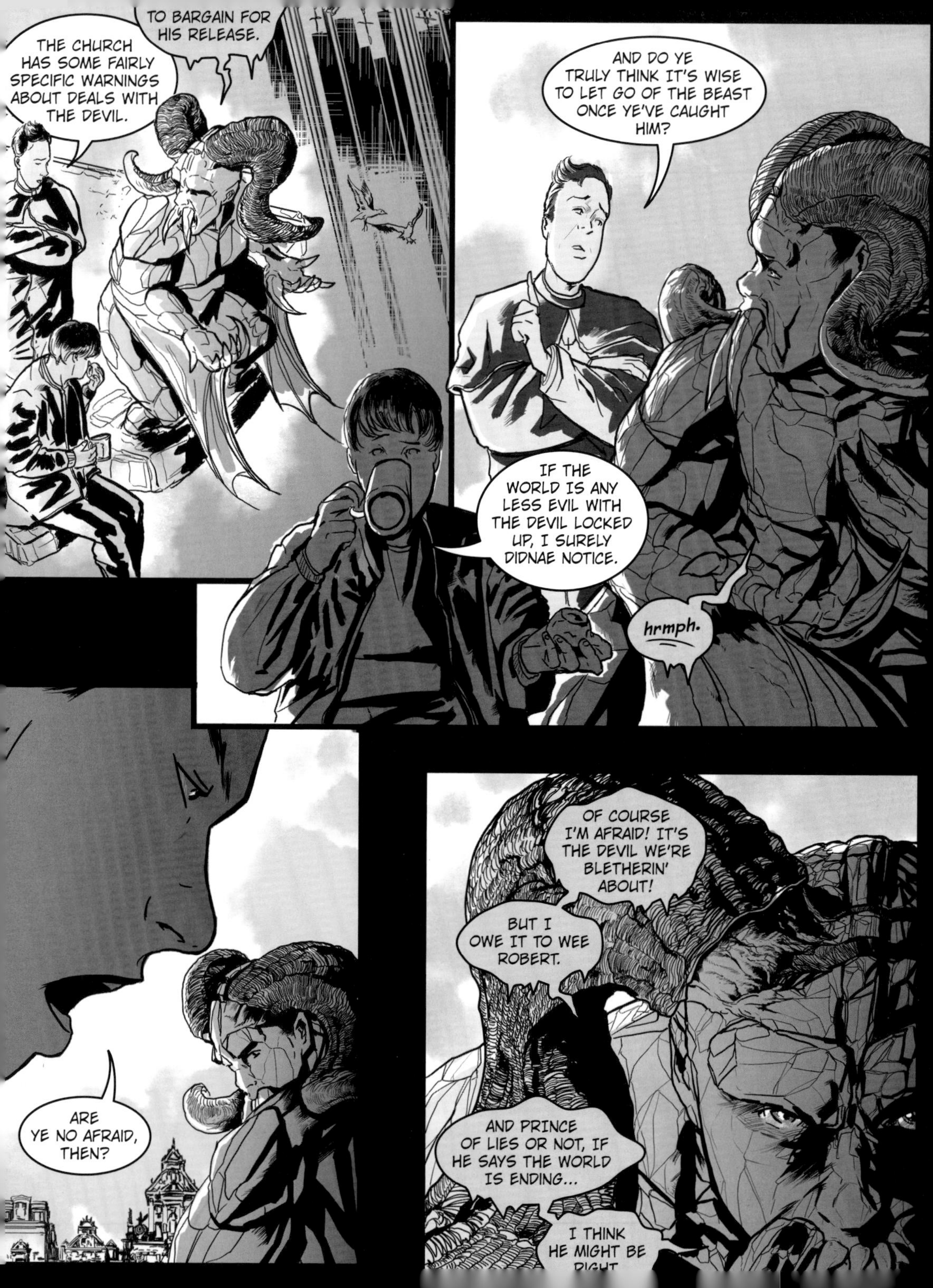
THE CHURCH HAS SOME FAIRLY SPECIFIC WARNINGS ABOUT DEALS WITH THE DEVIL.
TO BARGAIN FOR HIS RELEASE.
AND DO YE TRULY THINK IT'S WISE TO LET GO OF THE BEAST ONCE YE'VE CAUGHT HIM?
IF THE WORLD IS ANY LESS EVIL WITH THE DEVIL LOCKED UP, I SURELY DIDNAE NOTICE.
hrmph.
ARE YE NO AFRAID, THEN?
OF COURSE I'M AFRAID! IT'S THE DEVIL WE'RE BLETHERIN' ABOUT!
BUT I OWE IT TO WEE ROBERT.
AND PRINCE OF LIES OR NOT, IF HE SAYS THE WORLD IS ENDING...
I THINK HE MIGHT BE RIGHT.

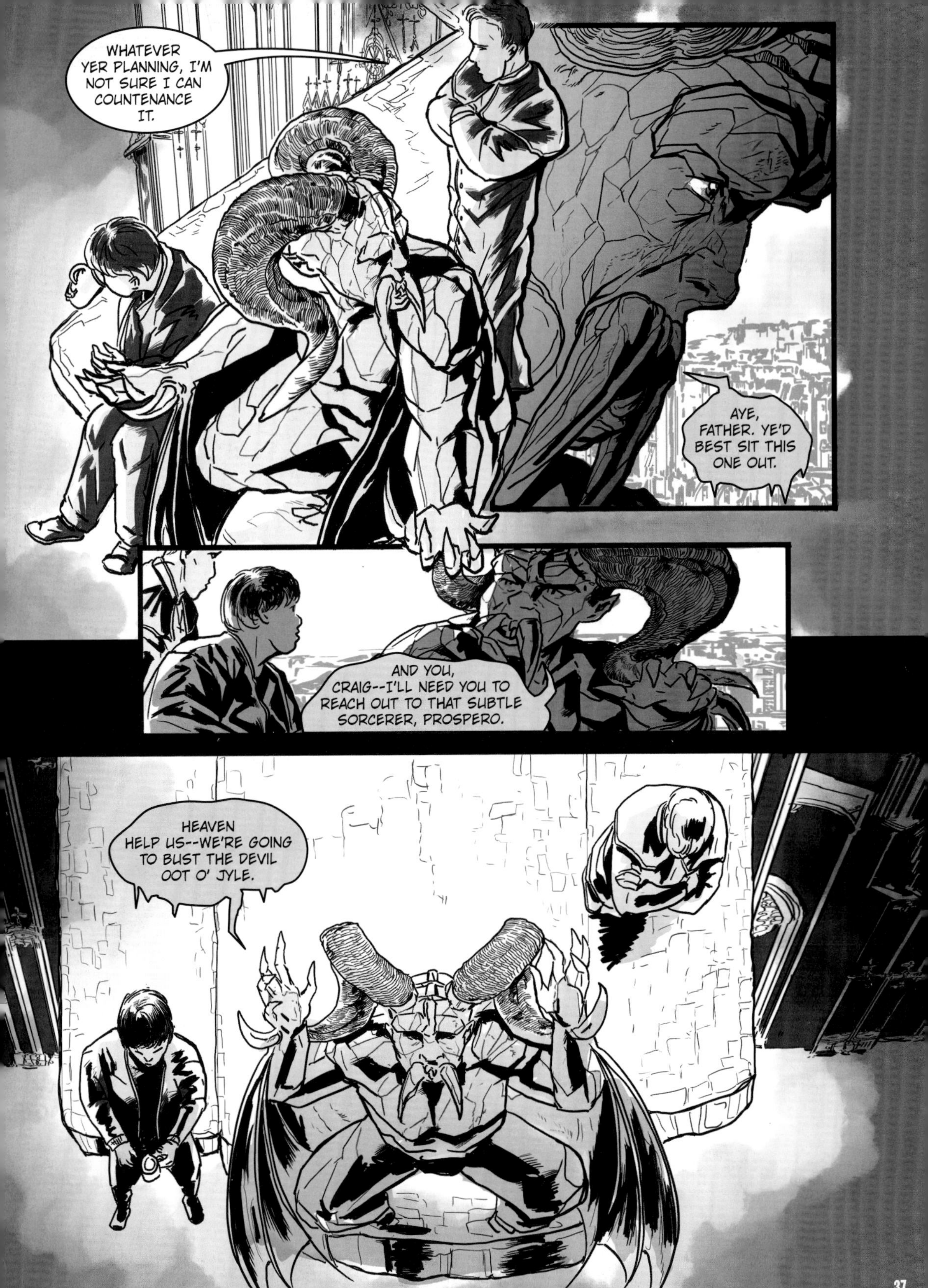
WHATEVER YER PLANNING, I'M NOT SURE I CAN COUNTENANCE IT.
AYE, FATHER. YE'D BEST SIT THIS ONE OUT.
AND YOU, CRAIG--I'LL NEED YOU TO REACH OUT TO THAT SUBTLE SORCERER, PROSPERO.
HEAVEN HELP US--WE'RE GOING TO BUST THE DEVIL OOT O' JYLE.

CHAPTER 5
A PROPOSITION

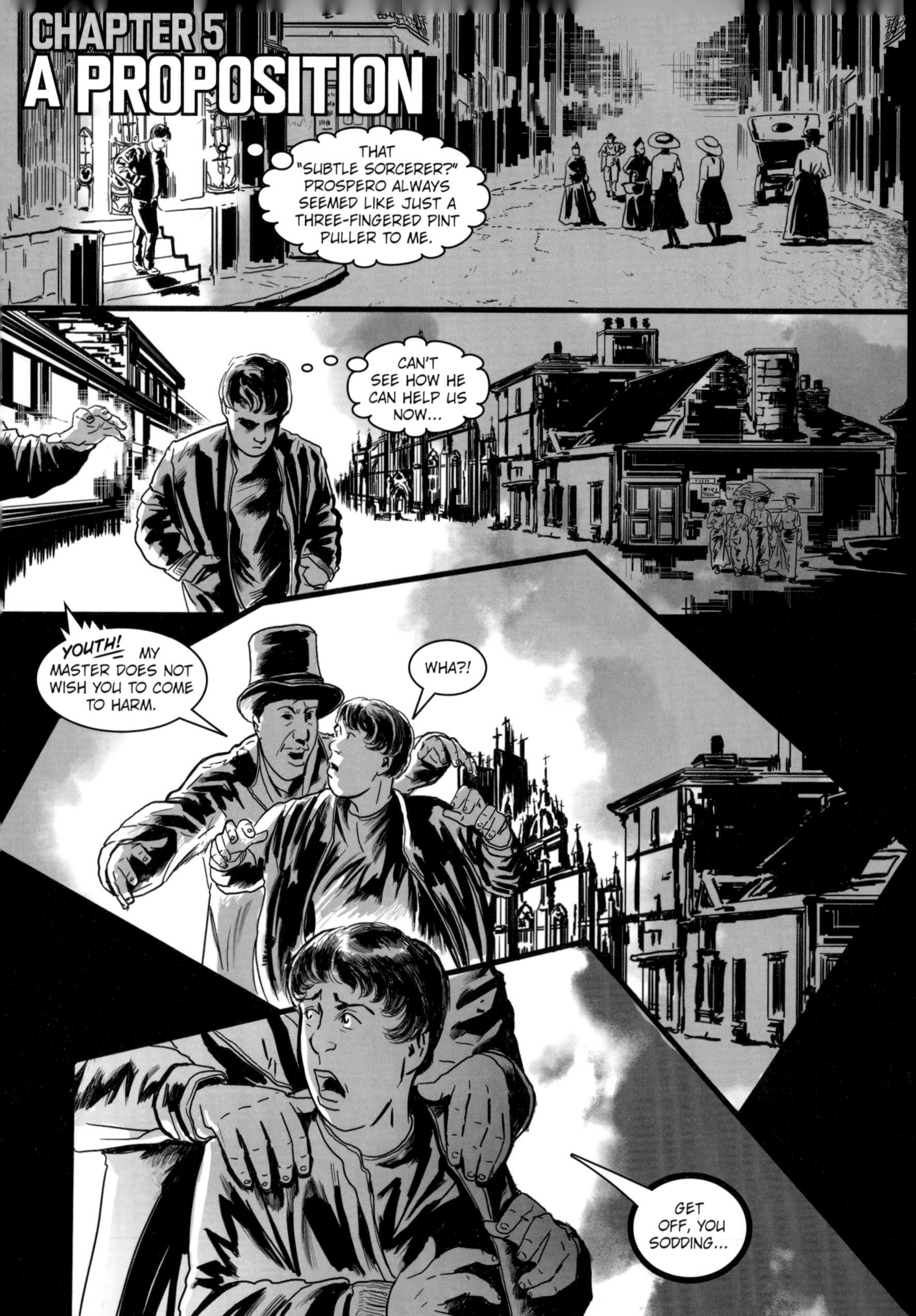
THAT "SUBTLE SORCERER?" PROSPERO ALWAYS SEEMED LIKE JUST A THREE-FINGERED PINT PULLER TO ME.
CAN'T SEE HOW HE CAN HELP US NOW...
YOUTH! MY MASTER DOES NOT WISH YOU TO COME TO HARM.
WHA?!
GET OFF, YOU SODDING...

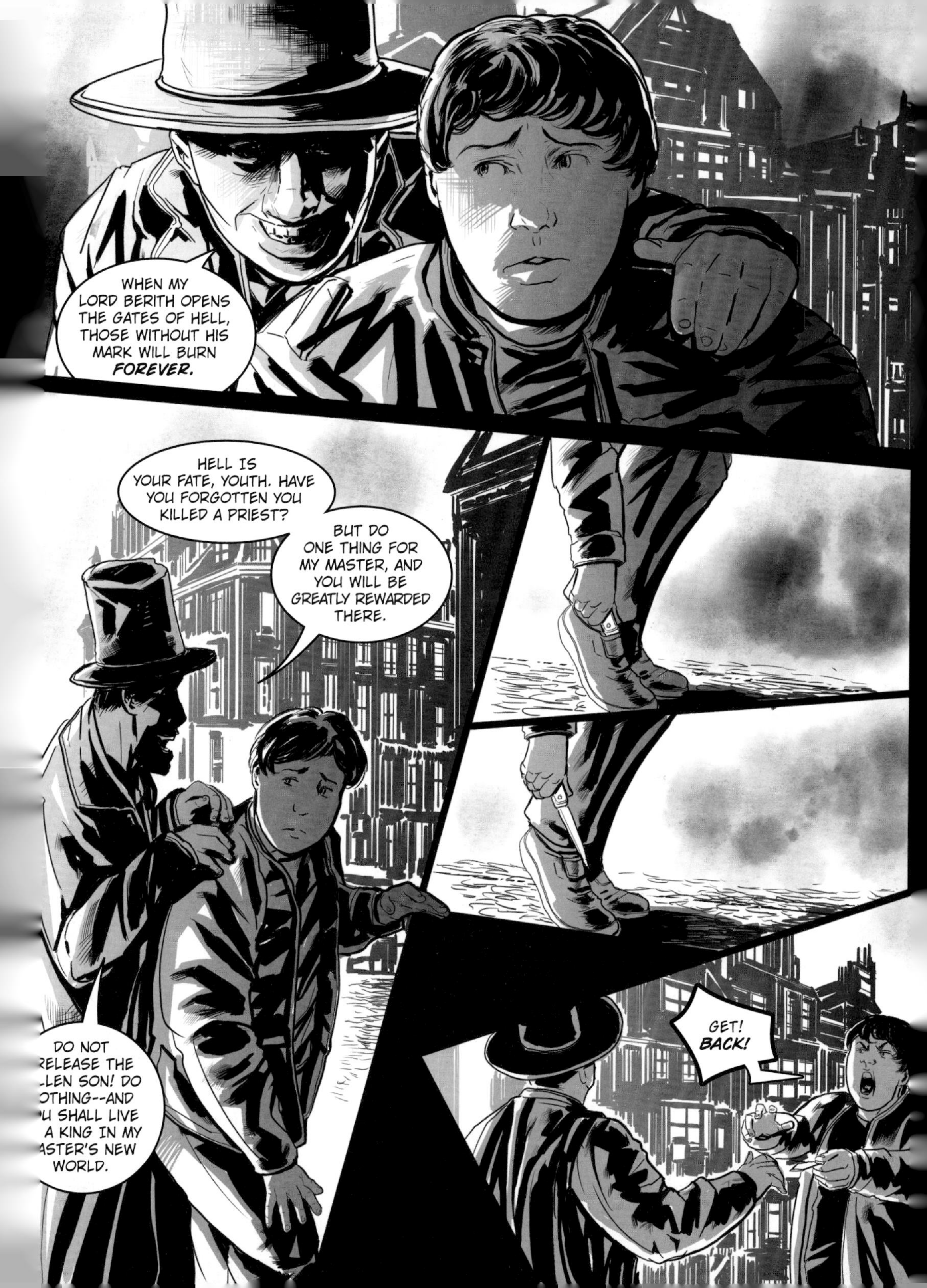
WHEN MY LORD BERITH OPENS THE GATES OF HELL, THOSE WITHOUT HIS MARK WILL BURN *FOREVER.*
HELL IS YOUR FATE, YOUTH. HAVE YOU FORGOTTEN YOU KILLED A PRIEST?
BUT DO ONE THING FOR MY MASTER, AND YOU WILL BE GREATLY REWARDED THERE.
DO NOT RELEASE THE -LEN SON! DO OTHING--AND U SHALL LIVE A KING IN MY ASTER'S NEW WORLD.
GET! *BACK!*

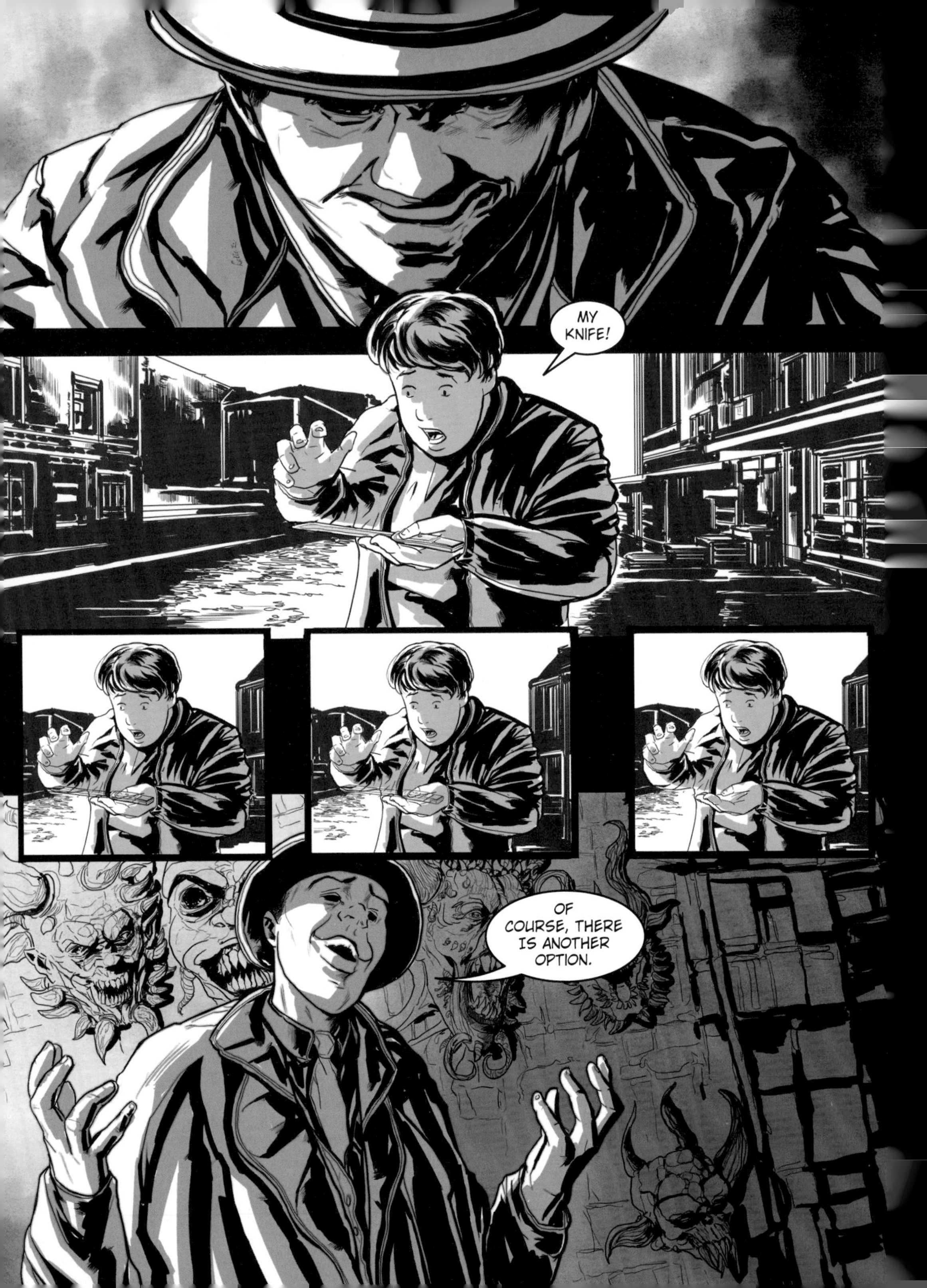
MY KNIFE!
OF COURSE, THERE IS ANOTHER OPTION.

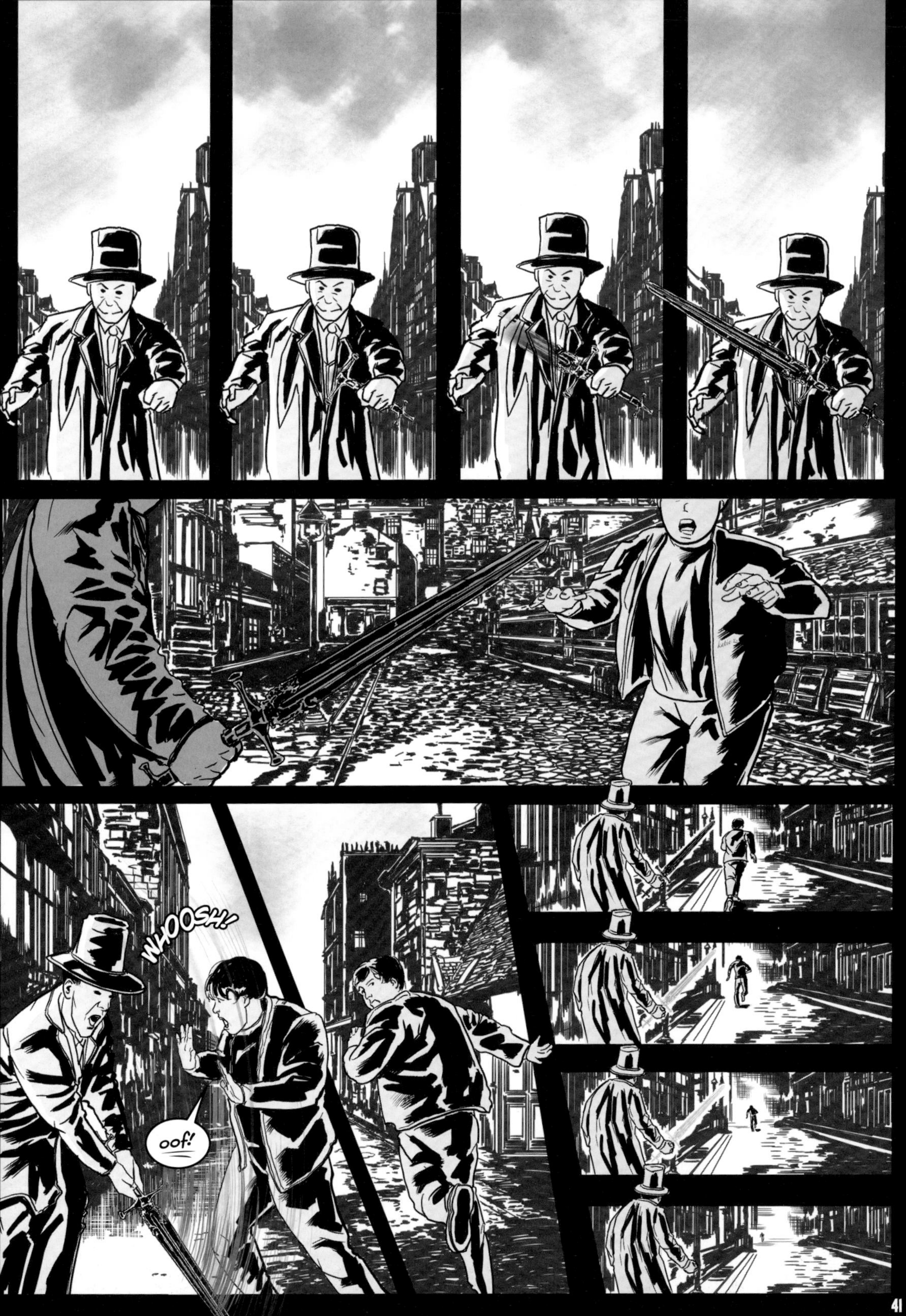
WHOOSH!
oof!

CHAPTER 6
CALLING IN A FAVOR

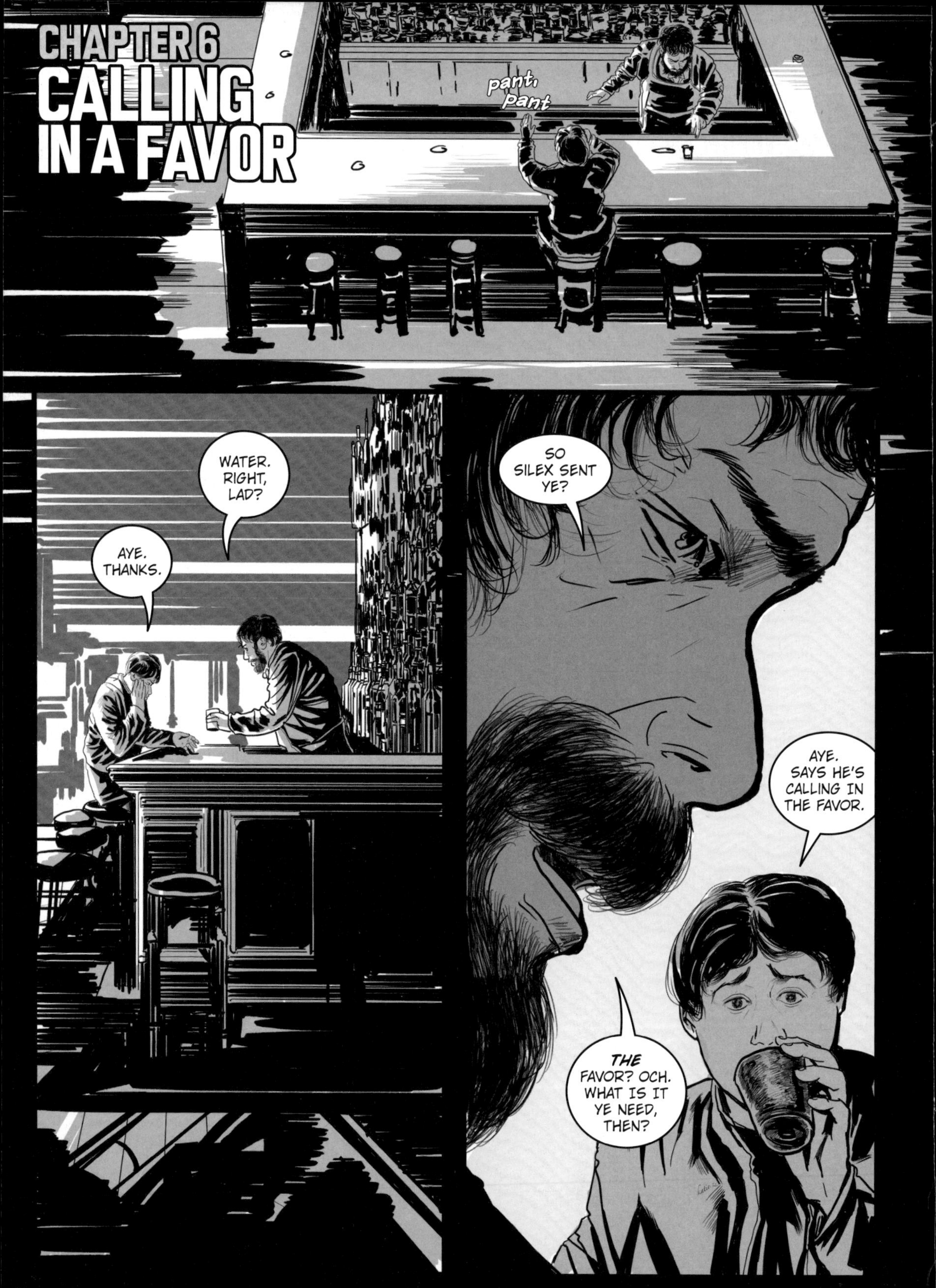
pant, pant
WATER. RIGHT, LAD?
AYE. THANKS.
SO SILEX SENT YE?
AYE. SAYS HE'S CALLING IN THE FAVOR.
THE FAVOR? OCH. WHAT IS IT YE NEED, THEN?

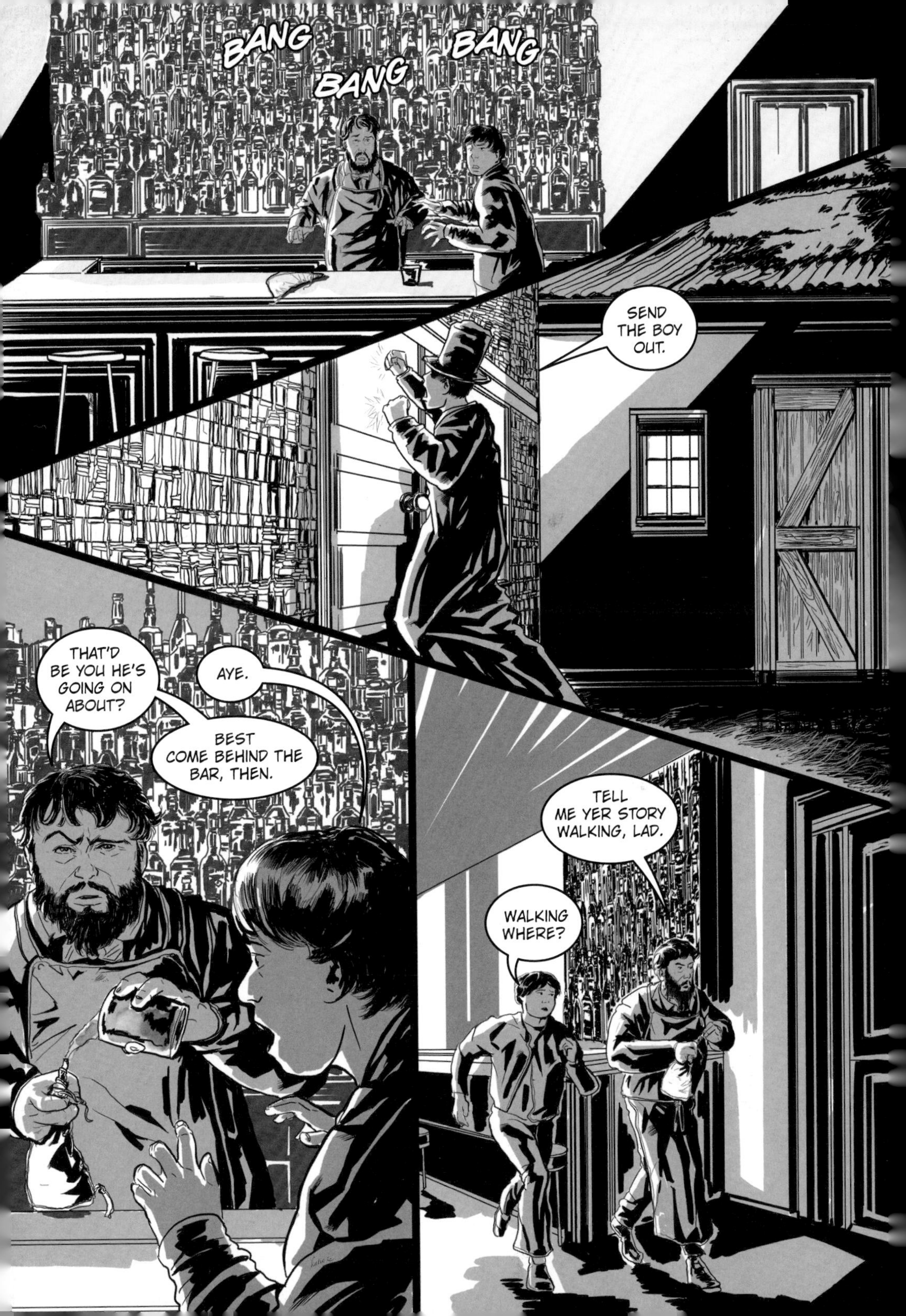
BANG
BANG
BANG
SEND THE BOY OUT.
THAT'D BE YOU HE'S GOING ON ABOUT?
AYE.
BEST COME BEHIND THE BAR, THEN.
TELL ME YER STORY WALKING, LAD.
WALKING WHERE?

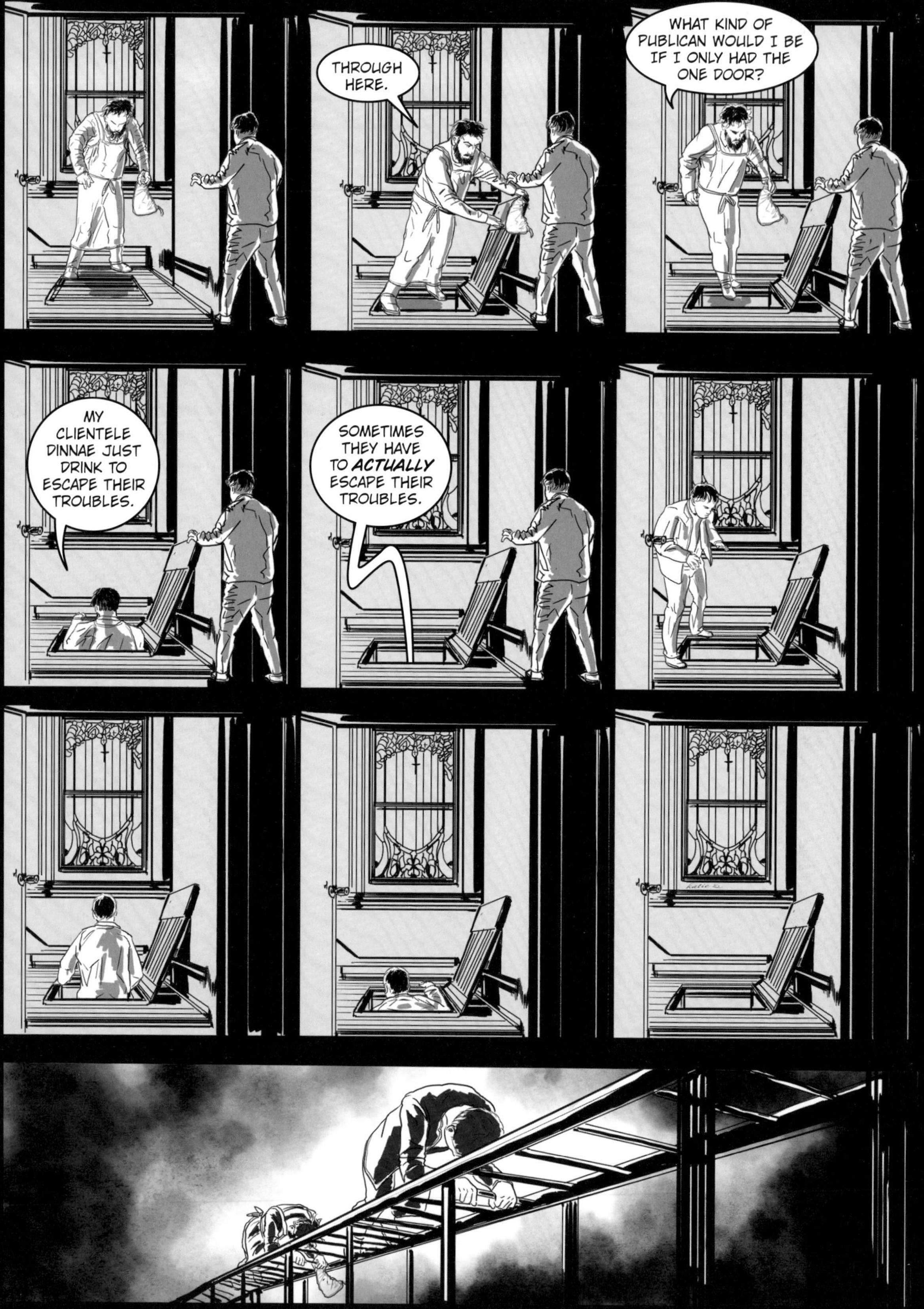
THROUGH HERE.
WHAT KIND OF PUBLICAN WOULD I BE IF I ONLY HAD THE ONE DOOR?
MY CLIENTELE DINNAE JUST DRINK TO ESCAPE THEIR TROUBLES.
SOMETIMES THEY HAVE TO ACTUALLY ESCAPE THEIR TROUBLES.

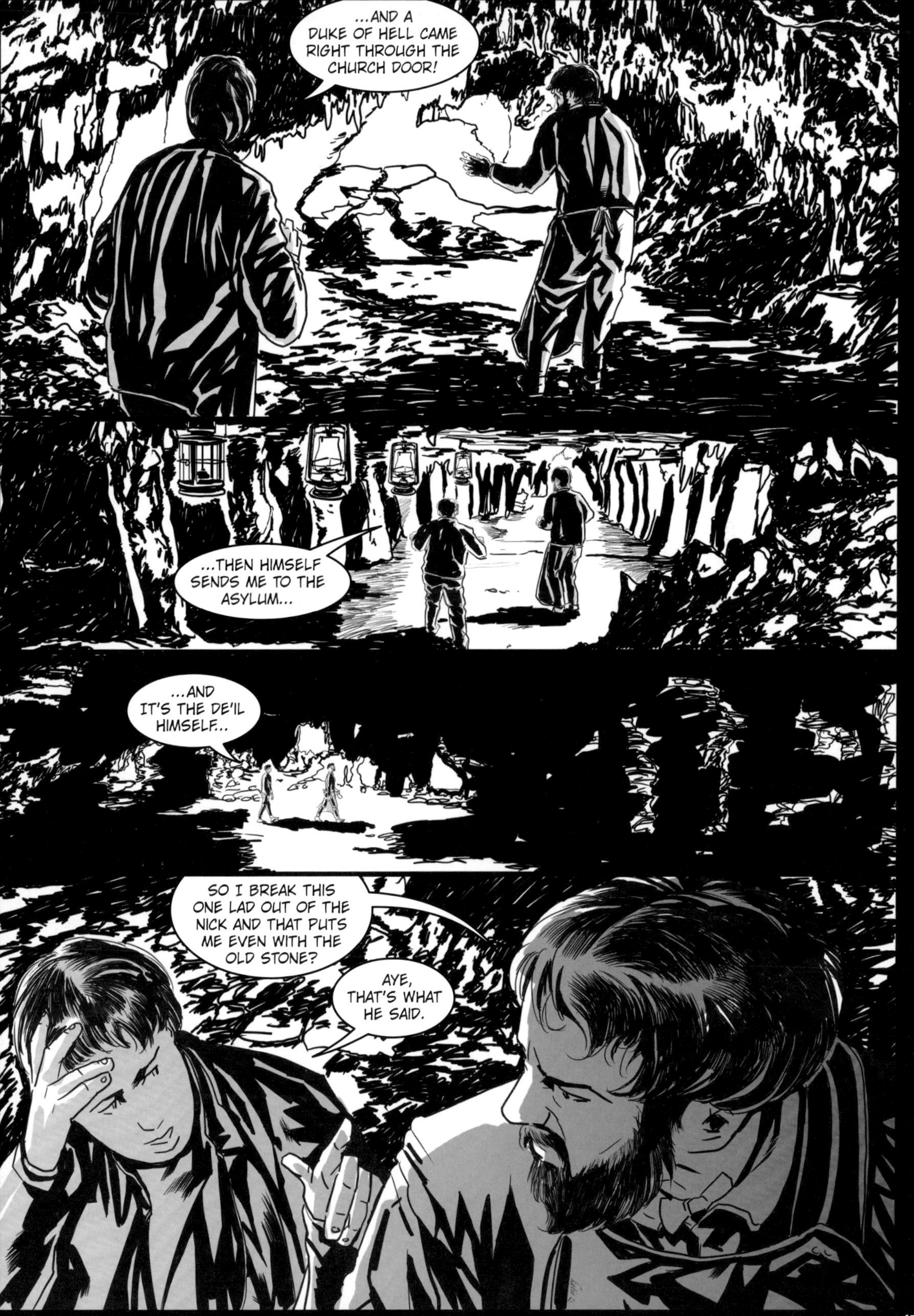
...AND A DUKE OF HELL CAME RIGHT THROUGH THE CHURCH DOOR!
...THEN HIMSELF SENDS ME TO THE ASYLUM...
...AND IT'S THE DE'IL HIMSELF...
SO I BREAK THIS ONE LAD OUT OF THE NICK AND THAT PUTS ME EVEN WITH THE OLD STONE?
AYE, THAT'S WHAT HE SAID.

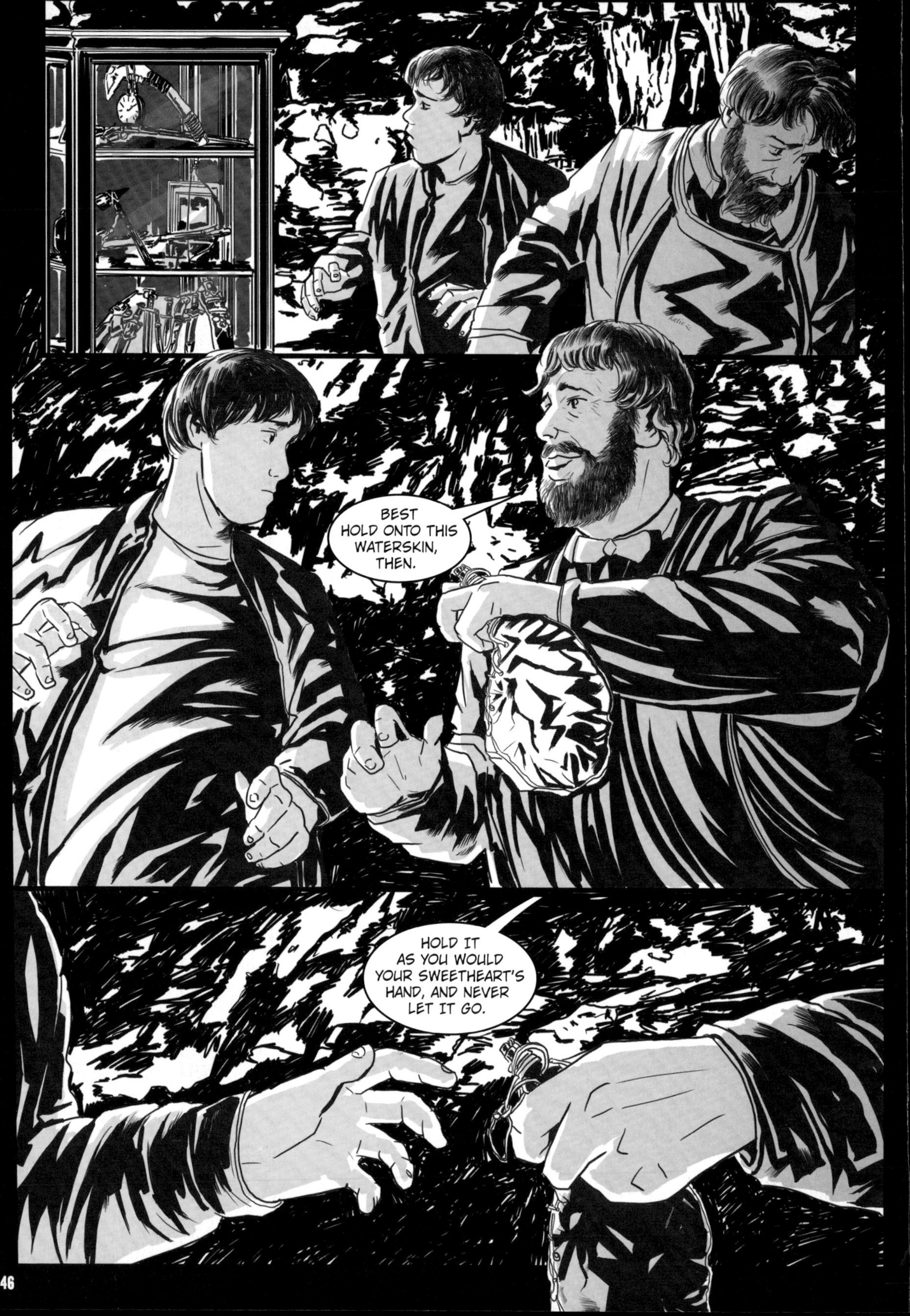
BEST HOLD ONTO THIS WATERSKIN, THEN.
HOLD IT AS YOU WOULD YOUR SWEETHEART'S HAND, AND NEVER LET IT GO.

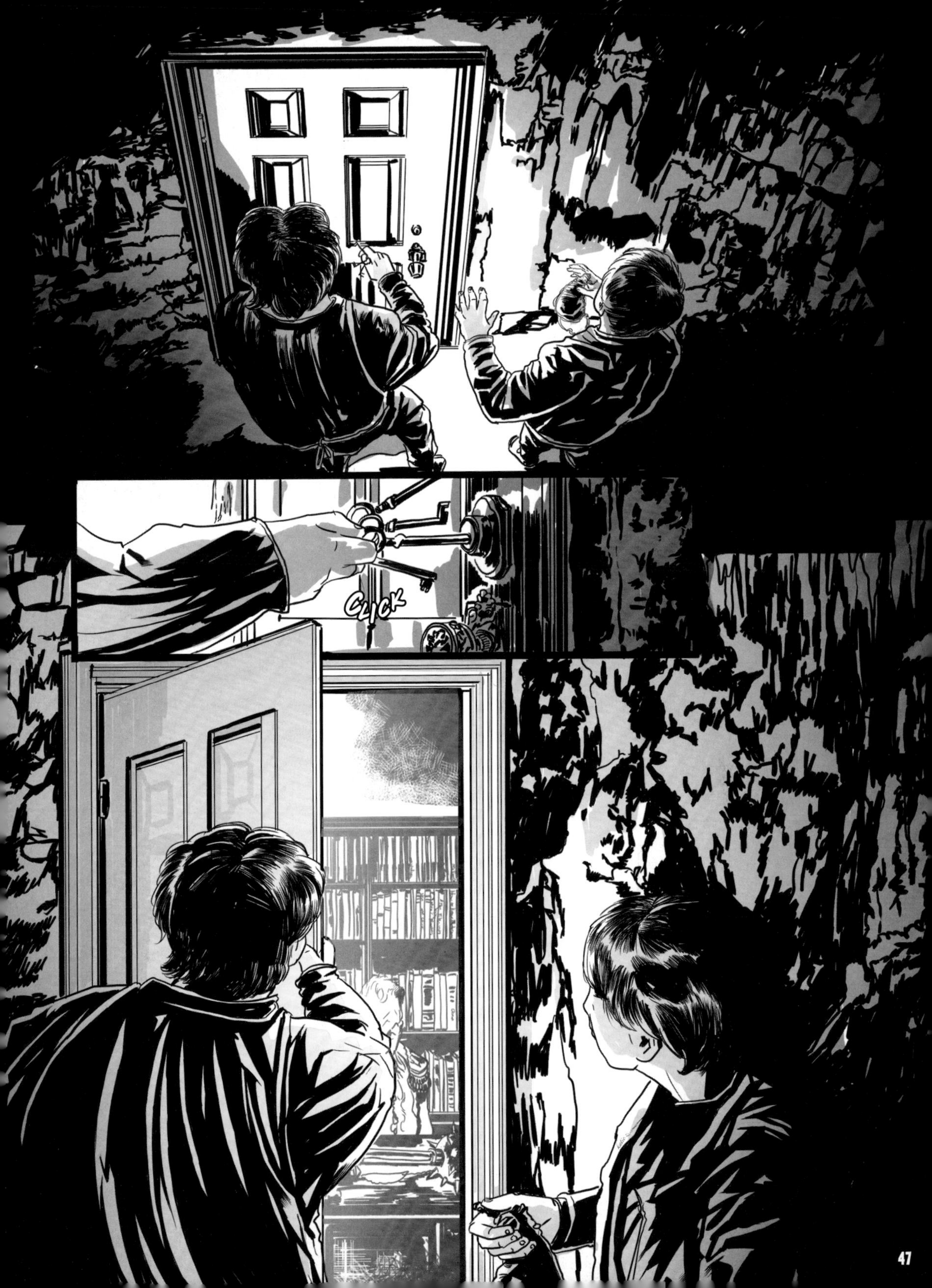
CLICK

CHAPTER 7
UP IN ARMS

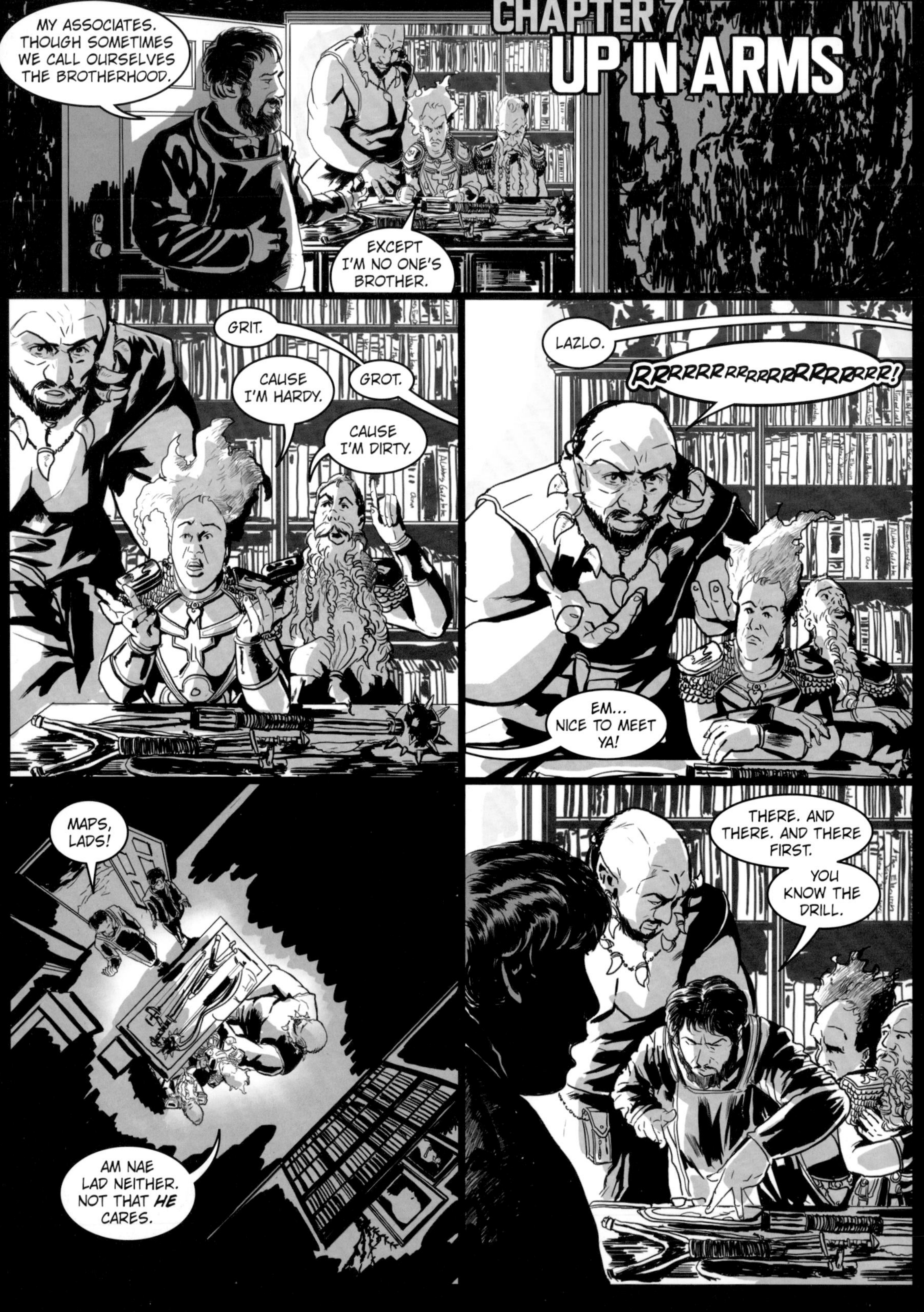
MY ASSOCIATES. THOUGH SOMETIMES WE CALL OURSELVES THE BROTHERHOOD.
EXCEPT I'M NO ONE'S BROTHER.
GRIT.
CAUSE I'M HARDY.
GROT.
CAUSE I'M DIRTY.
LAZLO.
RRRRRRRRRRRRRRRRRRRRR!
EM... NICE TO MEET YA!
MAPS, LADS!
AM NAE LAD NEITHER. NOT THAT *HE* CARES.
THERE. AND THERE. AND THERE FIRST.
YOU KNOW THE DRILL.

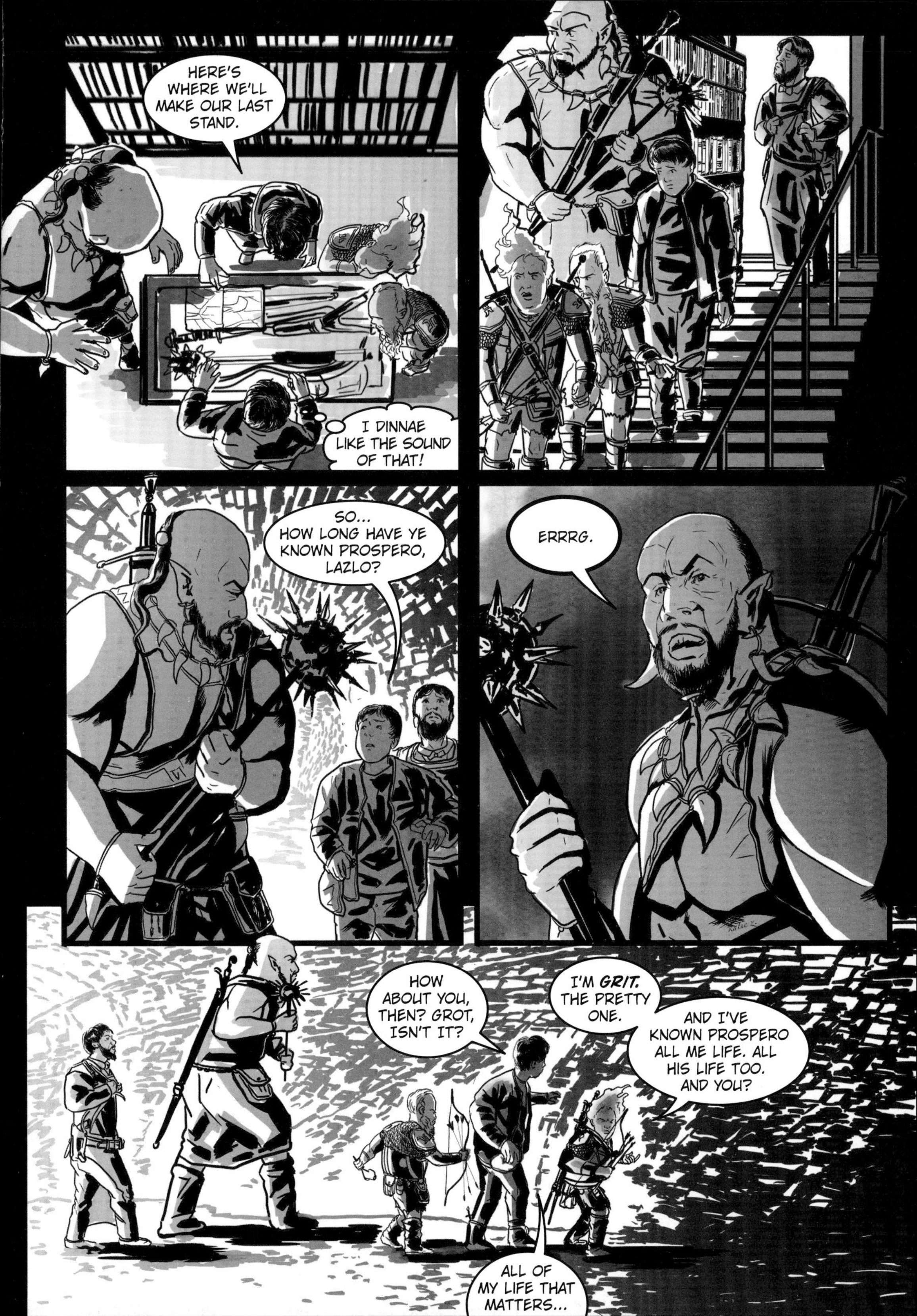
HERE'S WHERE WE'LL MAKE OUR LAST STAND.
I DINNAE LIKE THE SOUND OF THAT!
SO... HOW LONG HAVE YE KNOWN PROSPERO, LAZLO?
ERRRG.
HOW ABOUT YOU, THEN? GROT, ISN'T IT?
I'M GRIT. THE PRETTY ONE.
AND I'VE KNOWN PROSPERO ALL ME LIFE. ALL HIS LIFE TOO. AND YOU?
ALL OF MY LIFE THAT MATTERS...

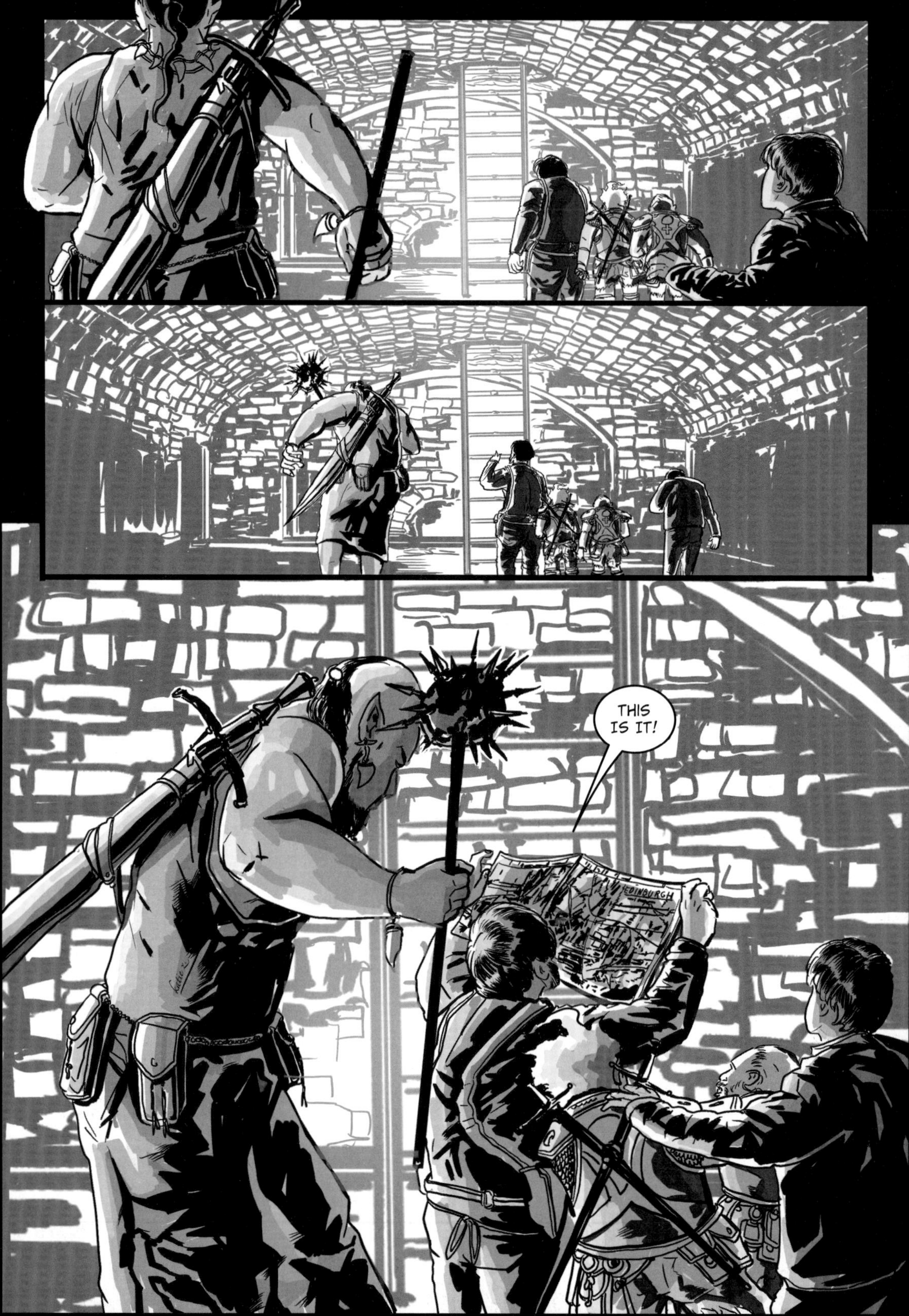
THIS IS IT!
EDINBURGH

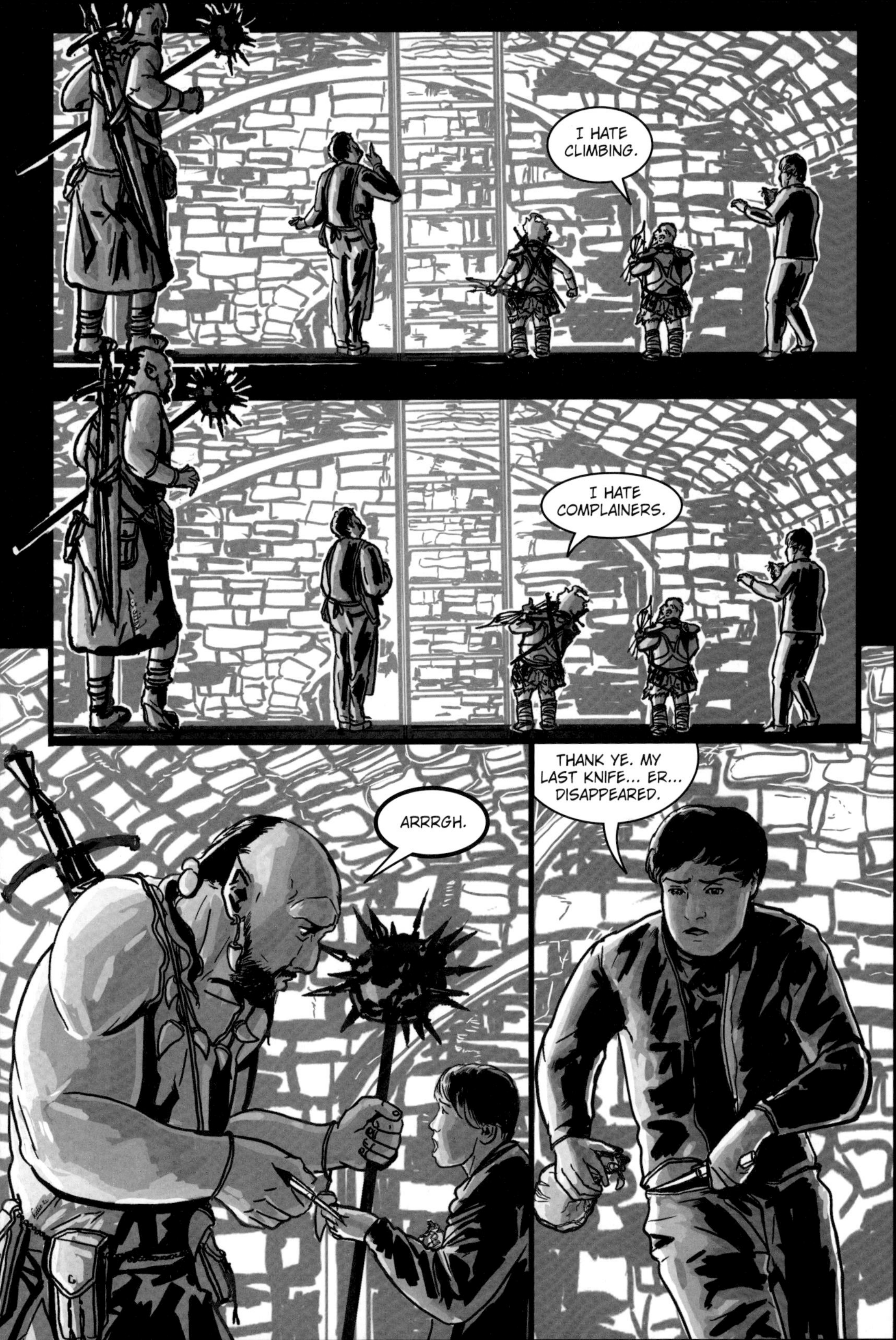
I HATE CLIMBING.
I HATE COMPLAINERS.
ARRRGH.
THANK YE. MY LAST KNIFE... ER... DISAPPEARED.

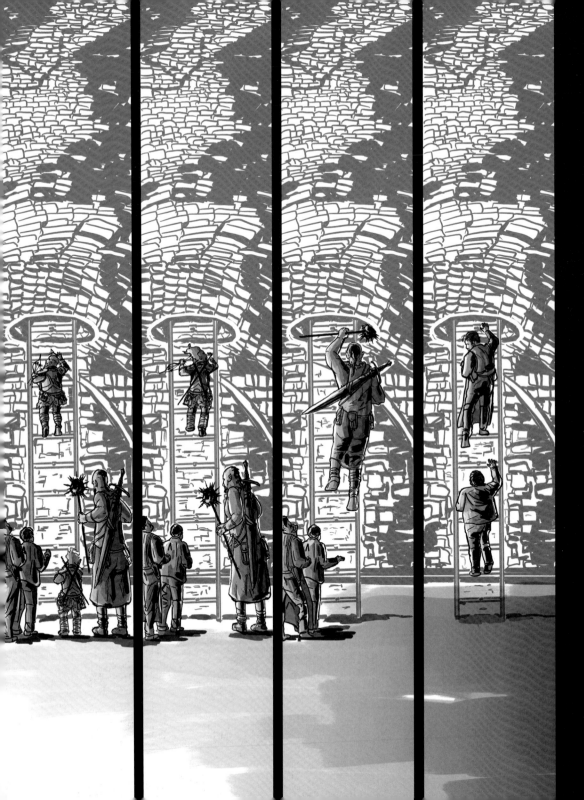

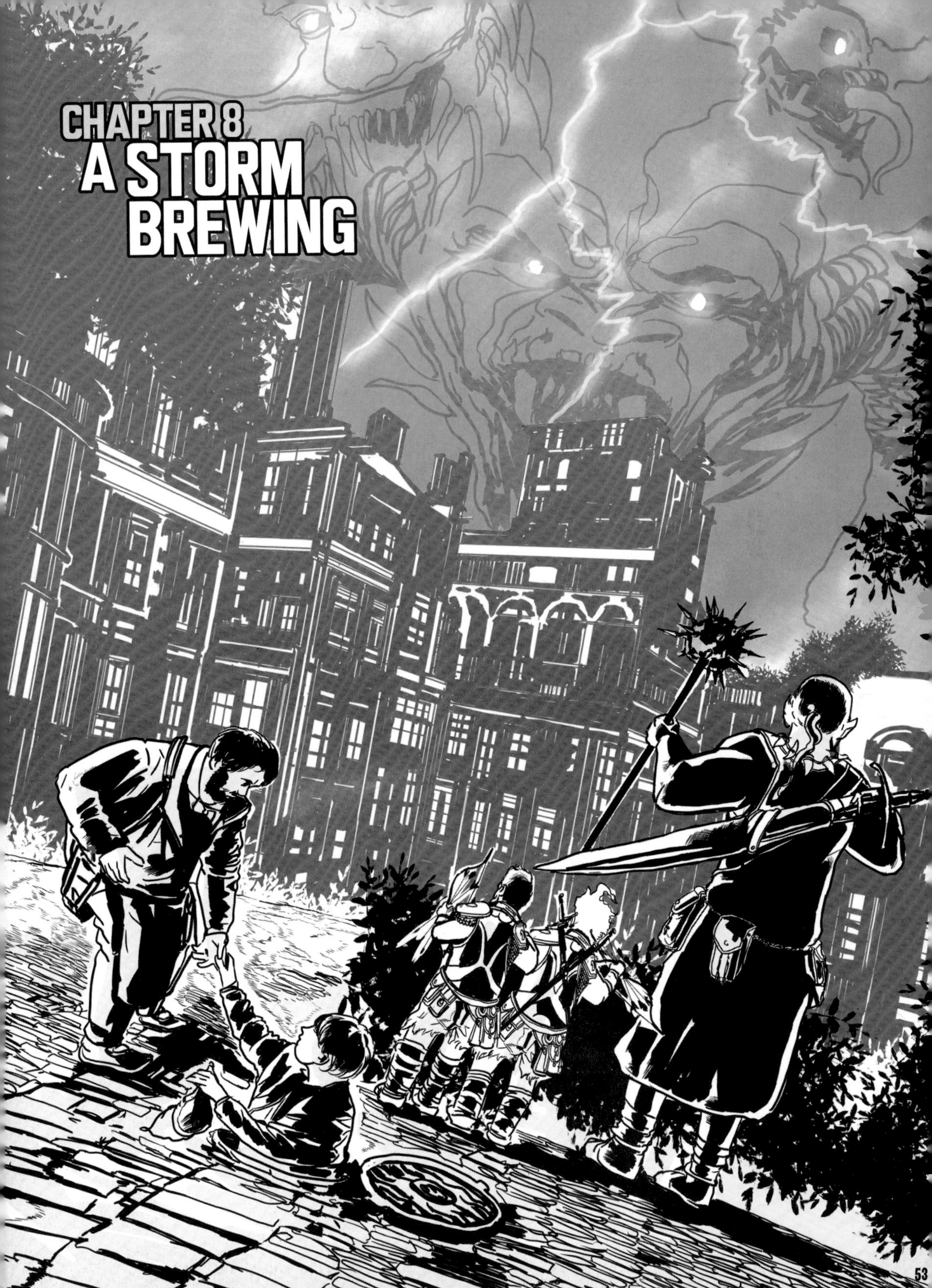
CHAPTER 8
A STORM BREWING

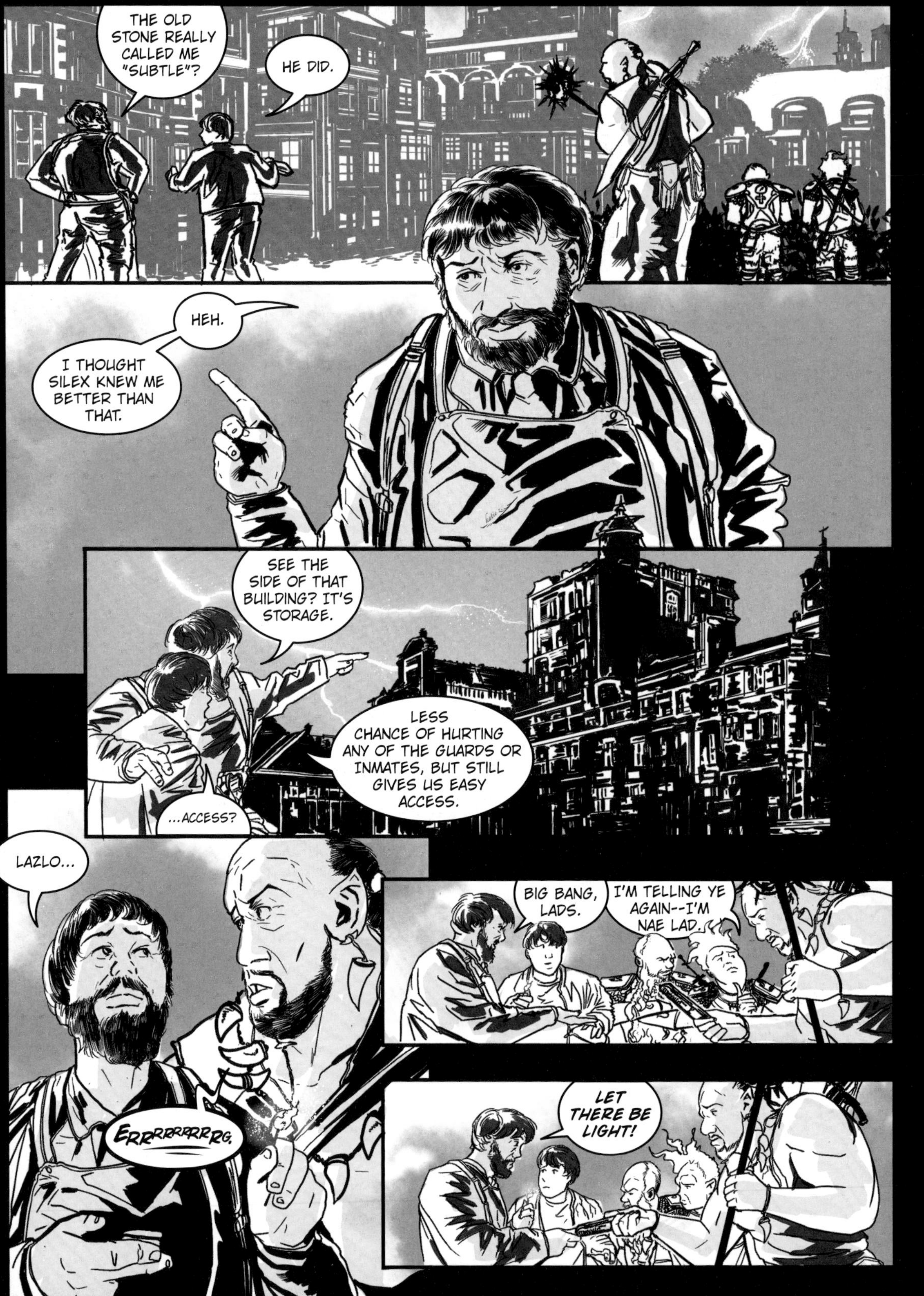
THE OLD STONE REALLY CALLED ME "SUBTLE"?
HE DID.
HEH.
I THOUGHT SILEX KNEW ME BETTER THAN THAT.
SEE THE SIDE OF THAT BUILDING? IT'S STORAGE.
LESS CHANCE OF HURTING ANY OF THE GUARDS OR INMATES, BUT STILL GIVES US EASY ACCESS.
...ACCESS?
LAZLO...
ERRRRRRRRRG.
BIG BANG, LADS.
I'M TELLING YE AGAIN--I'M NAE LAD.
LET THERE BE LIGHT!

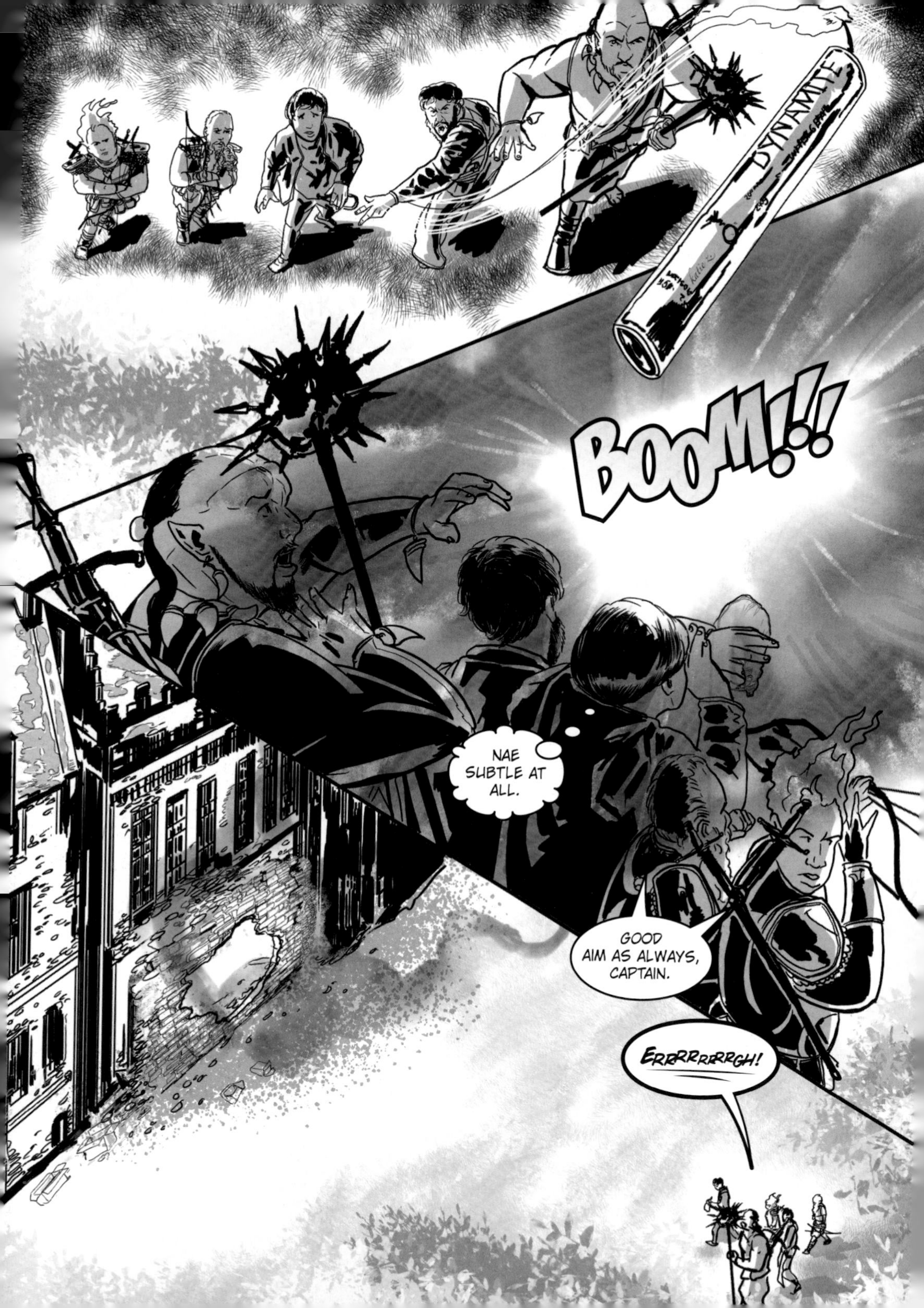
DYNAMITE
BOOM!!!
NAE SUBTLE AT ALL.
GOOD AIM AS ALWAYS, CAPTAIN.
ERRRRRRRRGH!

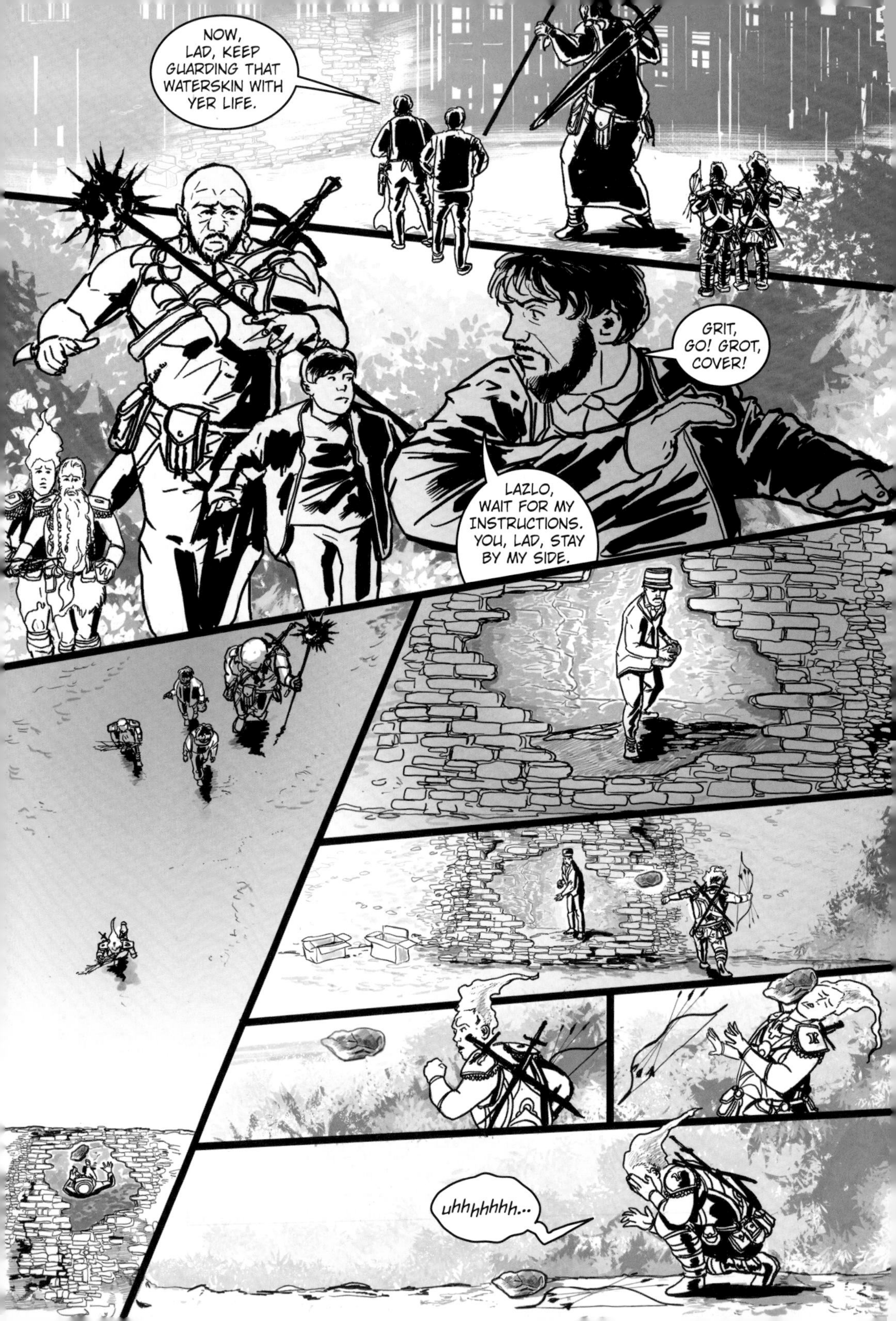
NOW, LAD, KEEP GUARDING THAT WATERSKIN WITH YER LIFE.
GRIT, GO! GROT, COVER!
LAZLO, WAIT FOR MY INSTRUCTIONS. YOU, LAD, STAY BY MY SIDE.
uhhhhhhh...

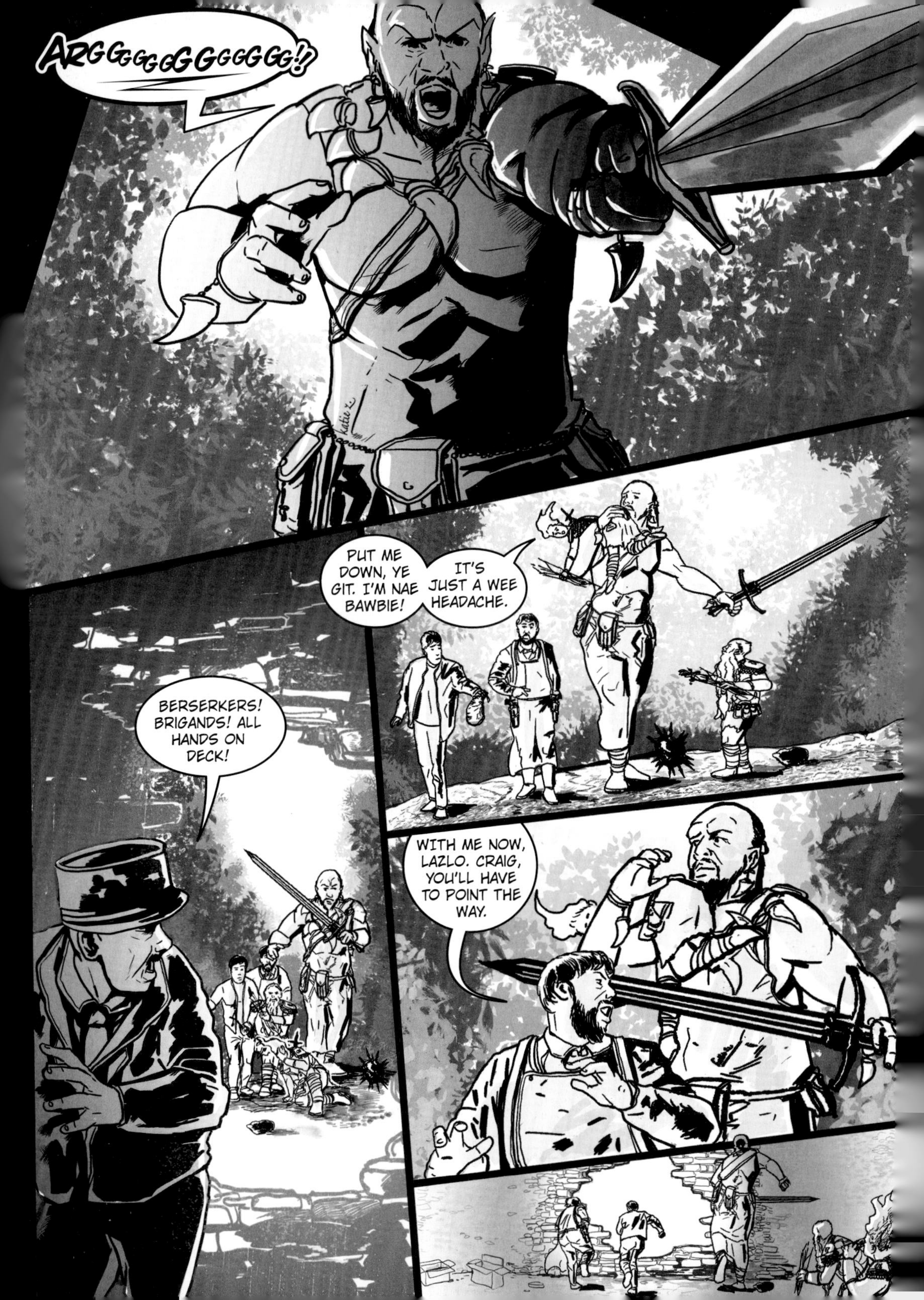
ARGGGGGGGGGGGG!?
PUT ME DOWN, YE GIT. I'M NAE BAWBIE!
IT'S JUST A WEE HEADACHE.
BERSERKERS! BRIGANDS! ALL HANDS ON DECK!
WITH ME NOW, LAZLO. CRAIG, YOU'LL HAVE TO POINT THE WAY.

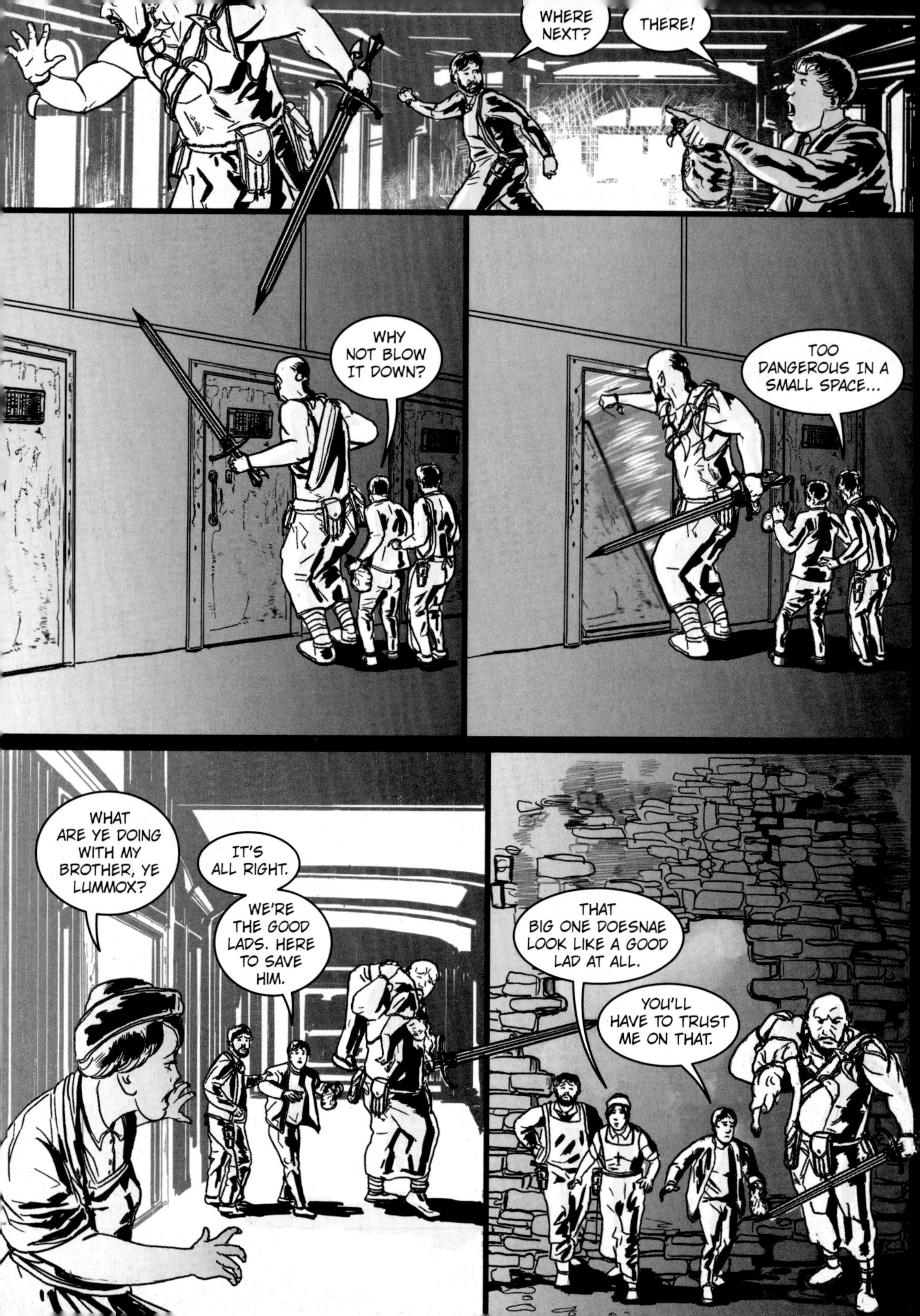
WHERE NEXT?
THERE!
WHY NOT BLOW IT DOWN?
TOO DANGEROUS IN A SMALL SPACE...
WHAT ARE YE DOING WITH MY BROTHER, YE LUMMOX?
IT'S ALL RIGHT.
WE'RE THE GOOD LADS. HERE TO SAVE HIM.
THAT BIG ONE DOESNAE LOOK LIKE A GOOD LAD AT ALL.
YOU'LL HAVE TO TRUST ME ON THAT.

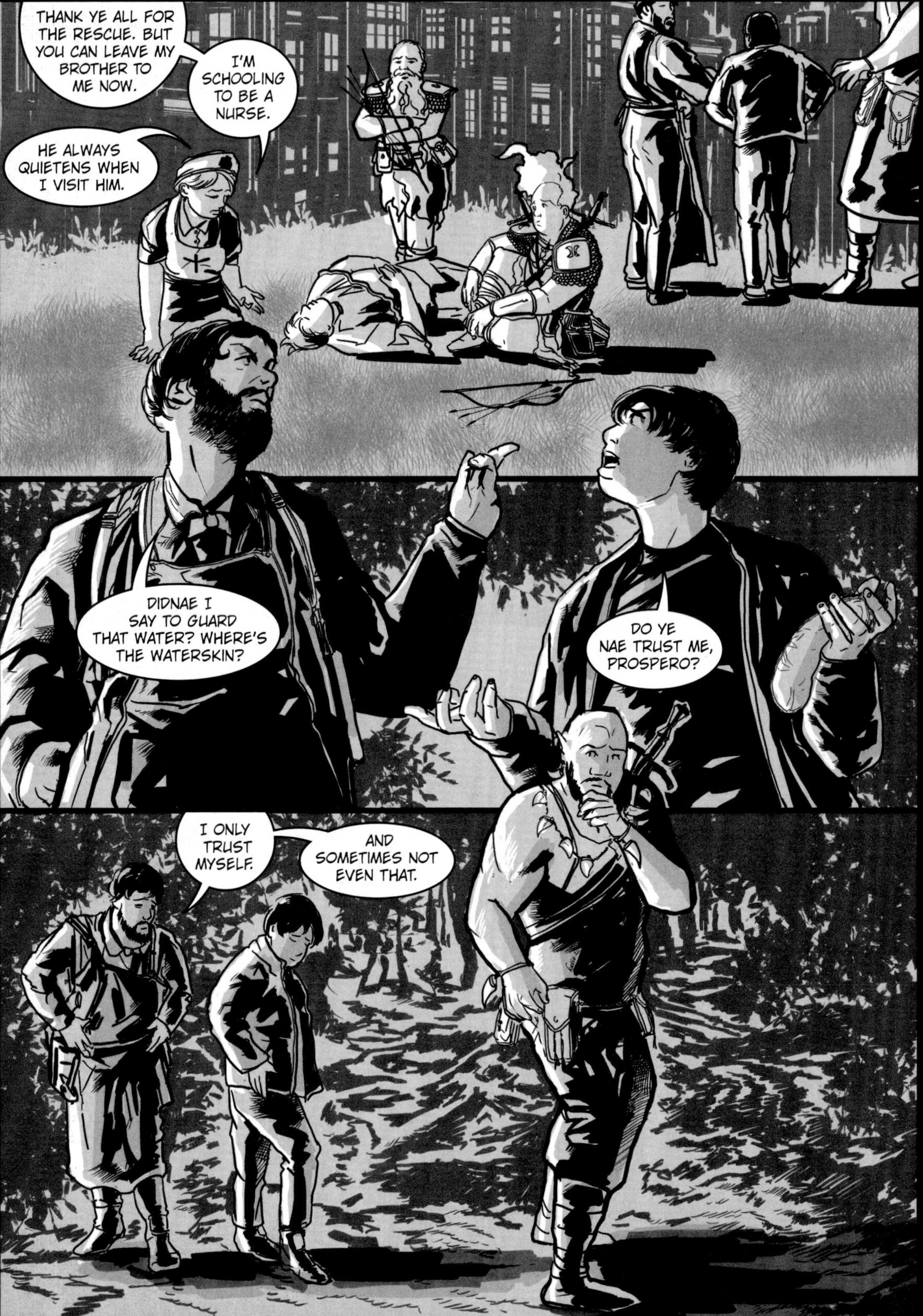
THANK YE ALL FOR THE RESCUE. BUT YOU CAN LEAVE MY BROTHER TO ME NOW.
I'M SCHOOLING TO BE A NURSE.
HE ALWAYS QUIETENS WHEN I VISIT HIM.
DIDNAE I SAY TO GUARD THAT WATER? WHERE'S THE WATERSKIN?
DO YE NAE TRUST ME, PROSPERO?
I ONLY TRUST MYSELF.
AND SOMETIMES NOT EVEN THAT.

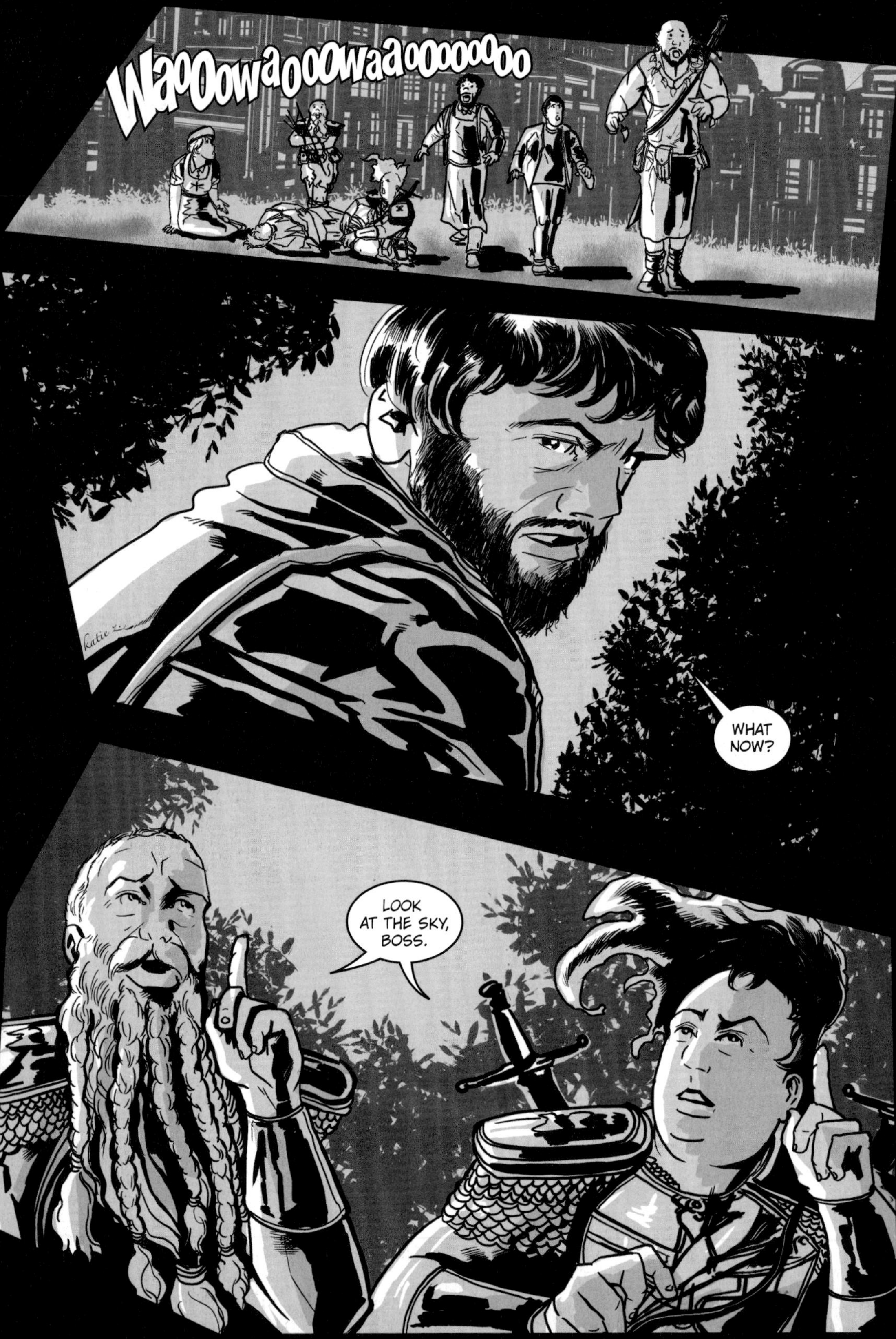
WAOOOWAOOOWAAOOOOOOOO
WHAT NOW?
LOOK AT THE SKY, BOSS.

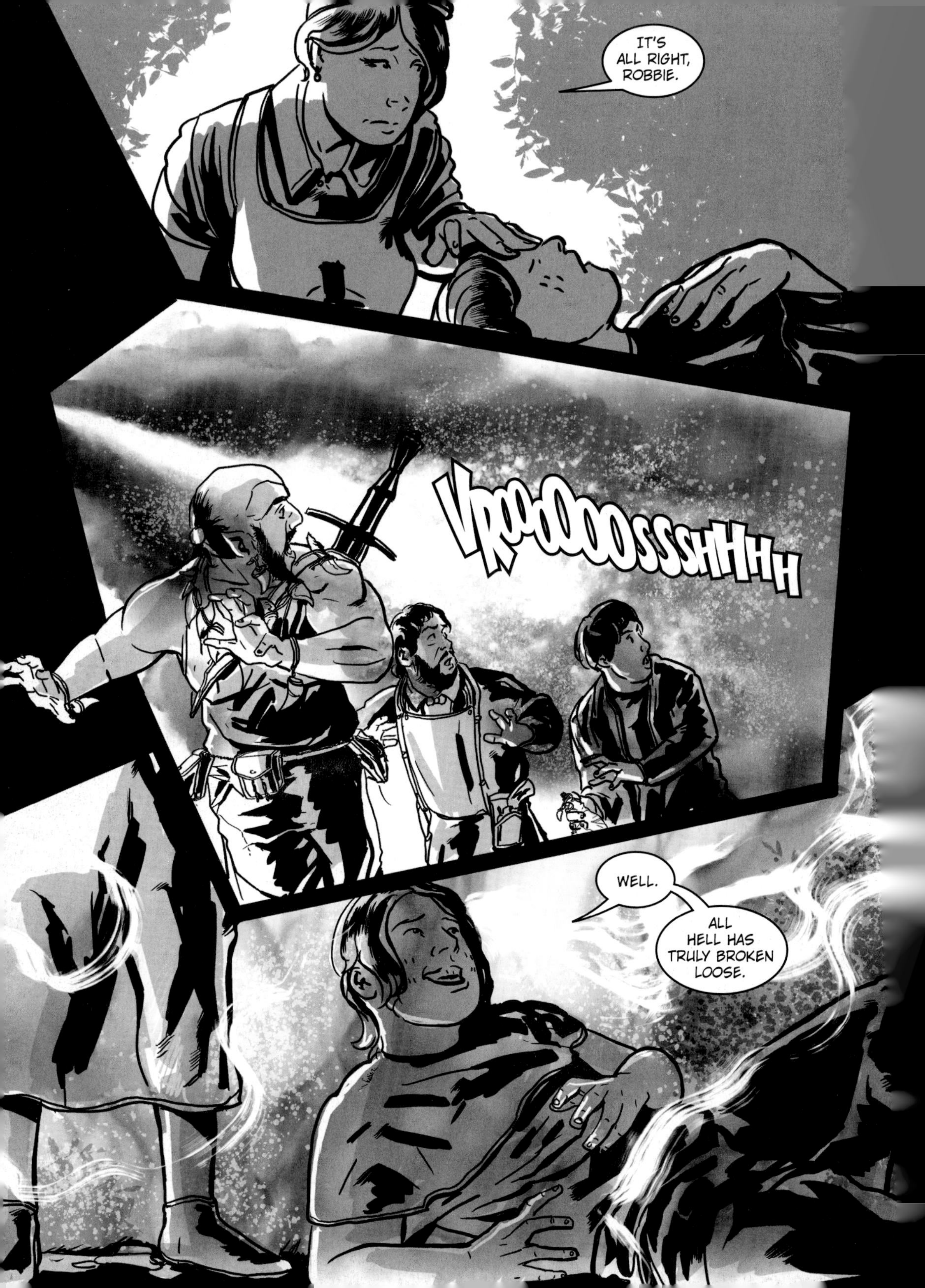
IT'S ALL RIGHT, ROBBIE.
VROOOOOOSSSHHHH
WELL.
ALL HELL HAS TRULY BROKEN LOOSE.

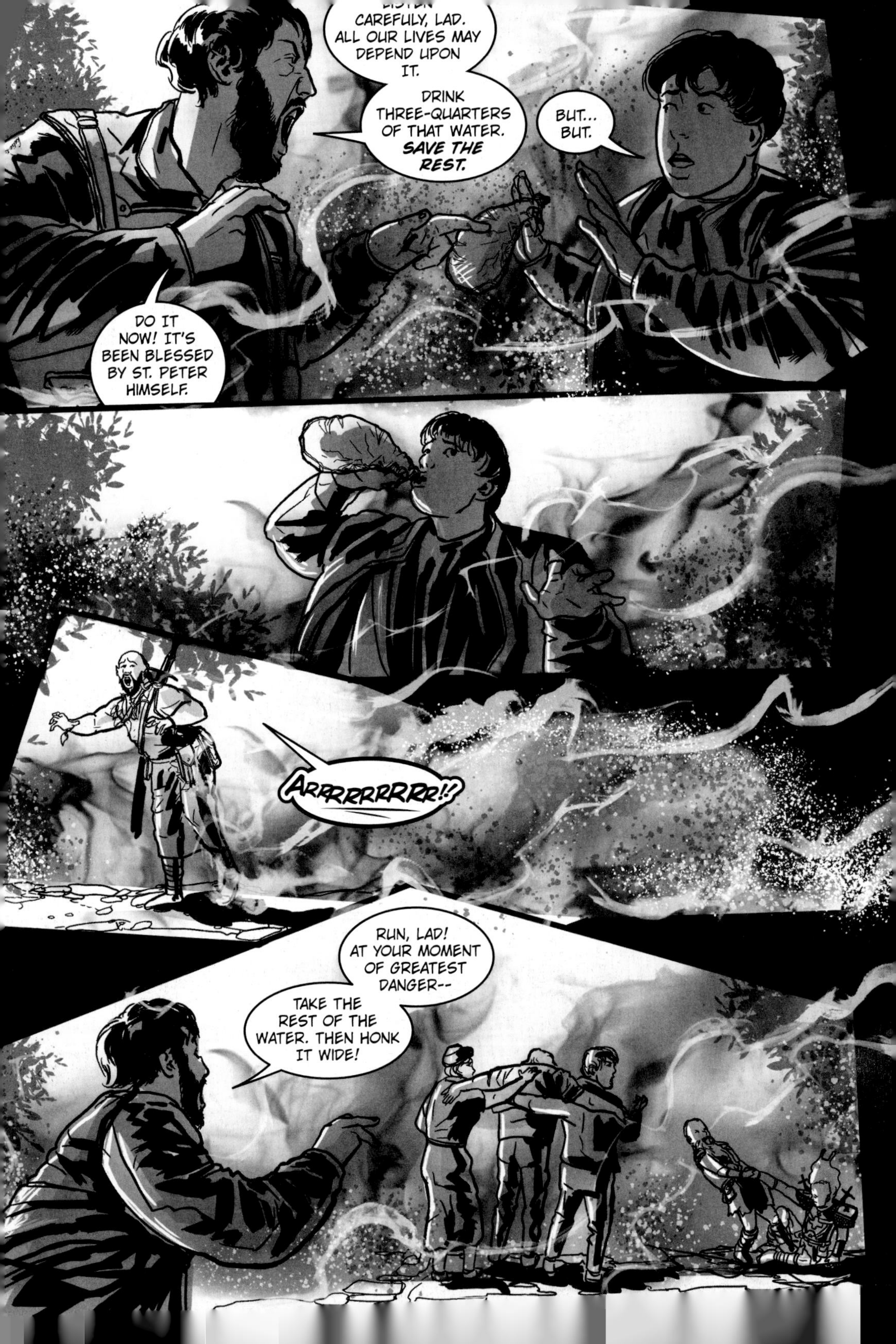
LISTEN CAREFULLY, LAD. ALL OUR LIVES MAY DEPEND UPON IT.
DRINK THREE-QUARTERS OF THAT WATER. *SAVE THE REST.*
BUT... BUT.
DO IT NOW! IT'S BEEN BLESSED BY ST. PETER HIMSELF.
ARRRRRRRRR!!
RUN, LAD! AT YOUR MOMENT OF GREATEST DANGER--
TAKE THE REST OF THE WATER. THEN HONK IT WIDE!

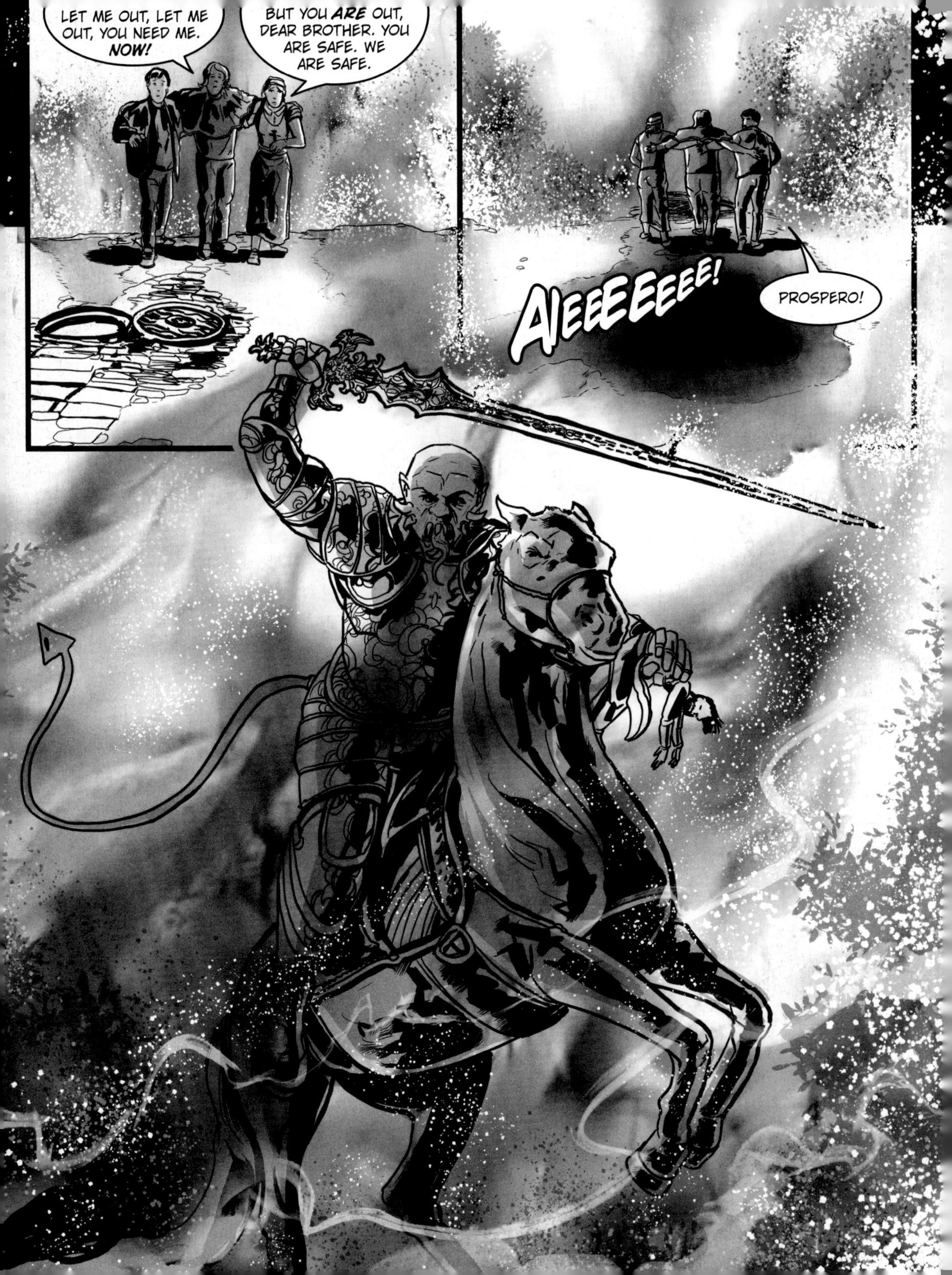

LET ME OUT, LET ME OUT, YOU NEED ME. **NOW!**
BUT YOU ***ARE*** OUT, DEAR BROTHER. YOU ARE SAFE. WE ARE SAFE.
AIEEEEEEE!
PROSPERO!

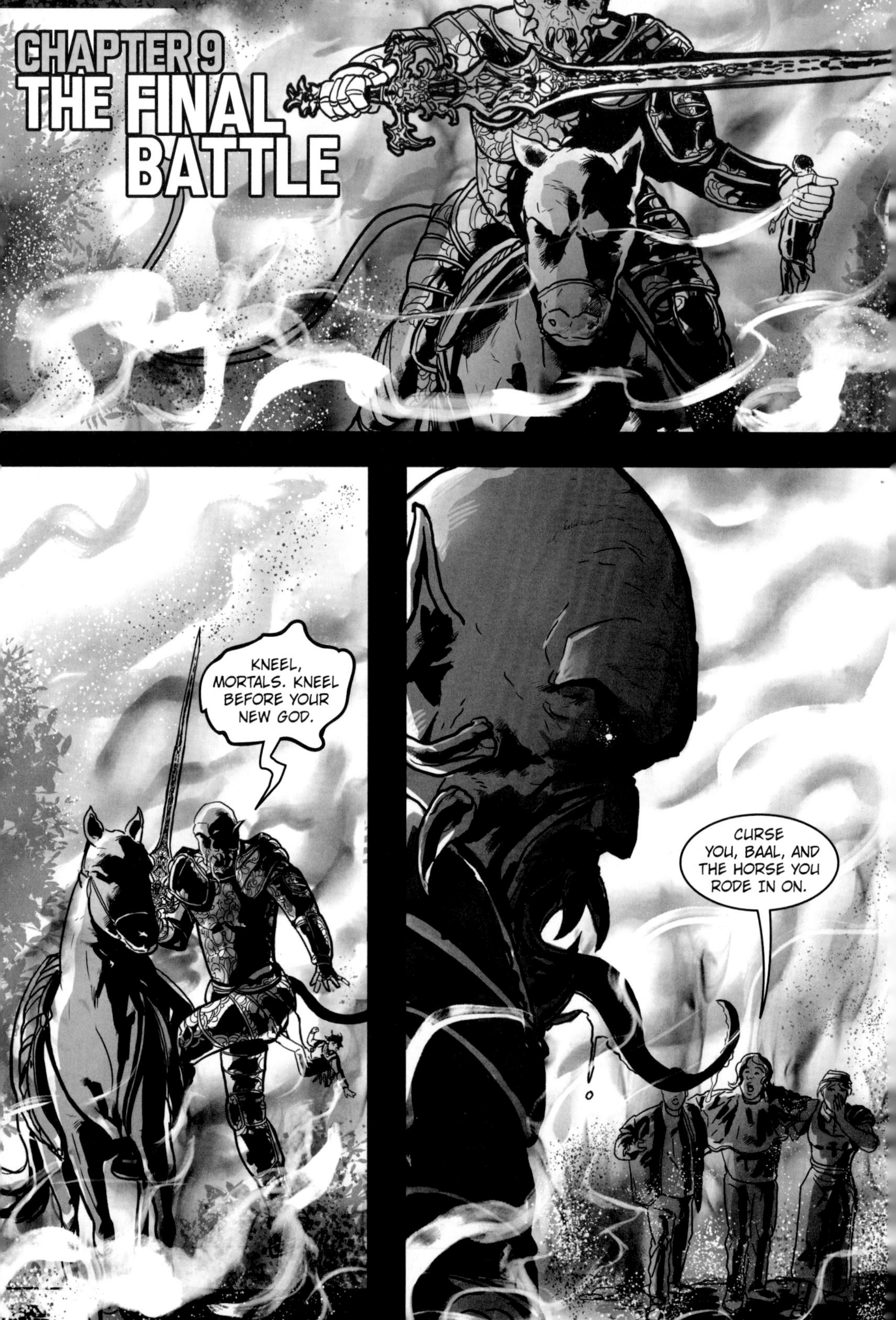
CHAPTER 9
THE FINAL BATTLE
KNEEL, MORTALS. KNEEL BEFORE YOUR NEW GOD.
CURSE YOU, BAAL, AND THE HORSE YOU RODE IN ON.

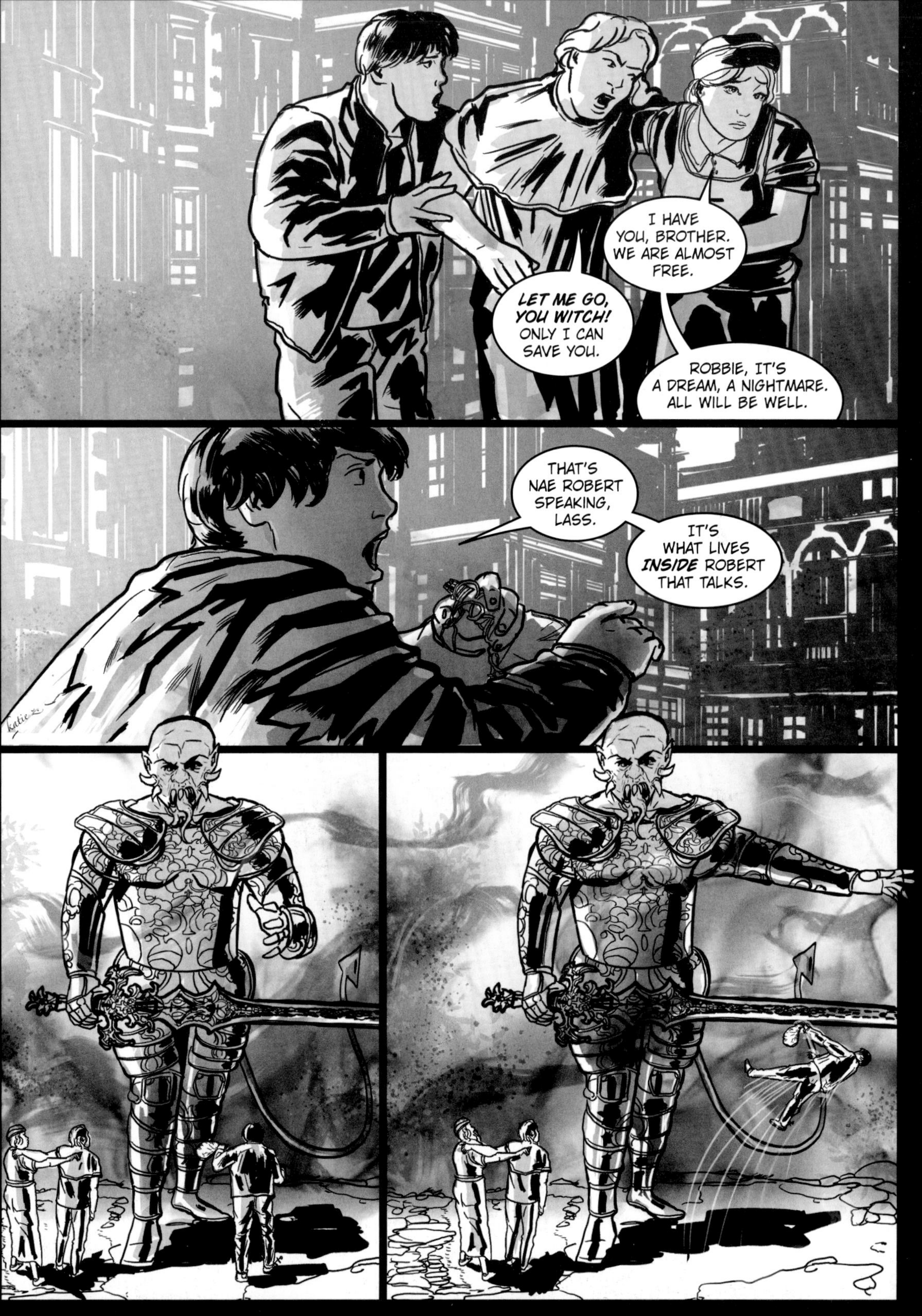
LET ME GO, YOU WITCH! ONLY I CAN SAVE YOU.
I HAVE YOU, BROTHER. WE ARE ALMOST FREE.
ROBBIE, IT'S A DREAM, A NIGHTMARE. ALL WILL BE WELL.
THAT'S NAE ROBERT SPEAKING, LASS.
IT'S WHAT LIVES INSIDE ROBERT THAT TALKS.
katie

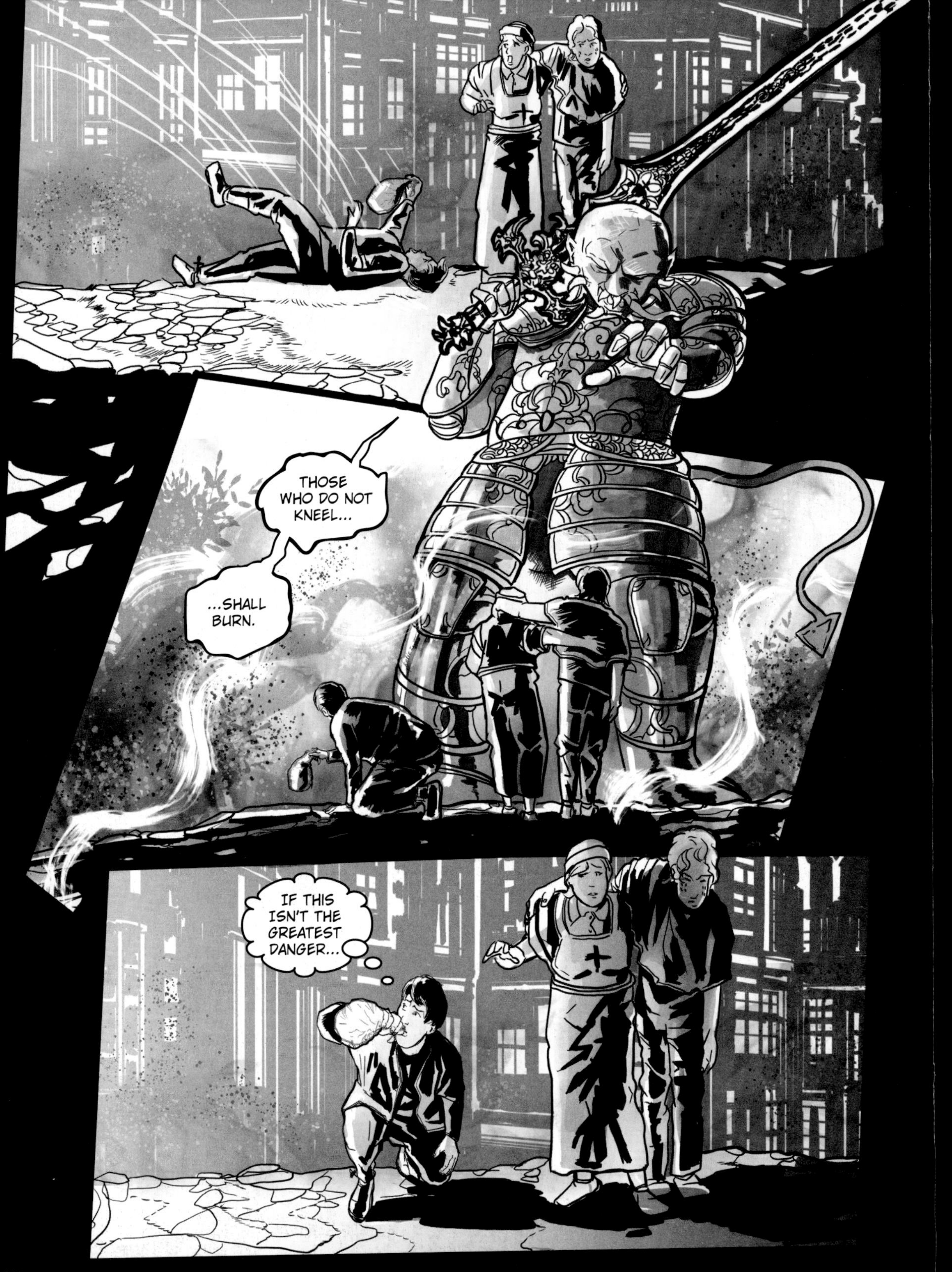
THOSE WHO DO NOT KNEEL...
...SHALL BURN.
IF THIS ISN'T THE GREATEST DANGER...

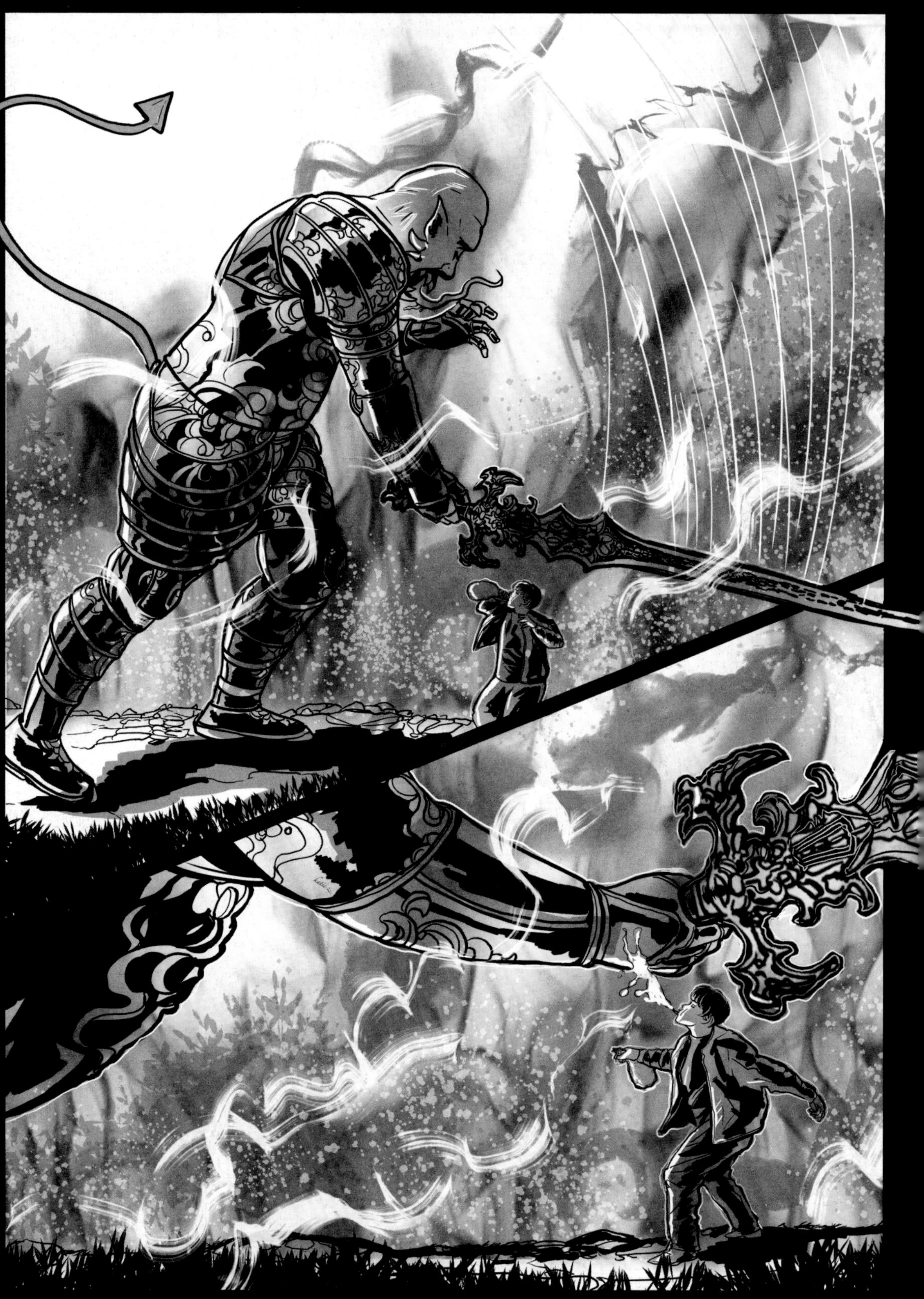

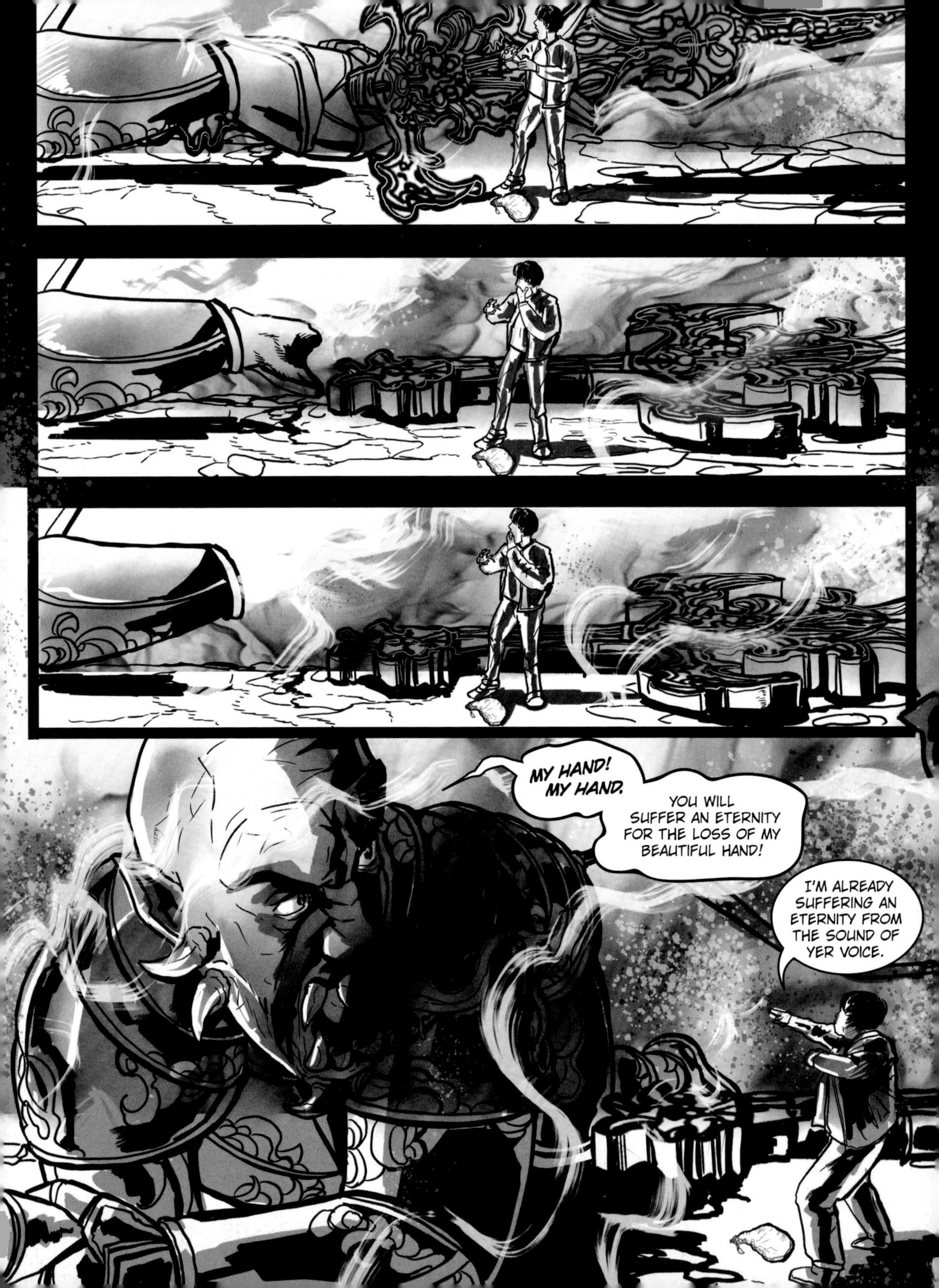
MY HAND! MY HAND.
YOU WILL SUFFER AN ETERNITY FOR THE LOSS OF MY BEAUTIFUL HAND!
I'M ALREADY SUFFERING AN ETERNITY FROM THE SOUND OF YER VOICE.

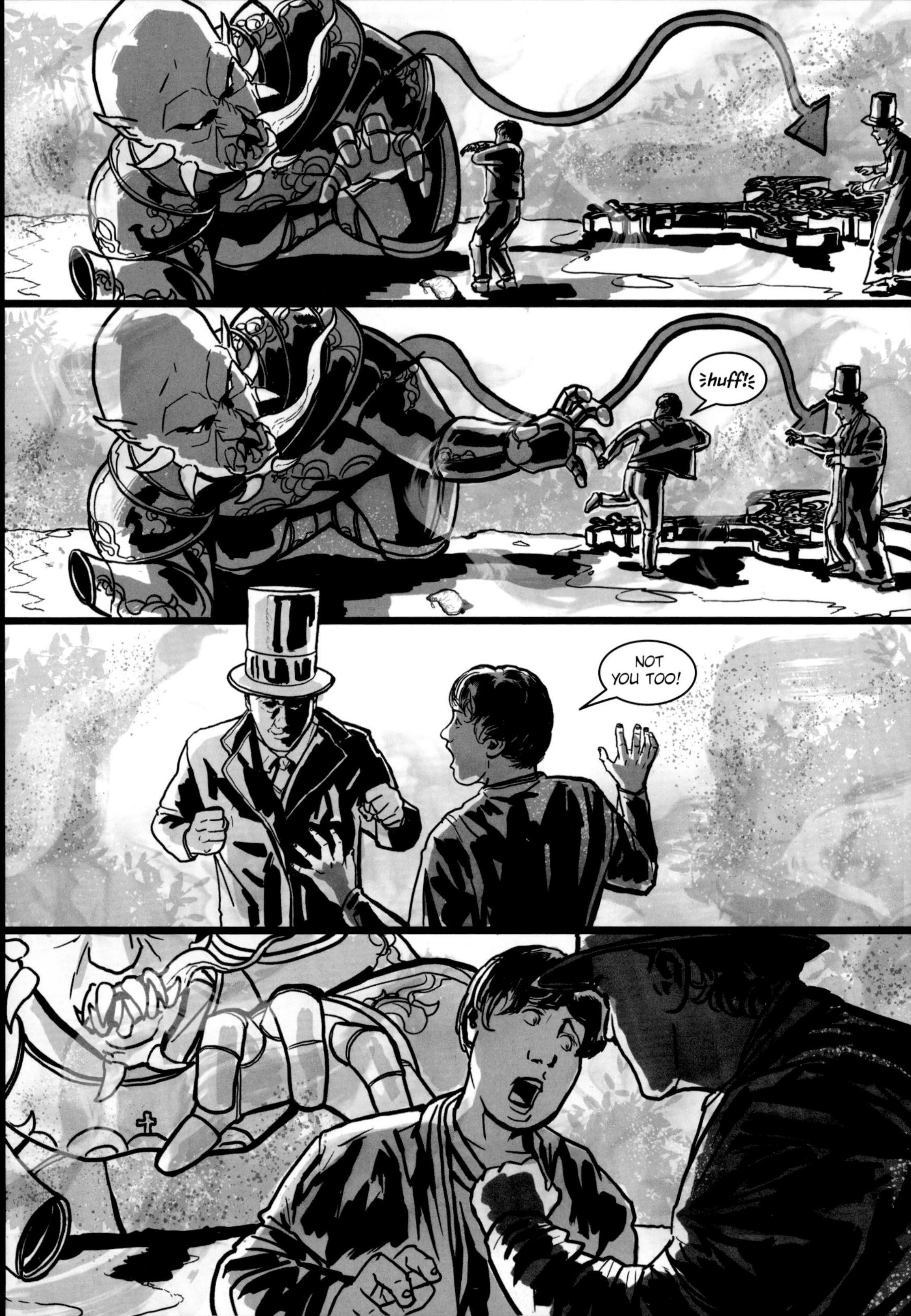
huff!
NOT YOU TOO!

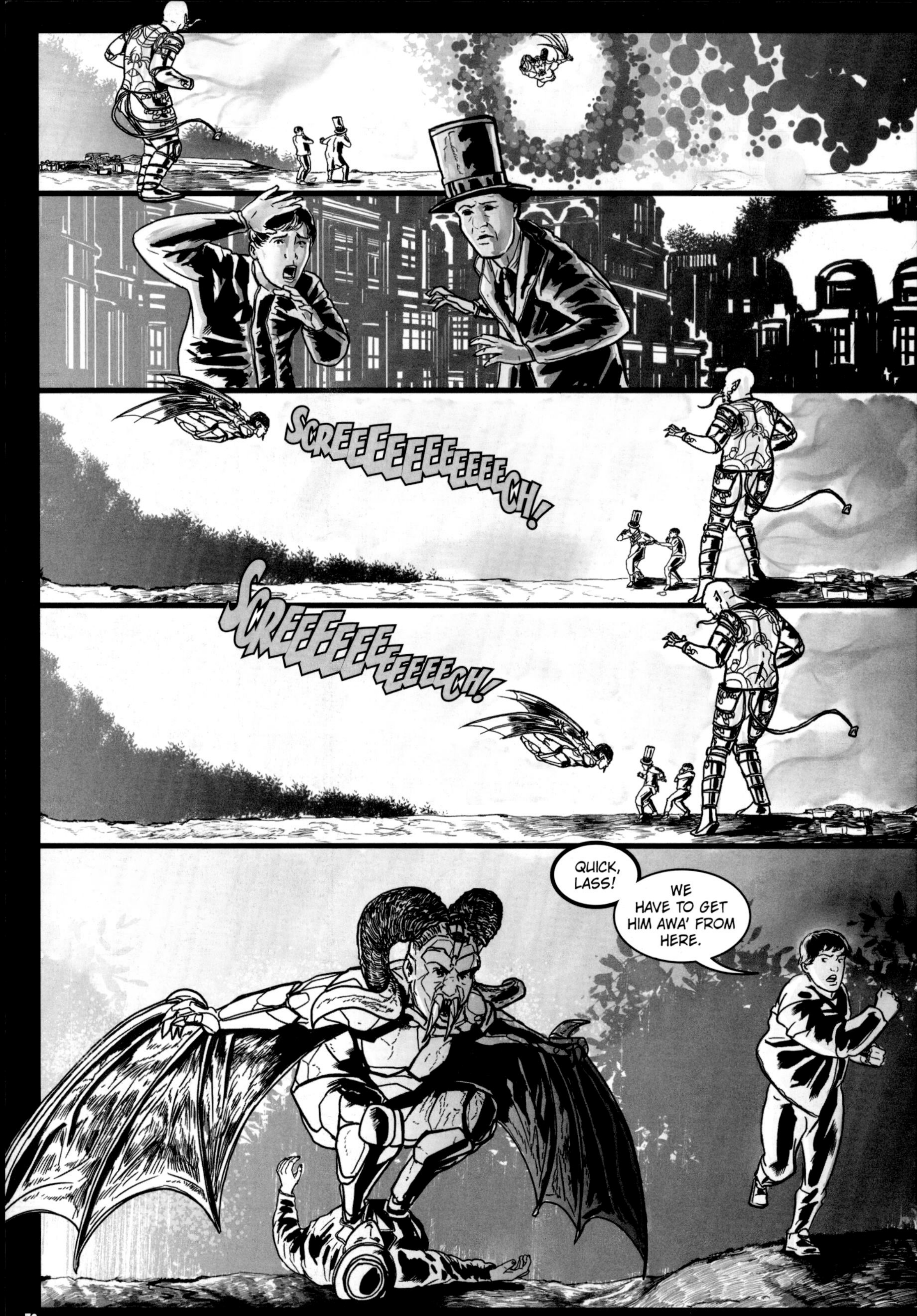

SCREEEEEEEEEEEEEECH!
SCREEEEEEEEEEEEEECH!
QUICK, LASS!
WE HAVE TO GET HIM AWA' FROM HERE.

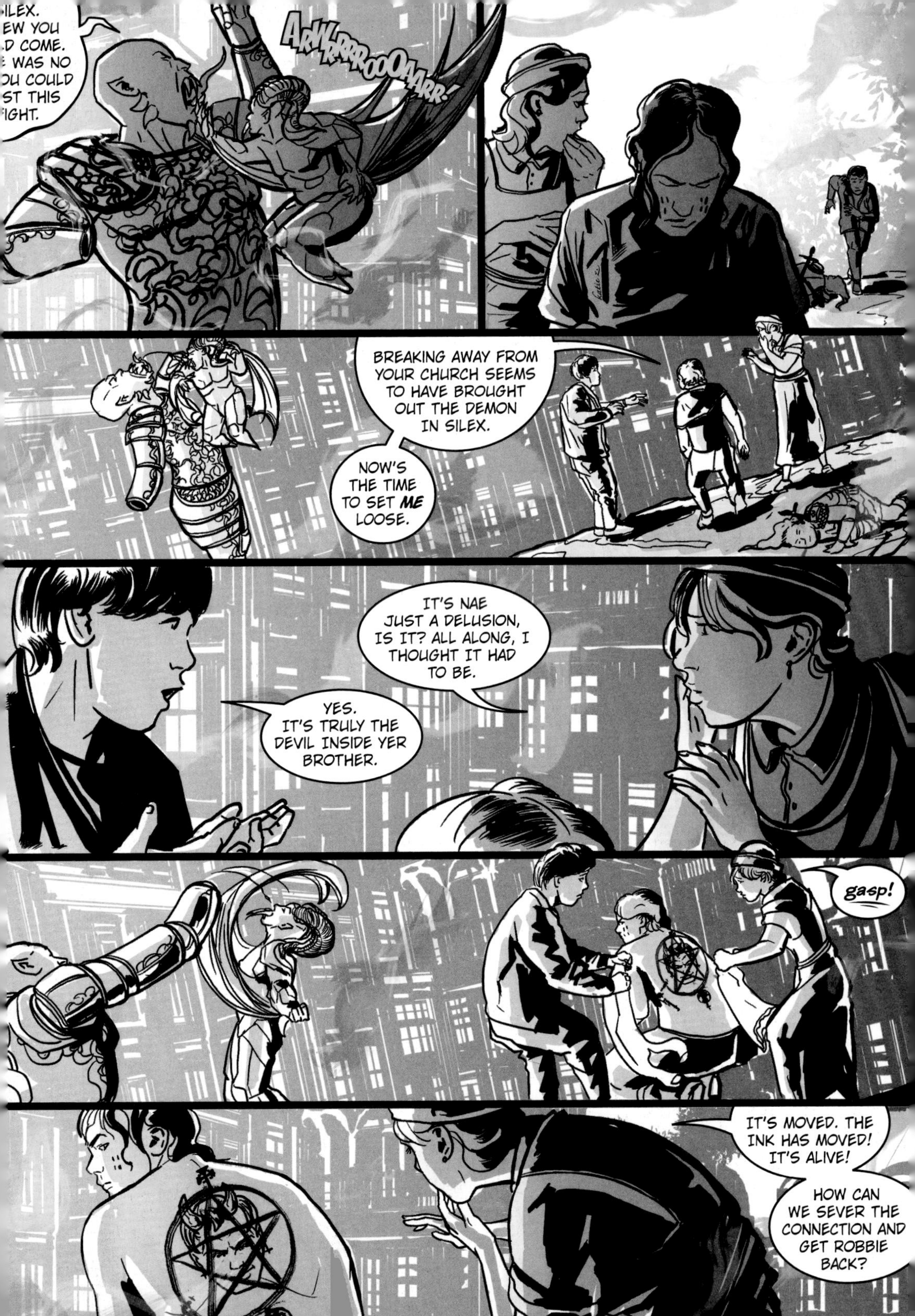
ILEX.
EW YOU
D COME.
WAS NO
U COULD
ST THIS
FIGHT.
ARWRRRROOOAARR!
BREAKING AWAY FROM YOUR CHURCH SEEMS TO HAVE BROUGHT OUT THE DEMON IN SILEX.
NOW'S THE TIME TO SET ME LOOSE.
IT'S NAE JUST A DELUSION, IS IT? ALL ALONG, I THOUGHT IT HAD TO BE.
YES. IT'S TRULY THE DEVIL INSIDE YER BROTHER.
gasp!
IT'S MOVED. THE INK HAS MOVED! IT'S ALIVE!
HOW CAN WE SEVER THE CONNECTION AND GET ROBBIE BACK?

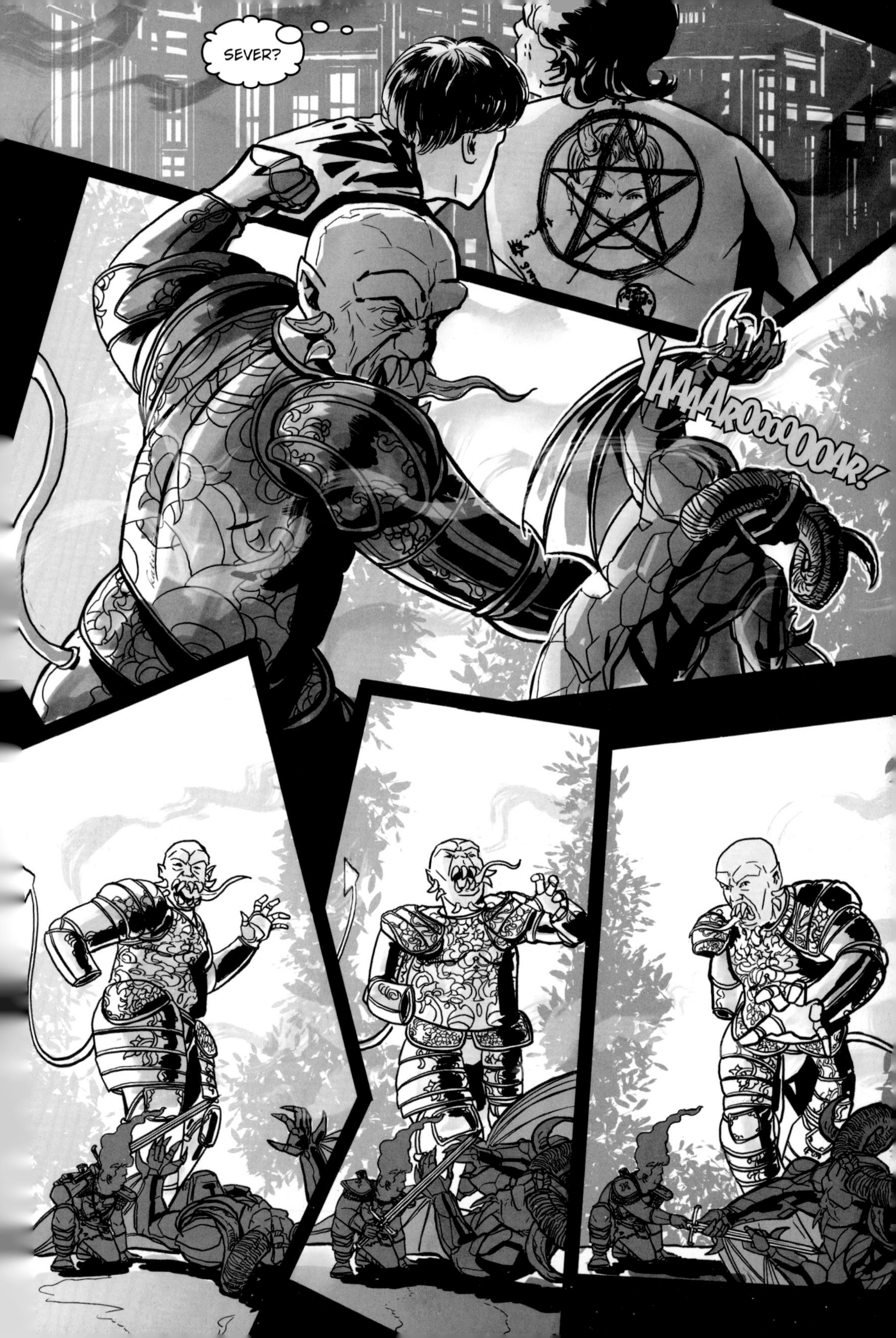
SEVER?
YAAAAROOOOOOOAR!

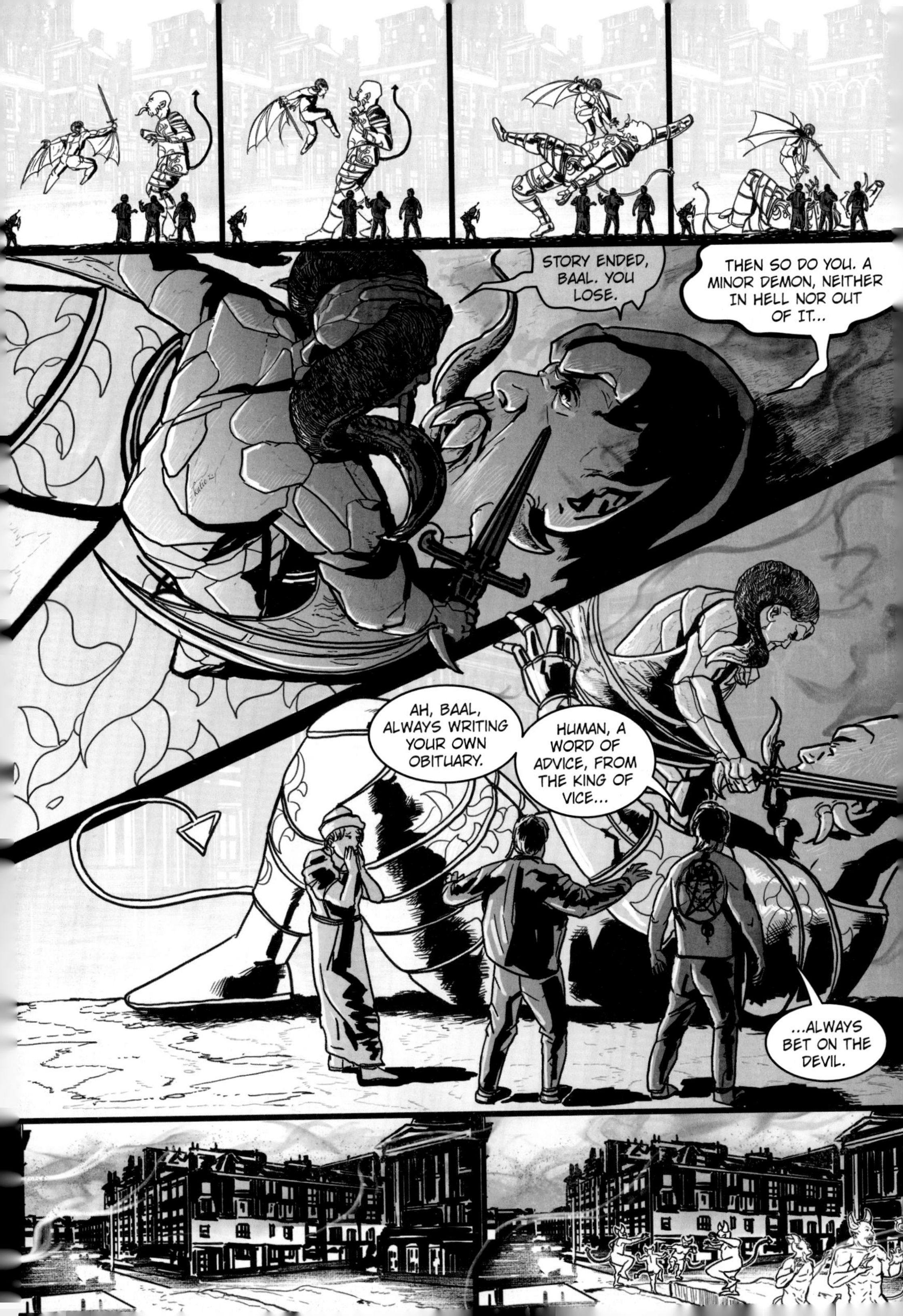
STORY ENDED, BAAL. YOU LOSE.
THEN SO DO YOU. A MINOR DEMON, NEITHER IN HELL NOR OUT OF IT...
AH, BAAL, ALWAYS WRITING YOUR OWN OBITUARY.
HUMAN, A WORD OF ADVICE, FROM THE KING OF VICE...
...ALWAYS BET ON THE DEVIL.

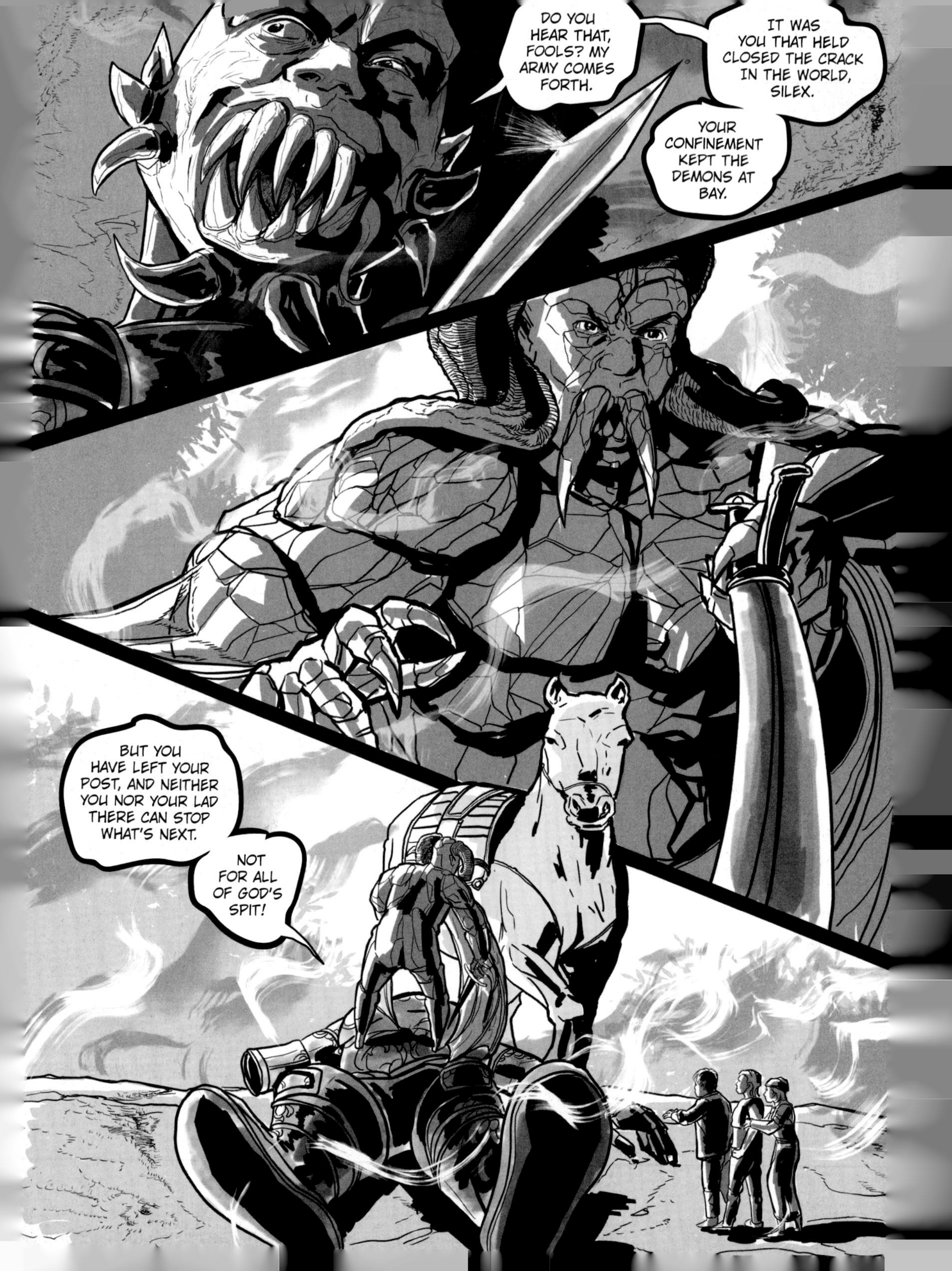
DO YOU HEAR THAT, FOOLS? MY ARMY COMES FORTH.
IT WAS YOU THAT HELD CLOSED THE CRACK IN THE WORLD, SILEX.
YOUR CONFINEMENT KEPT THE DEMONS AT BAY.
BUT YOU HAVE LEFT YOUR POST, AND NEITHER YOU NOR YOUR LAD THERE CAN STOP WHAT'S NEXT.
NOT FOR ALL OF GOD'S SPIT!

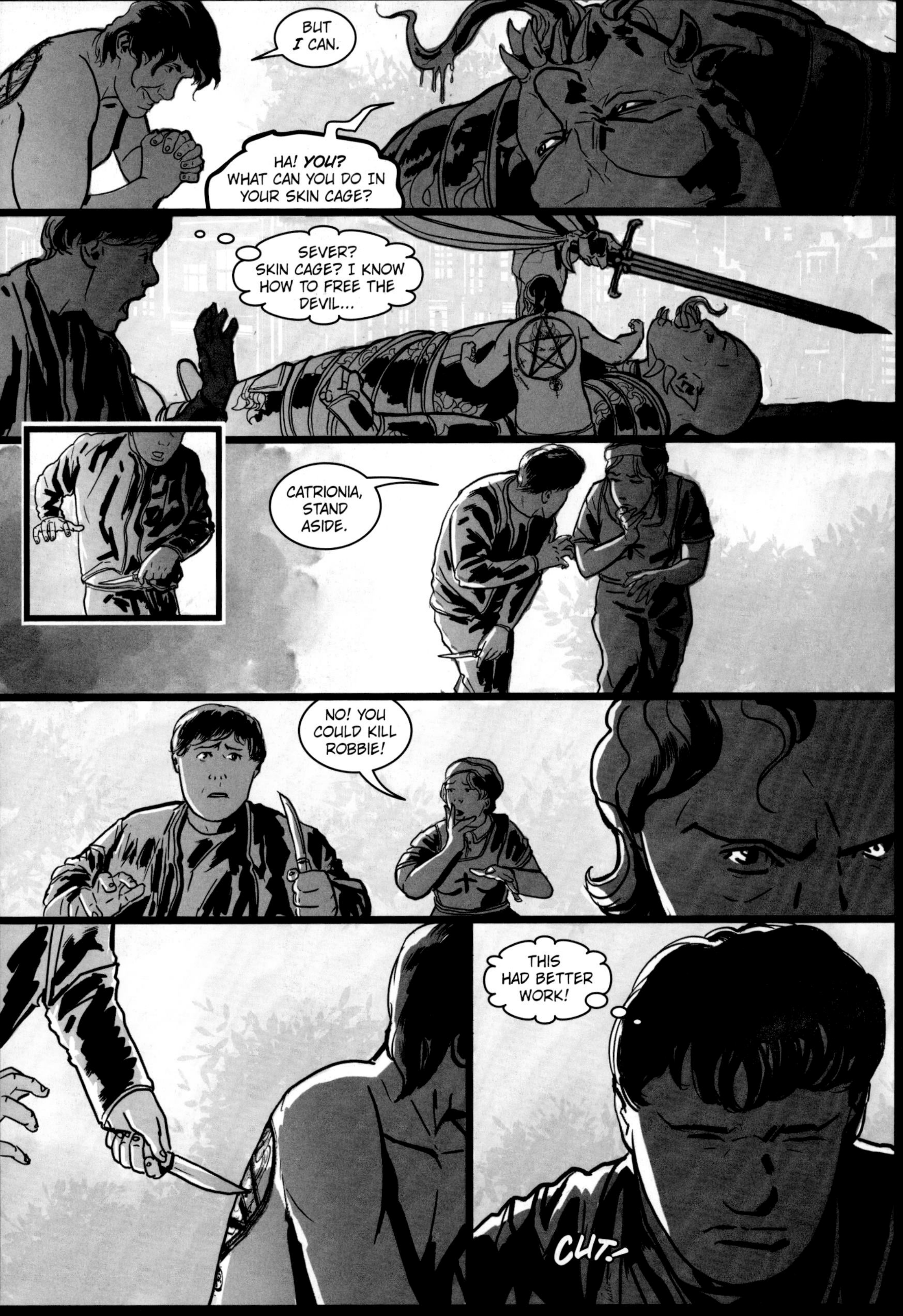
BUT
I CAN.
HA! YOU?
WHAT CAN YOU DO IN
YOUR SKIN CAGE?
SEVER?
SKIN CAGE? I KNOW
HOW TO FREE THE
DEVIL...
CATRIONIA,
STAND
ASIDE.
NO! YOU
COULD KILL
ROBBIE!
THIS
HAD BETTER
WORK!
CUT!

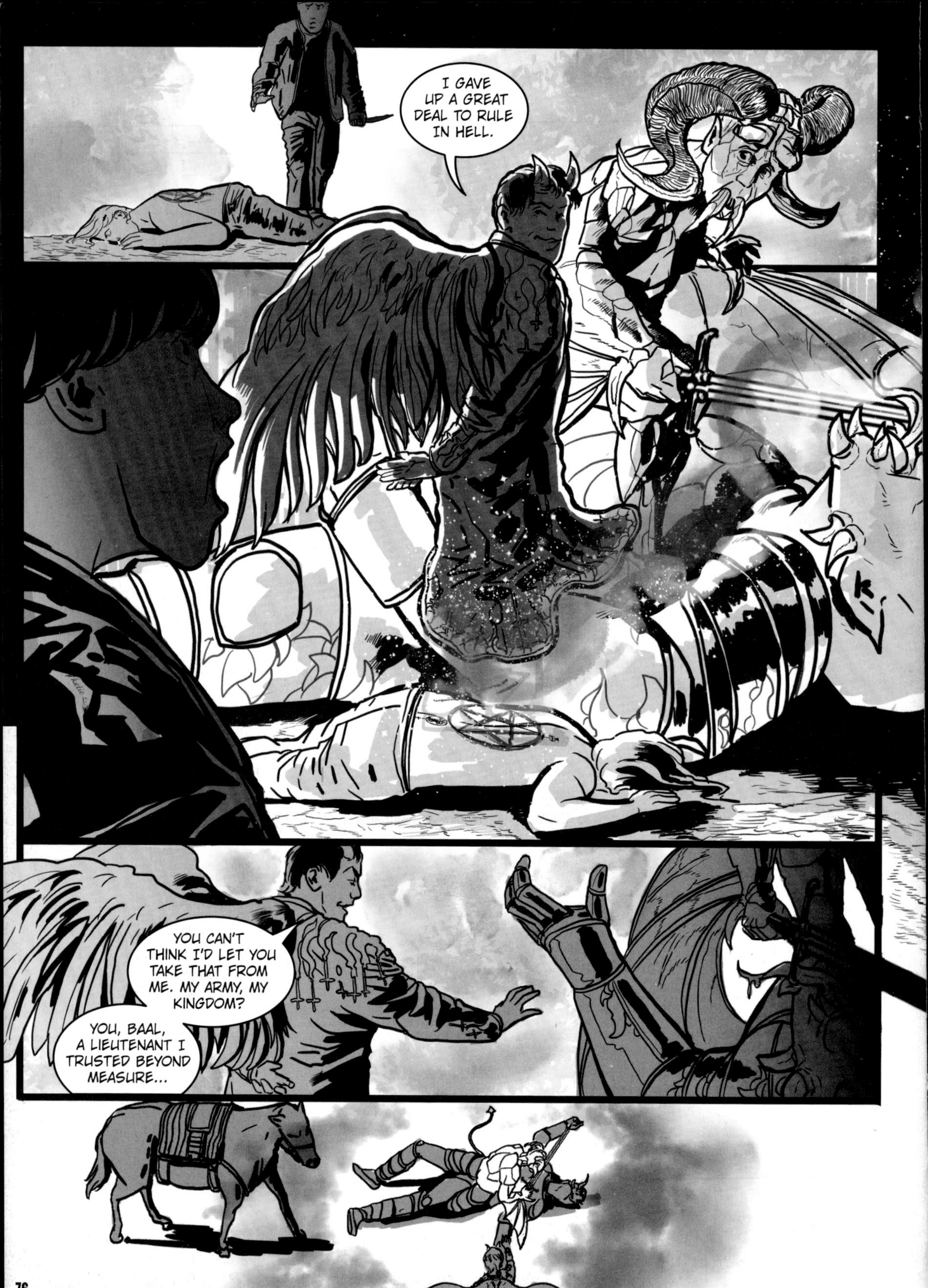

I GAVE UP A GREAT DEAL TO RULE IN HELL.
YOU CAN'T THINK I'D LET YOU TAKE THAT FROM ME. MY ARMY, MY KINGDOM?
YOU, BAAL, A LIEUTENANT I TRUSTED BEYOND MEASURE...

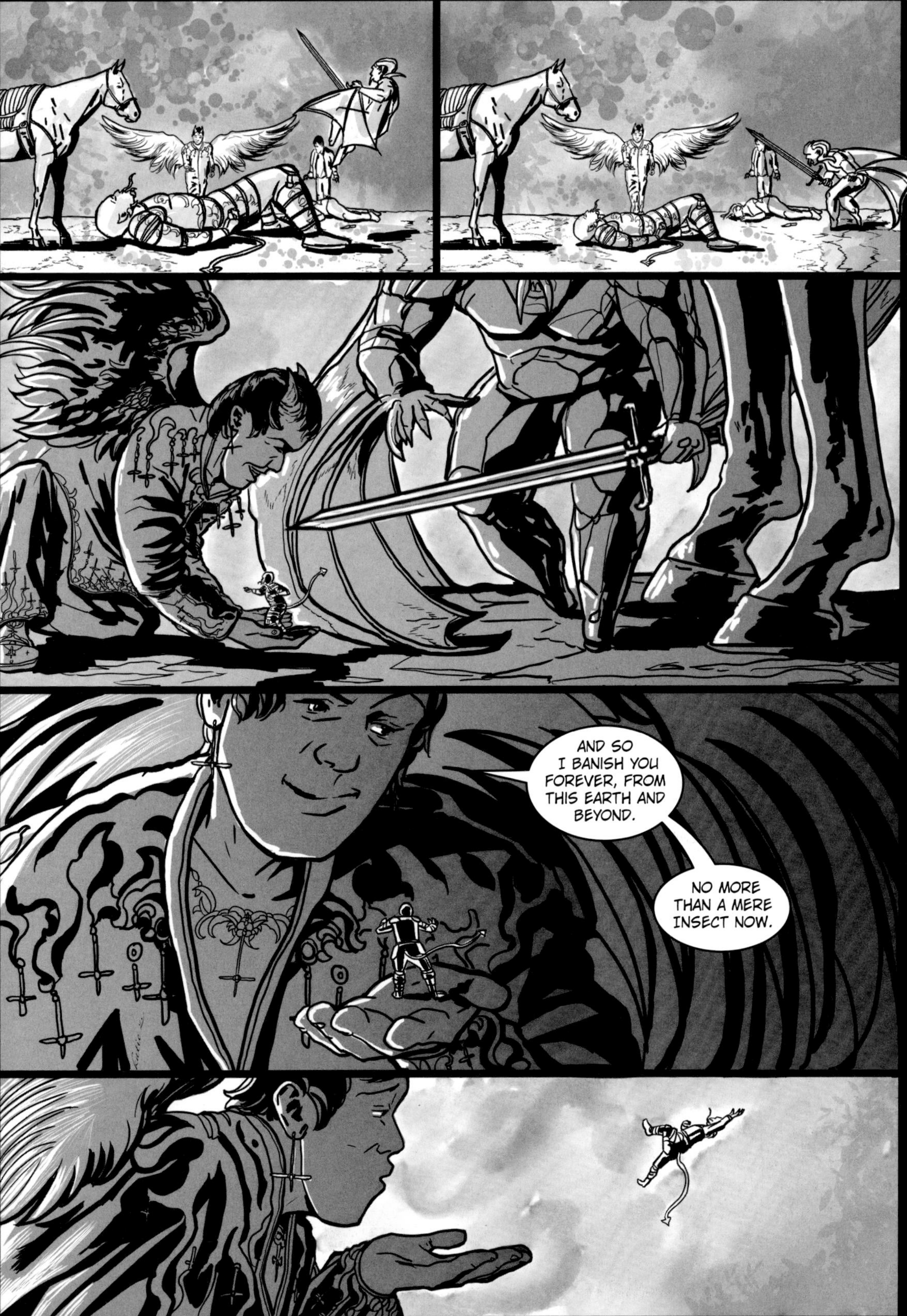
AND SO I BANISH YOU FOREVER, FROM THIS EARTH AND BEYOND.
NO MORE THAN A MERE INSECT NOW.

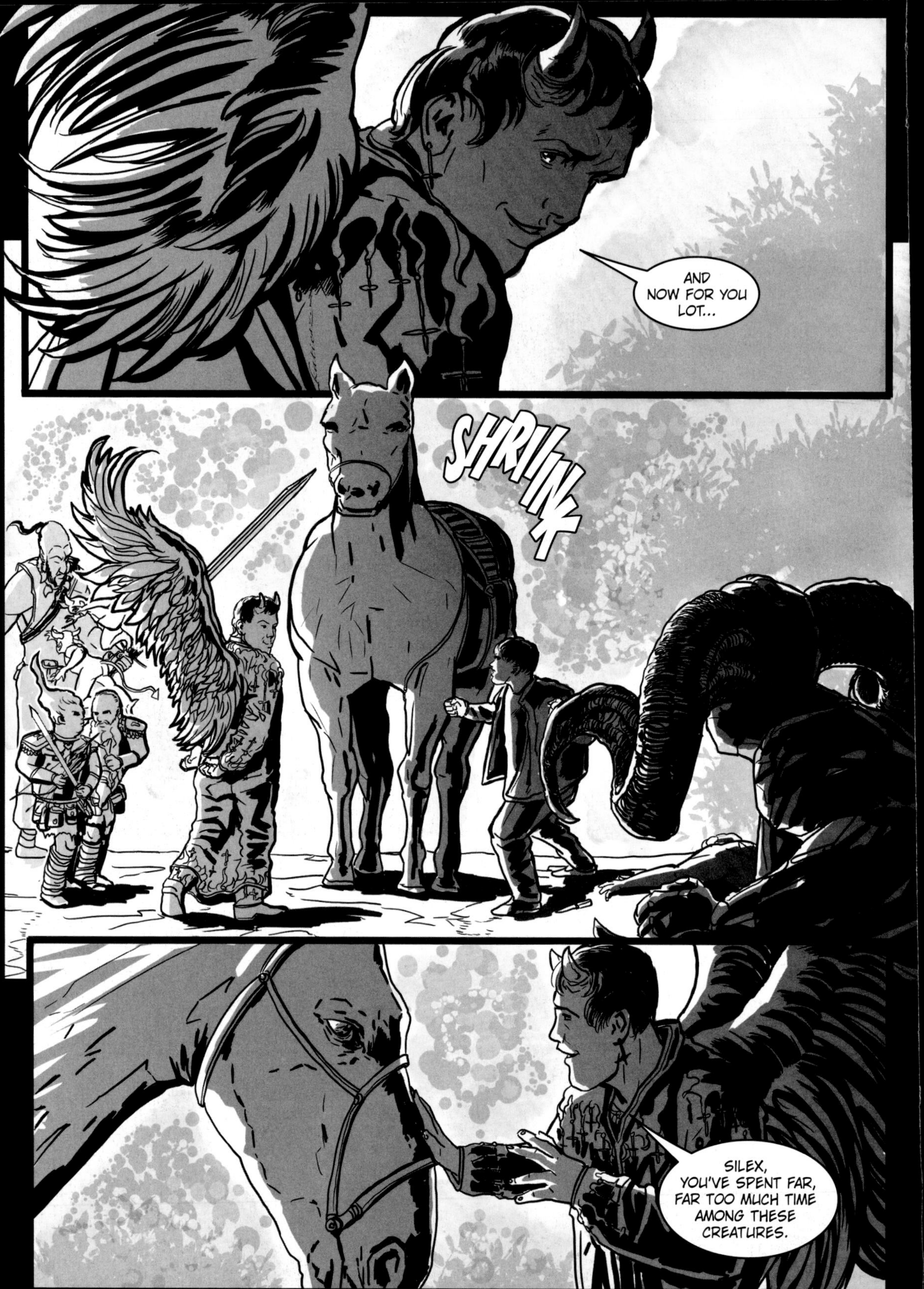
AND NOW FOR YOU LOT...
SHRIIINK
SILEX, YOU'VE SPENT FAR, FAR TOO MUCH TIME AMONG THESE CREATURES.

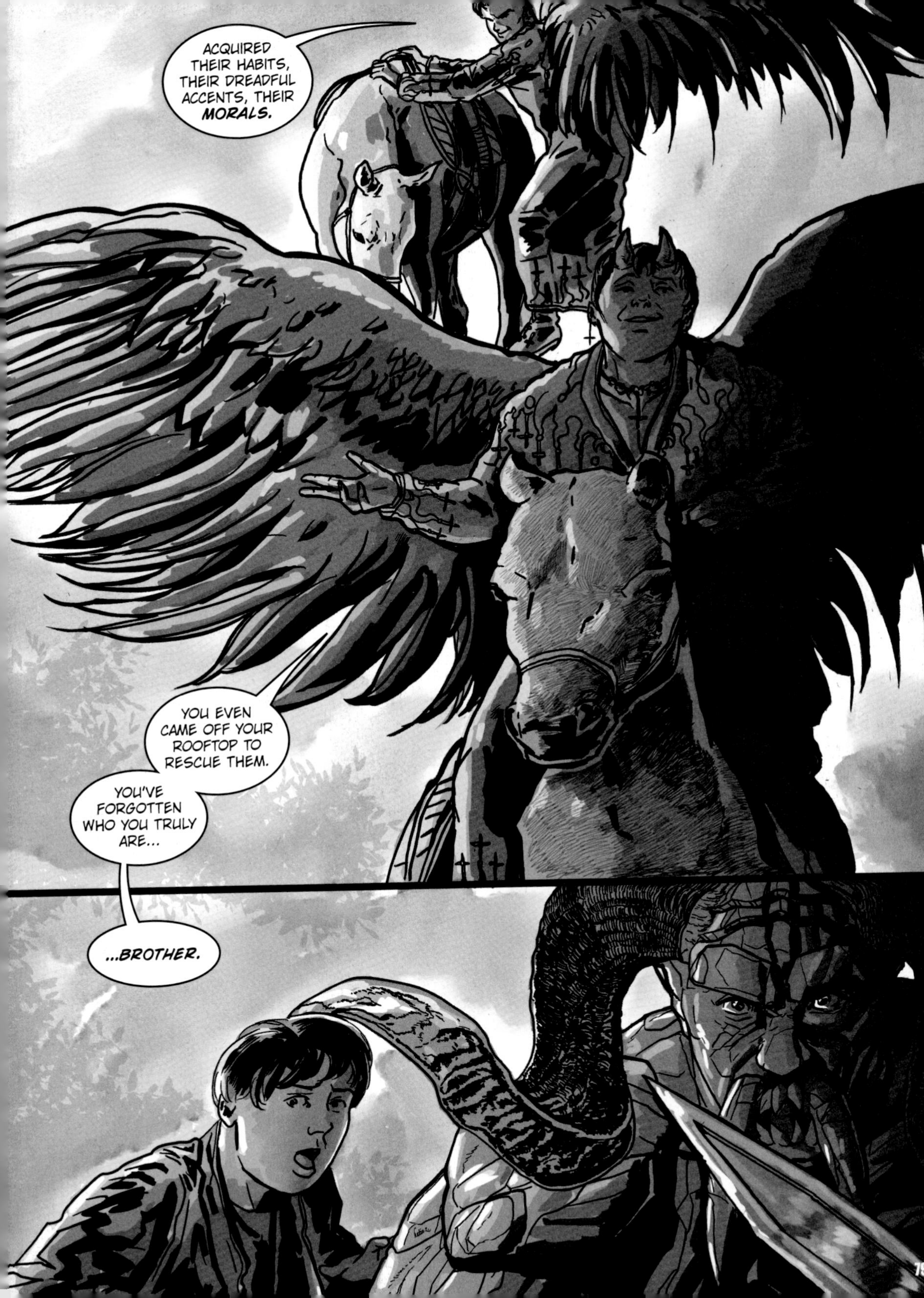
ACQUIRED THEIR HABITS, THEIR DREADFUL ACCENTS, THEIR MORALS.
YOU EVEN CAME OFF YOUR ROOFTOP TO RESCUE THEM.
YOU'VE FORGOTTEN WHO YOU TRULY ARE...
...BROTHER.

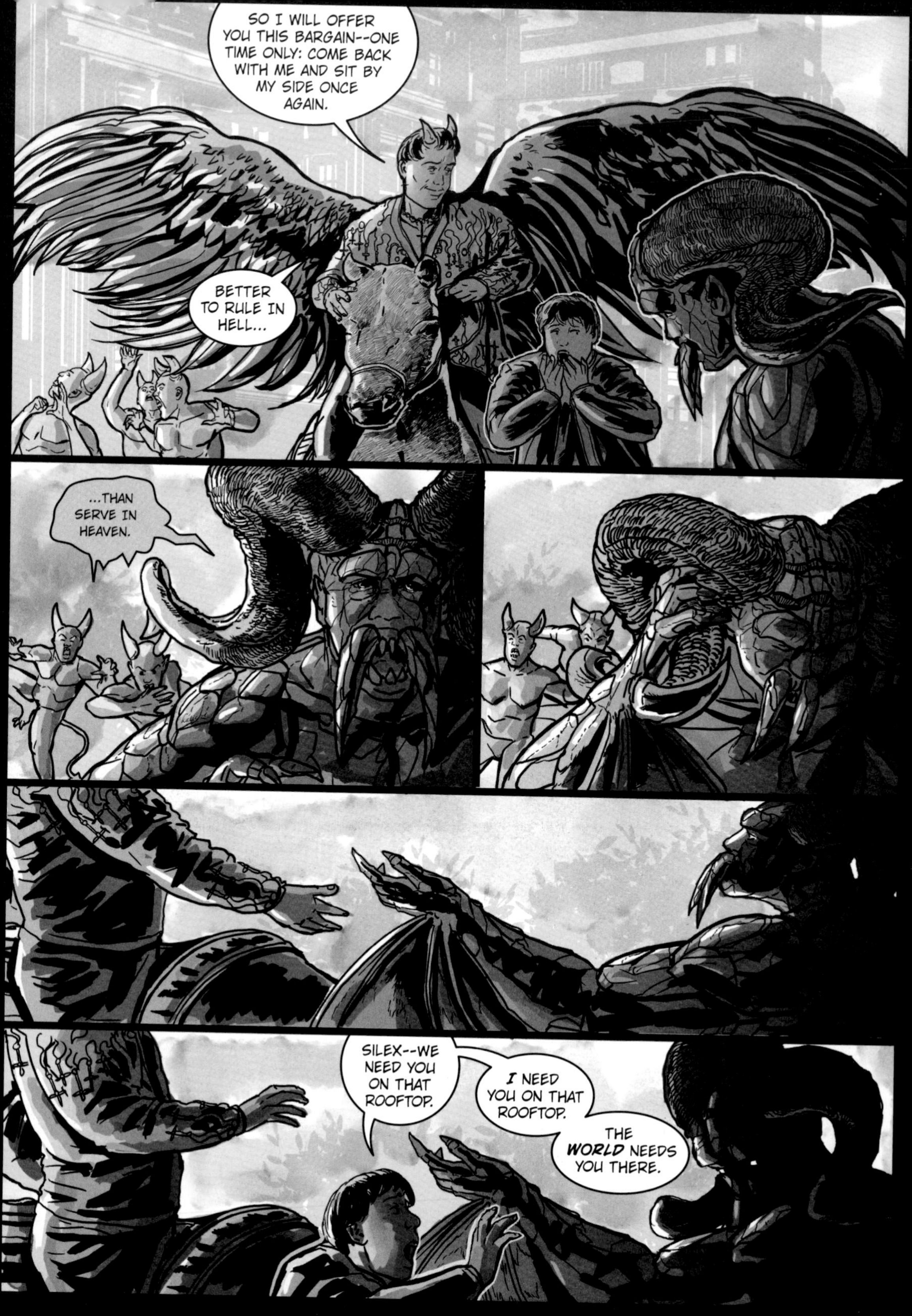
SO I WILL OFFER YOU THIS BARGAIN--ONE TIME ONLY: COME BACK WITH ME AND SIT BY MY SIDE ONCE AGAIN.
BETTER TO RULE IN HELL...
...THAN SERVE IN HEAVEN.
SILEX--WE NEED YOU ON THAT ROOFTOP.
I NEED YOU ON THAT ROOFTOP.
THE WORLD NEEDS YOU THERE.

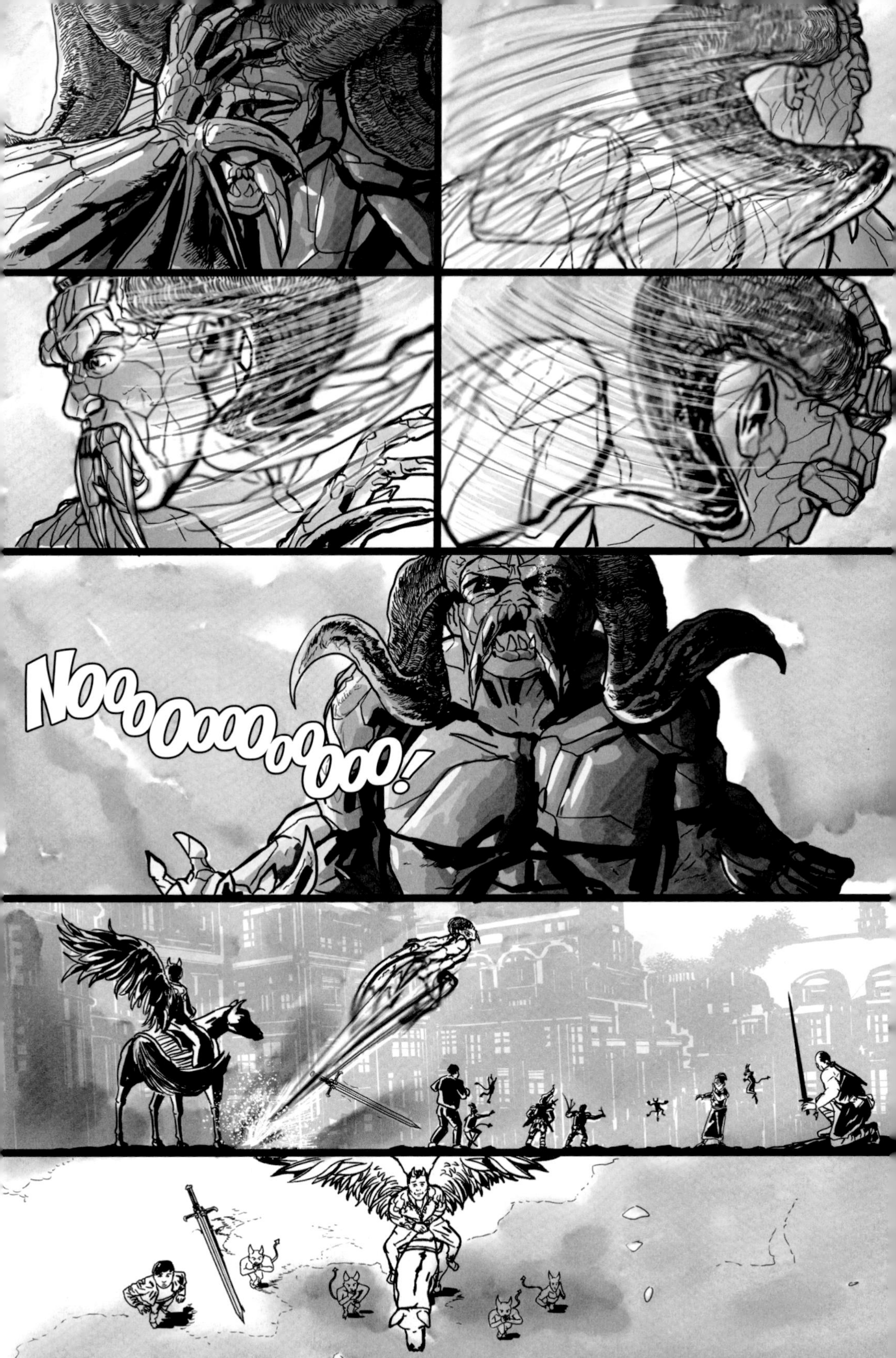
NOooOOOOooOOO!

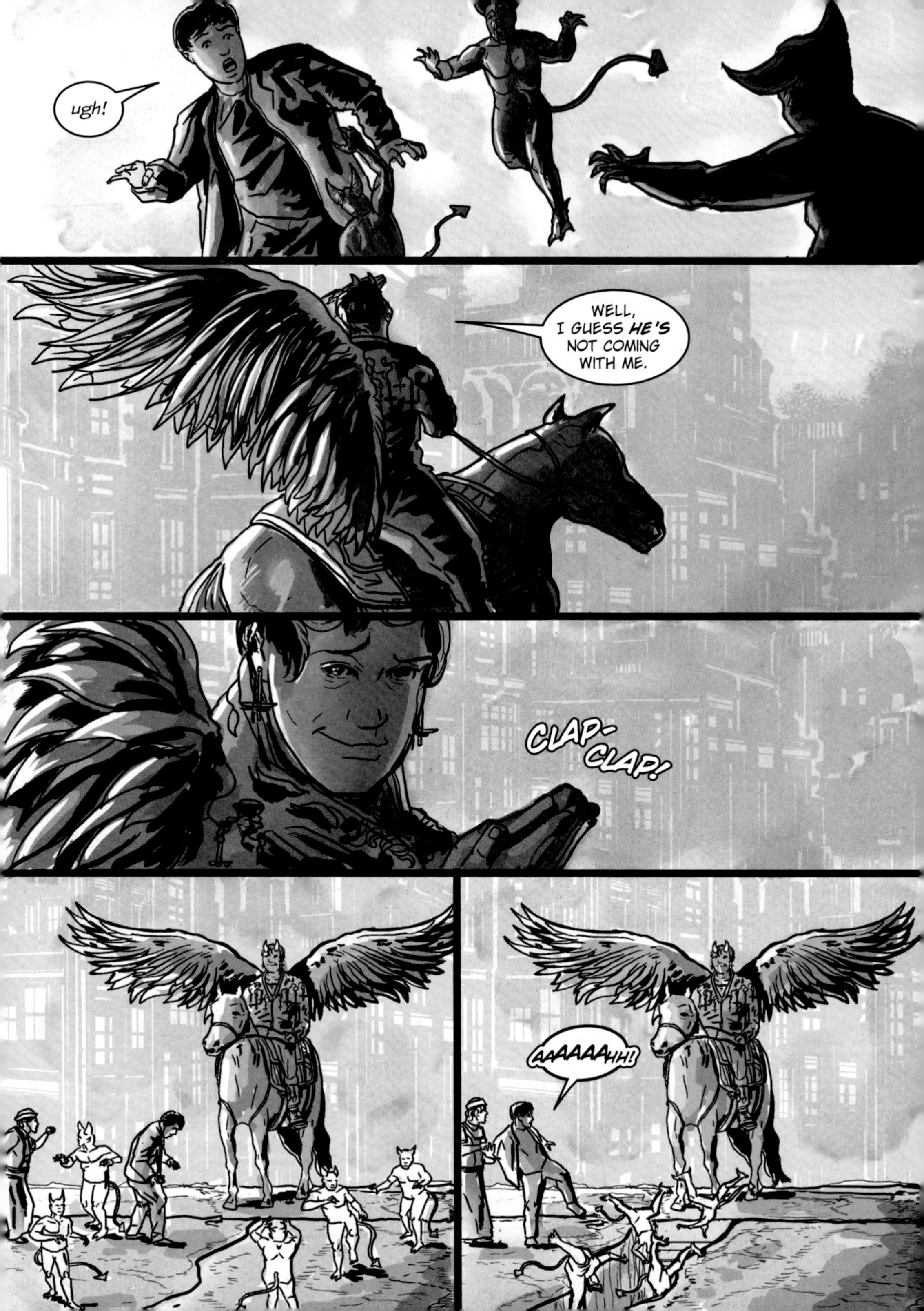
ugh!
WELL, I GUESS HE'S NOT COMING WITH ME.
CLAP-CLAP!
AAAAAAHH!

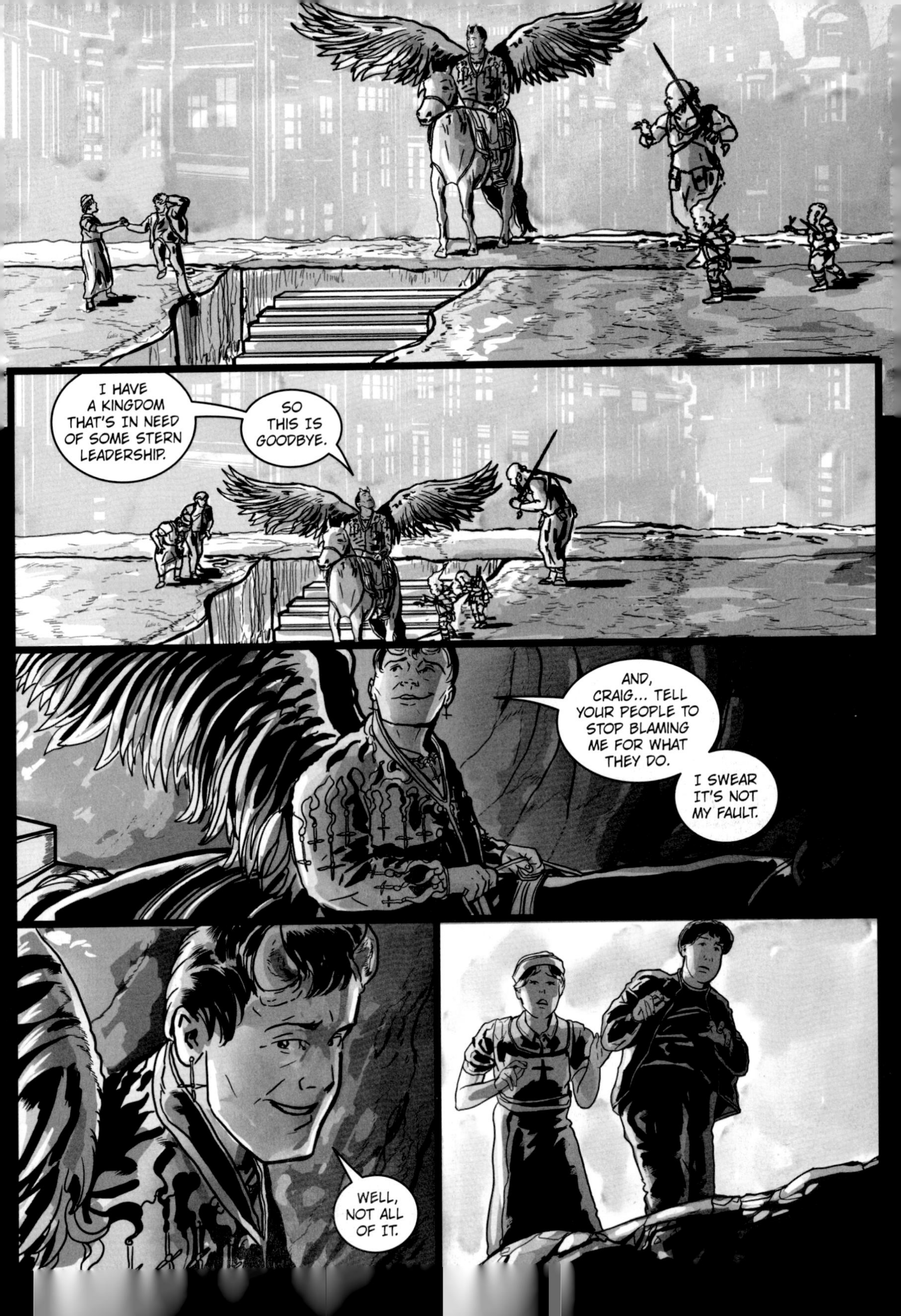
I HAVE A KINGDOM THAT'S IN NEED OF SOME STERN LEADERSHIP.
SO THIS IS GOODBYE.
AND, CRAIG... TELL YOUR PEOPLE TO STOP BLAMING ME FOR WHAT THEY DO.
I SWEAR IT'S NOT MY FAULT.
WELL, NOT ALL OF IT.

CHAPTER 10 AND AFTER

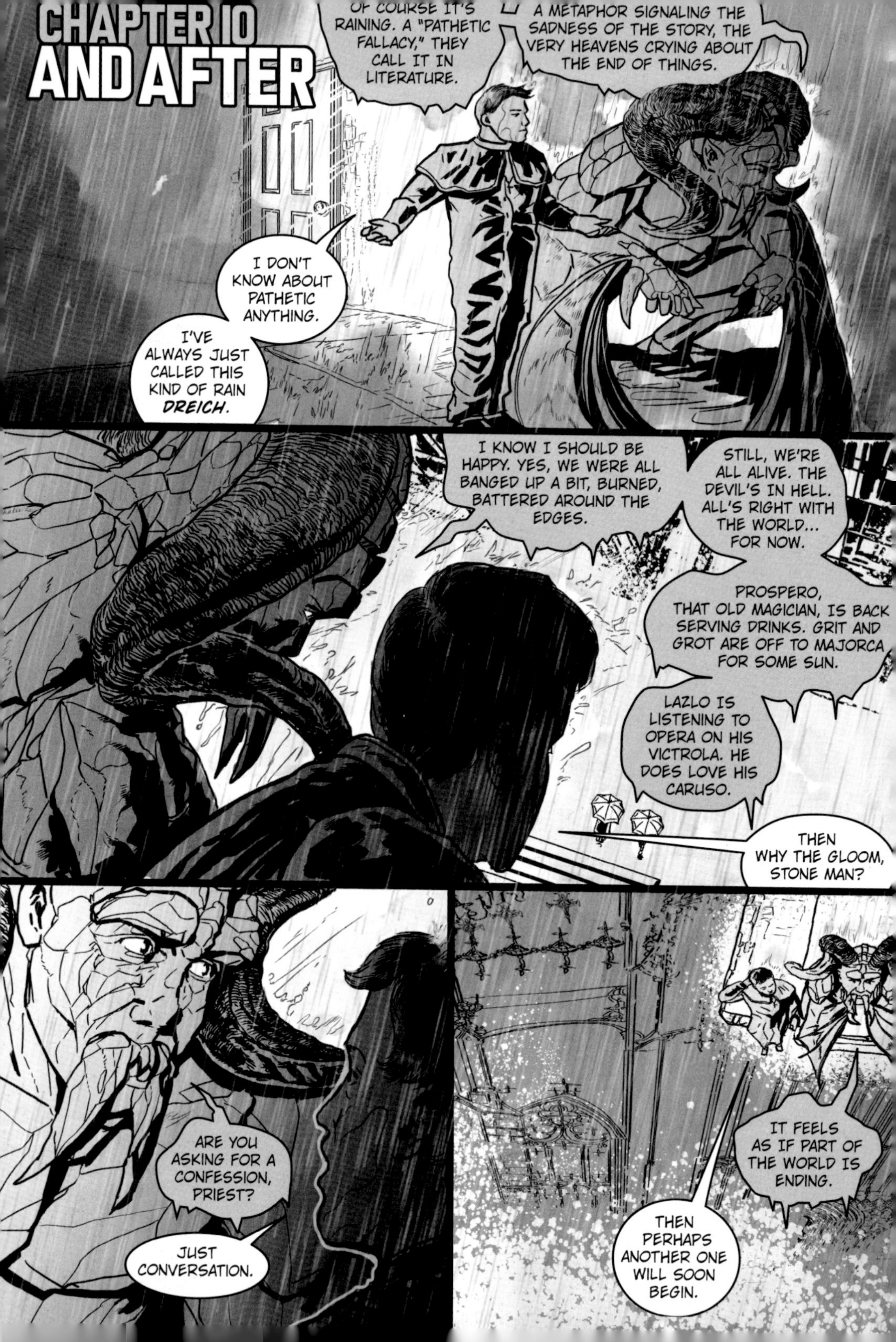

OF COURSE IT'S RAINING. A "PATHETIC FALLACY," THEY CALL IT IN LITERATURE.
A METAPHOR SIGNALING THE SADNESS OF THE STORY, THE VERY HEAVENS CRYING ABOUT THE END OF THINGS.
I DON'T KNOW ABOUT PATHETIC ANYTHING.
I'VE ALWAYS JUST CALLED THIS KIND OF RAIN DREICH.
I KNOW I SHOULD BE HAPPY. YES, WE WERE ALL BANGED UP A BIT, BURNED, BATTERED AROUND THE EDGES.
STILL, WE'RE ALL ALIVE. THE DEVIL'S IN HELL. ALL'S RIGHT WITH THE WORLD... FOR NOW.
PROSPERO, THAT OLD MAGICIAN, IS BACK SERVING DRINKS. GRIT AND GROT ARE OFF TO MAJORCA FOR SOME SUN.
LAZLO IS LISTENING TO OPERA ON HIS VICTROLA. HE DOES LOVE HIS CARUSO.
THEN WHY THE GLOOM, STONE MAN?
ARE YOU ASKING FOR A CONFESSION, PRIEST?
JUST CONVERSATION.
IT FEELS AS IF PART OF THE WORLD IS ENDING.
THEN PERHAPS ANOTHER ONE WILL SOON BEGIN.

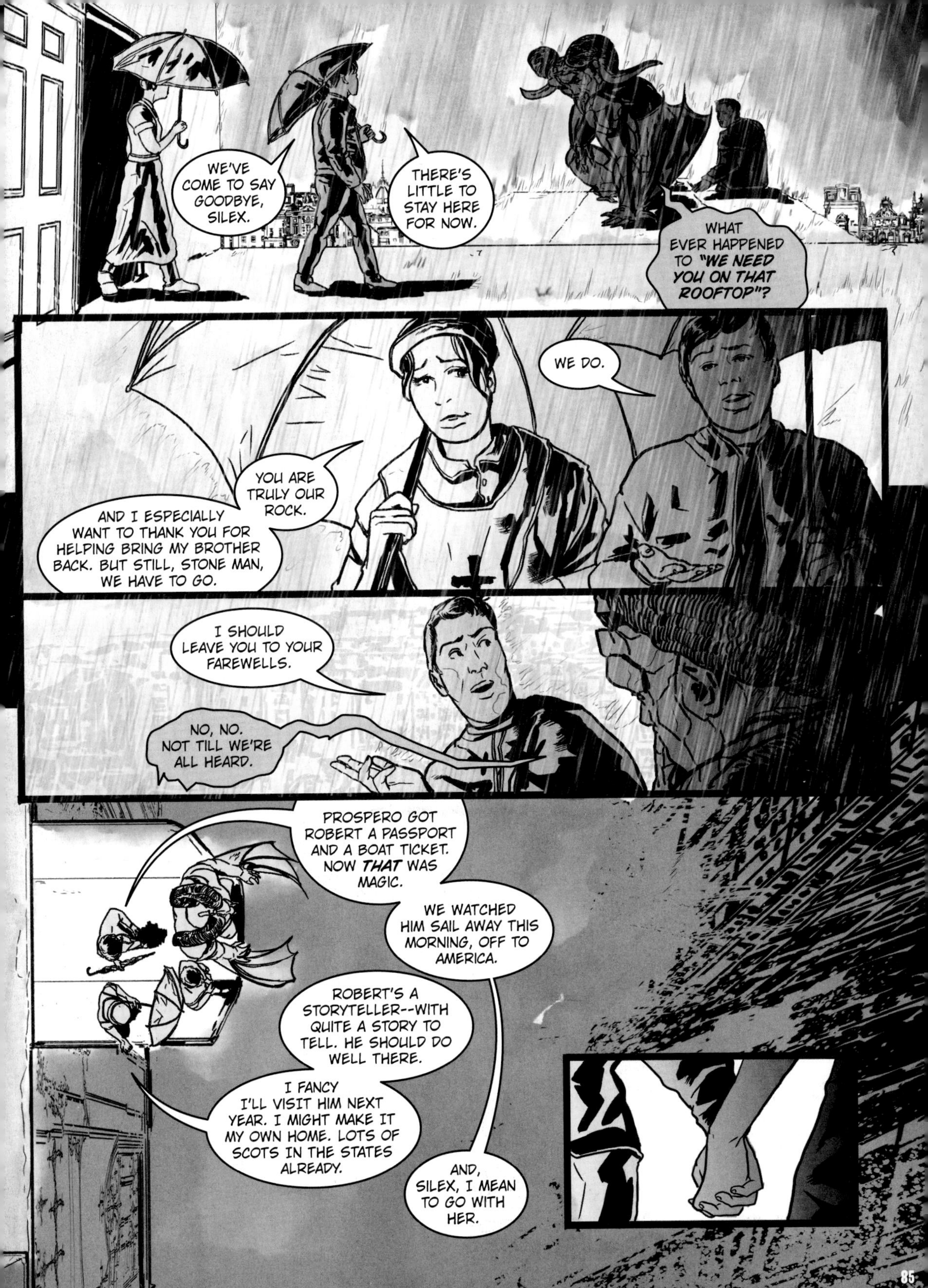
WE'VE COME TO SAY GOODBYE, SILEX.
THERE'S LITTLE TO STAY HERE FOR NOW.
WHAT EVER HAPPENED TO "WE NEED YOU ON THAT ROOFTOP"?
WE DO.
YOU ARE TRULY OUR ROCK.
AND I ESPECIALLY WANT TO THANK YOU FOR HELPING BRING MY BROTHER BACK. BUT STILL, STONE MAN, WE HAVE TO GO.
I SHOULD LEAVE YOU TO YOUR FAREWELLS.
NO, NO. NOT TILL WE'RE ALL HEARD.
PROSPERO GOT ROBERT A PASSPORT AND A BOAT TICKET. NOW THAT WAS MAGIC.
WE WATCHED HIM SAIL AWAY THIS MORNING, OFF TO AMERICA.
ROBERT'S A STORYTELLER--WITH QUITE A STORY TO TELL. HE SHOULD DO WELL THERE.
I FANCY I'LL VISIT HIM NEXT YEAR. I MIGHT MAKE IT MY OWN HOME. LOTS OF SCOTS IN THE STATES ALREADY.
AND, SILEX, I MEAN TO GO WITH HER.

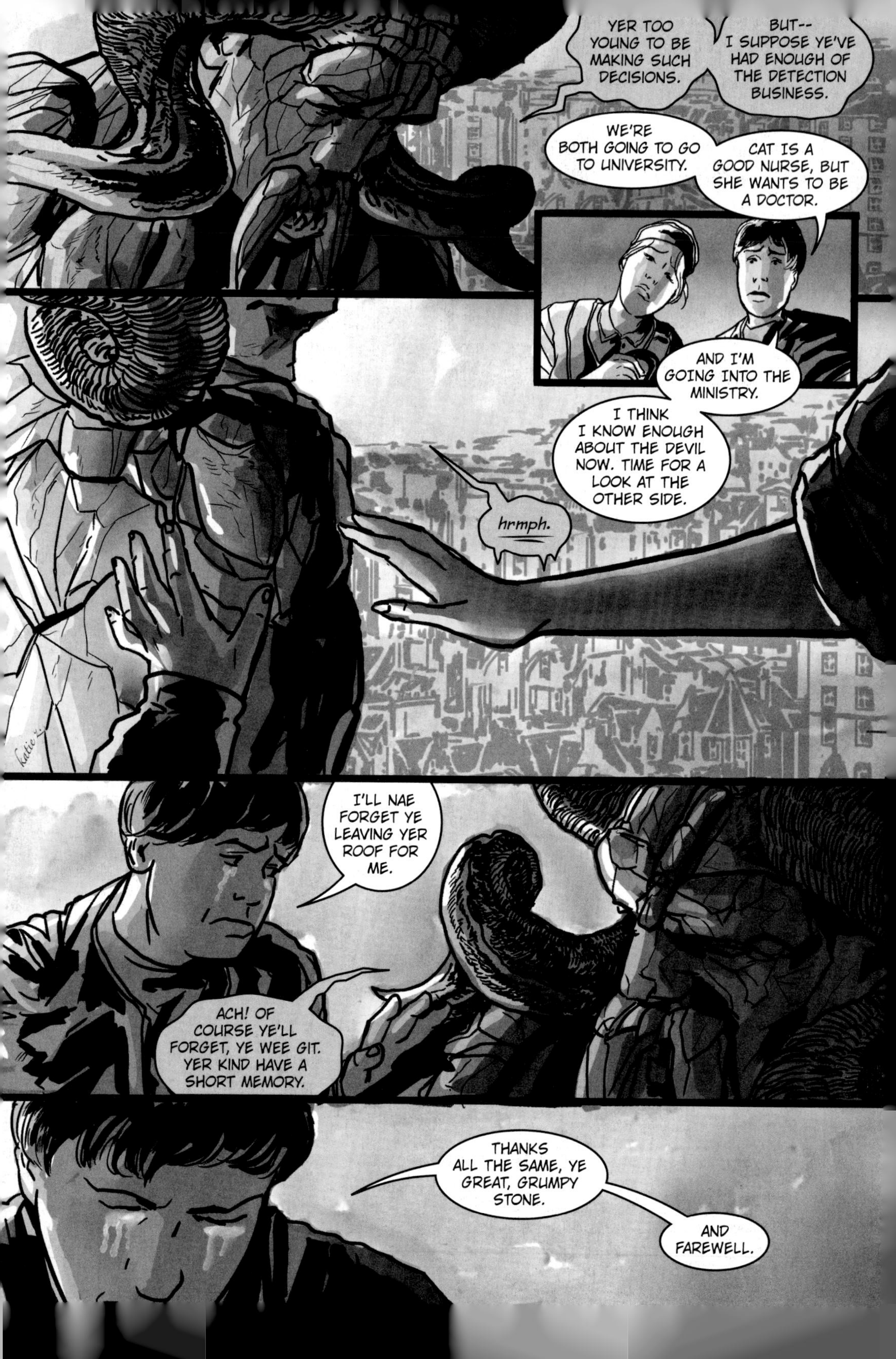
YER TOO YOUNG TO BE MAKING SUCH DECISIONS.
BUT-- I SUPPOSE YE'VE HAD ENOUGH OF THE DETECTION BUSINESS.
WE'RE BOTH GOING TO GO TO UNIVERSITY.
CAT IS A GOOD NURSE, BUT SHE WANTS TO BE A DOCTOR.
AND I'M GOING INTO THE MINISTRY.
I THINK I KNOW ENOUGH ABOUT THE DEVIL NOW. TIME FOR A LOOK AT THE OTHER SIDE.
hrmph.
I'LL NAE FORGET YE LEAVING YER ROOF FOR ME.
ACH! OF COURSE YE'LL FORGET, YE WEE GIT. YER KIND HAVE A SHORT MEMORY.
THANKS ALL THE SAME, YE GREAT, GRUMPY STONE.
AND FAREWELL.